Unrequited Love

The Secrets of Whispering Willows

Book 2

Caitlyn's Story

By: Mary Reason Theriot

Dedication

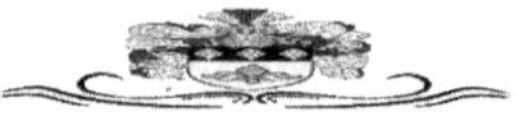

Without the love and support of my family and friends, I would not have pursued this new path in life. I would especially like to thank those who have proofread copy after copy, to give me their honest opinion of the books.

To my daughter Theresa, thank you so much for your continued encouragement.

To my wonderful husband Malwen, your continued love and support mean the world to me. I don't know what I would do without you in my life. All of my books wouldn't be what they are without you pushing me forward.

To my fans, I would like to offer a special thank you for your continued support.

ISBN-10: 1-945393-54-8
ISBN-13: 978-1-945393-54-9

Also Available by Mary Reason Theriot:

The Hideaway

The Traveler

Dr. Frankenstein

Above Suspicion

Horror in the Night

Deadly Seduction

Echoes on the Bayou

Seven Deadly Sins

A Kiss So Deadly

A Deadly Combination

CarnEvil of Souls

Seduced by Voodoo

www.maryreasontheriot.com

Prologue

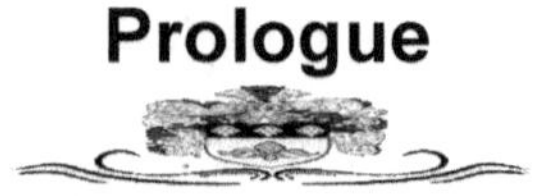

All of his planning, the risks he took, the preparations he made, and the lengths he went to were going to pay off. She would question his actions at first, but then she would realize this was the only way. Nothing else would have worked. There was no other way to spend eternity together. *Together in life and together in death.*

As he watched her enter the plantation, a smile turned up the corners of his mouth. Soon she would discover that love could transcend not only time but also space. He never considered himself to be a romantic. Some doubted whether someone as evil as he even had a heart.

Moving closer, he watched as her hips swayed from side to side. The woman was stunning, beautiful beyond compare. He could still recall her smelling of apple blossoms and summer. He remembered the way her laughter lingered in the air afterwards, soft and gentle. How he missed running his hands through her hair and kissing those luscious lips. His breath caught as she flipped her hair to the side, and a soft smile formed on her face. Perhaps she thought about him as she walked through the house.

He'd watched her intently these last few days and waited patiently for the perfect moment, the moment when he would change her life forever. Hopefully, he succeeded. The moment had not yet arisen; timing was crucial in what he had planned. He couldn't be reckless, he must wait.

She must understand why he did this for her. They were perfect for each other. He wanted to be with her forever, and he knew she wanted it. The only place to make her understand was here, at the plantation.

Chapter 1

Jean Paul Favre

Jean Paul Favre had a good life in Nova Scotia. A simple life, but a good life. He worked hard for the little money he received. In the blink of an eye, everything Jean Paul worked hard for was stolen from him. And there was nothing he could do about it. The men, young and old, were forced to attend the meeting in the church unarmed. Outside the church where they were held, they heard the roaring flames as their houses were burned to the ground. The British ignored the men's pleas to allow them to see their families once more, but instead, they were prodded with rifles onto waiting ships. Women and children rushed to the men, but they were held back by the soldiers. Tears streamed down their faces as the men were loaded onto the waiting ships.

Jean Paul was forced to leave his home in Nova Scotia on October 28, 1755 when he was only thirteen years old. At the age of twelve, his father considered him to be an adult and sent him off to work. Jean Paul was a blacksmith by trade in Nova Scotia, as was his father. On that fateful day in October, he was forced into exile on a small ship with other Acadians. His father was forced onto another vessel, and Jean Paul never saw him again.

The chill of winter had already begun to settle in as they set sail. The wintery air settled deep into their bones as fear overcame their minds. The sky and the sea were the same dreary gray, which matched their mood. Crashing waves sent salt spray over the bough as the ship continued its course and fierce winds picked up throughout the treacherous journey. Relentless storms battered them as the ships brought them to their uncertain future.

Life on the small ships was unforgiving; not everyone survived the harsh power of the waves and the wind. Their only rations were small amounts of dry bread and salt pork. Illness broke out and took the lives of most of the exiled. No comforts could be found on the ships; they slept out on the decks or huddled together below in the most unsanitary of conditions. It was then, Jean Paul vowed to never set foot on a boat again once they reached land.

Each time they landed at a port, disappointment filled their hearts. Once again, they were turned away and forced to find another port that might allow them entry. Being a different nationality, no one saw reason to welcome the Acadians. The further south they traveled, the more welcoming the ports became. Jean Paul and those on the ship with him were brought to Louisiana. The waterfront was littered with crates, barrels, and rough looking dockhands. A score of ships lined the river; their masts bobbed up and down in the water as they waited to take commerce to other ports.

As Jean Paul and the others prepared to disembark the ship, the smell of the yard assaulted their senses. Although the smell was far better than what they'd endured these last few months, it still reeked of grease, horse manure, and fish. He carefully stretched his legs as apprehension took over his body.

As they disembarked the ship by a gangplank, Jean Paul took in the sights in front of him. The docks were extremely busy. "It must be easy for thieves to pilfer here," he thought to himself. At one end of the docks, he noticed black men; he presumed them to be slaves, busy loading and unloading barrels of rum, sacks of sugar, coffee, and a multitude of bales of cotton.

All around him were hundreds of laborers, roustabouts, and some of the roughest riverboat men. Black and mulatto women, with their heads wrapped in brightly colored tigons, sold all sorts of sugary concoctions. Their tantalizing aromas drifted through the air to lure passersby into purchasing their goods.

***

As Celeste looked around the dock, she recalled her horrid childhood. At barely ten years old, Celeste had been ripped from her loving mother's arms and sold to an ugly spirited man in New Orleans. Every morning, he ordered the women to the docks to sell pralines, rice cakes, and other concoctions that they cooked to those coming from or getting on the steamboats. The master took no heed in the dangers there and if they returned with the incorrect amount of money, they would be dealt a lash of the whip. So they kept the money and goods close to their bodies to prevent theft.

After making it back to the plantation later that afternoon, the women prepared more baked goods to sell the next day. Today was bread baking day. It was Celeste's turn to scrub out the big pots that they mixed the dough in. She dipped the wooden bucket into the rain barrel and filled it with water. It took all of her strength to haul it back to the cookhouse. She carried buckets upon buckets of water to the pots so that she could scrub them clean. The air had a harsh chill to it; winter had set in. Her feet were wrapped in cloths and quickly became soaking wet, which made the chill seem even worse. For a moment, she considered removing the threadbare cloths on her feet, but she thought better of it. At least the wet cloth gave her poor soles some protection.

Clouds passed over to hide the sun, making the day even colder. She began to scrub the gooey flour that clung to the sides of the pots. As she scrubbed, she passed the time by thinking back to the group of children and men she saw escorted off the ship, much like slaves. Would they be sold as slaves as she had been or would they be granted freedom?   For some unknown reason, this group of people intrigued her. They were not dark like the other slaves, but more like her caramel coloring. Could it be that they were mulattos such as she? They spoke in a foreign tongue, so perhaps these people were kin to the Creoles living in New Orleans. One young boy caught her eye, but she diverted her gaze before anyone noticed her looking. But he looked as forlorn as she did.

She looked at her surroundings and cursed this life they lived. The master treated his dogs better than any of them. Working the docks was better than working the fields though. The work in the fields was hot, and the bugs were plentiful.

***

Around Jean Paul, the city throbbed with its own importance. Conversations occurred around them as they tried to decide where to go from here. In the distance, a whistle from a steamship caught his attention.

Some of the Acadians considered themselves lucky to be in Louisiana. At least here, their language was spoken. Upon his arrival, he worked in New Orleans for five years. During that time, Jean Paul fell in love with the young slave woman, Celeste. Celeste worked on one of the plantations that Jean Paul did blacksmith work for. She also worked the docks in New Orleans selling baked goods for her master. Whenever he could spare some change, Jean Paul purchased a praline or two just from her. They both knew that their love for each other would never be accepted.

Celeste's light coloring meant one of her parents had to be white, more than likely her father. She was so strikingly beautiful. Jean Paul could imagine the stir she caused around the plantation. He suspected that the slaves and the owner were captivated by her beauty. Celeste never mentioned her life on the plantation, but he had seen her move slowly at times and feared what she was forced to endure. Yet, she served her master diligently with no grief.

Jean Paul saw how owners treated their slaves. He did not understand why these sins were committed or allowed. One day while on the dock, he became nauseated when he witnessed a slave being tied to a ship's mast and whipped to the point of death. The punishment was for failing to load a delivery fast enough. He quickly learned that some of the masters were cruel and unjust in their treatment of the slaves. Surely something could be done about the unfair and unjust treatment of these people. Unfortunately, most people here treated them as if they were no better than cattle. They acted as if these poor slaves had no feelings. How could one human being own another?

Unable to live without Celeste's love any longer, they made plans to run away. For his love of this woman, he would risk his freedom. He opened his heart to a woman he could never legally marry, but still, he found the kind of love he could only dream of. It tore at his heart to watch as the love of his life was insulted, beaten, overworked, and starved. She lived in fear that at any time she could be raped or sold away.

It was a dangerous attempt for freedom, but the two young lovers were willing to take on the endeavor. They lived in New Orleans for another year where Jean Paul worked hard and saved his money. He overheard that land was being sold for cheap in Point Creole. A few Acadians settled there, and he had great hopes that there they could live in hiding. Jean Paul had enough money set aside and was ready to sneak his lover out of New Orleans and to Point Creole.

Celeste whispered to her secret lover, "Jean Paul..."

The catch in her voice broke his heart, "No. Don't say it."

Her eyes glittered with tears, "We are such fools. You are free, and I am a slave. I am..."

Silencing her with a finger to her lips, he said, "Hush now. You are the woman I love. I am your slave."

Trying to stay strong, she whispered, "I am wrong for you."

"I have been yours for a very long time now cher. We will find a place for us to love each other freely."

Celeste looked in his eyes, "You are too much of a romantic."

He had already stayed here longer than he should, but soon, they would leave this place. They would be together, forever. He would make her his. They would have babies together and live happily ever after.

***

A soft moon shined down on the bayou as he maneuvered the bateau in the thicket of shrubs and vines that hung low on an enormous oak tree. Under its canopy, the swamp was alive with nocturnal creatures.

A snake slithered up the tree and curled itself around a thick limb as it watched for prey. A swamp rat scurried into a hole in the ground. The crickets mating call filled the night as they rubbed their knees frantically, calling out for their mates.

His heart pounded in his ears as he tried to calm his nerves. His eyes stayed sharp and alert. It would be too dangerous to travel by day. When morning came, they would discover Celeste missing and send out the dogs. Traveling by water, they would not leave tracks, but still, someone may see the boat move along the water.

Celeste could barely contain her fear as she slipped into the night. Biting her bottom lip as she waited to make sure no one followed her; if she were discovered, she would be beaten to death. It seemed as if an eternity passed before she made her way to where Jean Paul waited for her. As she left the plantation, a few slaves completed last minute chores before tomorrow's big gala event.

Perspiration slowly made its way down her body. The stress of what she was doing did little to dampen her mood. She had never been out this late. She became frantically aware of her surroundings, worried that someone might find her. It amazed her how different her surroundings looked in the darkness of the night. The area now looked foreign and foreboding. Every furry animal, slithering reptile, crawling insect, and flicker of light sent her heart racing. Every few steps, she stopped to listen, waiting to hear the baying of the hounds as they echoed through the stagnant swamp air. She pulled the raggedy shawl closer around her shoulders. Despite the sweat bathing her body, she shivered in fear with agonizing doubt and an irreversible destiny.

She quickened her steps as she rushed to see her one true love. She tripped, landing hard on the ground as her foot caught on a fallen branch. Angry tears welled up as she feared that she would never meet up with Jean Paul. She kept moving as she surveyed the area. A menacing symphony of night sounds bombarded her ears. The discordant voices of a myriad of frogs echoed through the night. A splash sounded in the distance as an alligator slipped into the water, and a hair-raising shriek of an owl caused her heart to race even faster. The incessant whine of the mosquitoes told her she was near the water.

The air reeked of decay and mold. As she moved deeper into the swamps, she recalled the warnings about destitute and desperate slave masters who preferred to steal slaves rather than buy their own. Now she feared this was more than a scare tactic as the darkness closed in on her. Not only could she be captured, but she could catch the dreaded swamp fever as she breathed in the stagnant night air. Any such mortal danger paled in comparison to the reward.

The full moon hung high overhead; its silvery lights penetrated the tree branches and created eerie shadows along the way. Finally, she saw the landing where she was to meet Jean Paul. He planned to hide her in a small bateau that he had. They would move along the bayou in the darkness of the night until they could no longer travel by water.

She rushed into his arms as soon as she saw her beloved. His calloused fingers closed around hers in a gentle but firm grip as he pulled her into the bateau. She looked deeply into his eyes and felt his love flow like a current into her heart.

They made the treacherous journey in constant fear that they would be discovered. Along the way, he found an impressive piece of land on the bayou. Immediately, they knew this was where they wanted to raise their family. No one else seemed to want the desolate piece of land, so the price was relatively cheap. The Mississippi River wasn't far away. If he planned his plantation correctly, the barge boats could take the crops straight from the land, down the bayou to the river and directly to New Orleans.

Point Creole was like nothing they had ever seen. It had fertile soil, a subtropical climate, and picturesque swamps. Jean Paul had never seen trees as big as the huge oaks that grew on the property. There were also cypress, maple, and gum trees as far as one could see. He began clearing the land to build his lover the house of her dreams. Locals never asked why he kept to himself, and very few locals even attempted to venture out that way.

Getting involved in the Underground Railroad movement was an easy decision for the two of them. He did not consider himself to be a hero, but merely wanted to deliver the slaves from the tyranny of their owners. He took Celeste into his warm embrace and voiced his desires, "My love, if you don't want me to do this, I will abide by your wishes."

She looked deep in his eyes and responded, "Evil can only prevail when good men like you do nothing. By the grace of God, I pray that He keeps my family safe." They both were aware of the dangers; they must be extremely careful. When runaway slaves were involved, Jean Paul often feared that even the trees had ears. As he built Whispering Willows Plantation, Jean Paul personally made sure that his family could be hidden within the walls. He lived in constant fear that one day someone would find out about Celeste and his ever growing family.

With that simple decision, their course in life was laid out. The method of escape that he advocated was one person at a time. They both had strong feelings about freeing the slaves from their plight. It was worth the risk, and any punishment that would happen, he must endure. Unfortunately, Celeste still carried many scars from the whippings she received over the years from her master. Jean Paul shuddered at the thought of what she had endured.

To keep up appearances, Jean Paul had slaves as well, but unlike others, he freed his slaves. Only a few people knew what went on at his plantation. He treated his slaves so well that they did not care to leave. If a slave wanted to leave, no one forced him to stay.

This arrangement was dangerous for not only the slaves, but also stationmasters along the Underground Railroad. Slaves caught escaping were punished severely before being killed. Some were still willing to take the risk, especially the slaves of cruel masters.

Some people involved in the Underground Railroad you would never suspect of helping smuggle slaves to Canada. Most of those helping did not want their involvement known. This smuggling was done right under most master's noses. They had to be careful; some would betray you for a small piece of silver. Unfortunately, you never knew who it could be.

Most of the slaves coming through their doors had nothing more than an old flour sack to wear for clothes. Celeste spent her spare time ensuring that they had spare clothes on hand. In the hidden tunnels, she kept clothes and diapers for those traveling on. As each slave left their house, they prayed for their safe journey to freedom.

Several slaves had no idea what to think about people openly wanting to help them. They had learned not to trust anyone, and Jean Paul didn't find fault with their thinking. Sometimes, though, you have to trust the Lord to take you to safety. The slaves believed God would look out for them during their journey.

Boats and wagons were built with secret compartments to aid in the transfer of slaves. It was handy having Whispering Willows built on the river. In the darkness of the night, slaves were transported to the awaiting steamboats. Once they left the safety of his house, Jean Paul didn't always know who would be next in line to help them along their way to freedom. This mission had turned into a fight of good versus evil.

As time went on, it became more and more dangerous when transporting slaves from Whispering Willows. The cash reward for returning runaway slaves to their owners was too tempting for most men. It became imperative for them to dig tunnels, and more of the land had to be cleared for the timbers that were needed. There were even several tunnels that ran underneath the town. The dirt had to be removed, which caused the biggest problem. Celeste came up with an ingenious idea for Jean Paul to market his own "manure" blend in which he could make money by selling the dirt mixed with manure. They purchased cattle and chickens, which gave them the extra milk and eggs they needed. No one questioned why a single man with a few slaves needed such an excess of cows and chickens. They assumed it was another of Jean Paul Favre's business ventures.

By the age of thirty-five, Jean Paul Favre had made a name for himself along the river, and the plantation was booming. Jean Paul became worried when not too far from where they resided, another plantation was built, Cottonwood Plantation. Jean Paul feared that having new neighbors could mean that Celeste would be discovered. Over the years, Celeste gave him three children, but Jean Paul knew that their love and children were still unaccepted. They had a happy life on the plantation, but his children never knew of a life outside the walls of their home. He and Celeste kept them sheltered from the hatred that would be cast upon them.

Night had long since fallen; Jean Paul was in his study working on the books while Celeste sat in a far corner embroidering. His good friend and confidant, Isaac, knocked gently on the door before entering, "Mr. Andre Picou is asking questions again, sir. Jeddah got word to me earlier."

The creaking of Celeste's rocking chair stopped, as did the needle in mid air. "Did he ask any of the right questions?" She asked.

Isaac quickly replied, "No, ma'am."

Jean Paul shifted in his seat and began to worry about their neighbor. He purchased the neighboring plantation a few months ago and was already getting too nosey. He recently asked if Jean Paul would sell him Whispering Willows. When Jean Paul declined his offer, he asked about using the dock. Jean Paul had to be careful about how he handled this man. He didn't want the man on his property, but he also didn't want him snooping around either. Denying him the use of the dock would make the man curious.

Several months passed with no incident, then late one night as Jean Paul worked in his study and Celeste was busy embroidering there was a loud, incessant knock at the door. Just as Celeste entered her secret room, Andre Picou came barging into the room. "I am sorry to bother you this late mon ami, but I must know if any of your slaves ran off of late."

Jean Paul looked the man directly in his eyes, "Mais non. I had one slave to disappear, and he was found later that night down by the bayou."

Andre let out an exasperated sigh, "Somebody living amongst us has to be leading the slaves right out of the cane fields. My overseer watches the slaves like a hawk. He swore that one minute they were there and then gone the next. It was as if the ground just opened up and sucked them in."

"Mais, I will have to keep an eye out then." Jean Paul walked over to the bar, "Would you care to accompany me for a drink?"

Andre shook his head, "Mais non. We are watching the slave cabins closely tonight hoping to find one attempting to sneak out. I suggest you do the same, as you are more than likely the next to be hit. Unlike you, mon ami, I cannot afford to shell out one thousand dollars per lost slave."

The years passed by quickly. During Mardi Gras in 1780, Celeste talked Jean Paul into throwing a Mardi Gras Ball in the house. She saw this as the perfect opportunity to blend in with the other citizens of Point Creole.

As their guests left, Jean Paul was called to the landing. A steamboat captain wished to speak to him for a few moments. As Jean Paul headed to the boat, he kissed Celeste, "Go on to bed. I will join you as soon as I can."

Jean Paul let the moon guide him to the landing. Upon his arrival, he found no one wishing to speak with him. A shiver moved across his body. The indigo night went eerily still, and not even a bullfrog's deep throated croak broke the ominous silence of the night. All thoughts of the enjoyable evening he had just experienced vanished. Goosebumps made their way up his arms.

Fear gripped him as he rushed toward the house. He threw open the kitchen door and ran through the house until he found her on the porch. An anguished cry escaped his lips as he saw his Celeste's body. His Celeste, always full of love for him and their children, would never smile, laugh or even cry ever again. How could he live without her? Who did this to her? The guilty person would know his unyielding vengeance.

Deep purple bruises covered the once rich caramel skin of Celeste's delicate neck. Thick black rivers of mascara streaked across her high cheekbones and along her jaw before dripping onto the billowing skirt of her gown. A thin stream of blood escaped her plump, reddened bottom lip. He carefully removed the mask that hid her true identity, and he gasped at the sight of her lifeless eyes staring back at him.

He must cut her down. He didn't want his children to walk in and see their momma like this. A noise at the end of the porch caught his attention. He went to call out and ask for help when the moonlight glinted on an object. Before he could react, a puff of smoke caught his attention. Blood began to color the front of his shirt as it spread rapidly. He fell to his knees, and his blood turned to ice as his life slipped away. He tried to draw air into his lungs, but couldn't find the strength to call out. He must warn his children; they must not come outside. They must stay hidden. As his murderer looked down on him, his life faded away. All he could do was gasp and gurgle. Tonight, he saw the extent of evil in this man.

Chapter 2

Andre Picou

Andre Picou had big dreams. He wanted to own a sprawling plantation, large enough to harvest both cane and cotton. Whispering Willows Plantation was by far the largest here, and no matter how much money Andre offered Jean Paul Favre the man refused to sell. Hate and anger rose in him like an insurmountable tidal wave as he thought of that man sitting in his large home counting his money. It may be time for Andre to remind the people of this town that no matter how much money he had he could not hide his parentage. Andre scowled at the fact that this man was nothing more than a peasant in rich man's clothing.

The hour grew late, but he couldn't sleep. Bloody hell! The stubborn Acadian had refused to sell the plantation to him, and would not budge on the cost to use his dock. Andre needed to get the cotton to New Orleans. The man could be stubborn at times. It was as if Jean Paul Favre didn't want him near his property.

Worse, he had problems with his slaves running away. They would be there one minute and the next they were gone. So far, he had five escapees. If it wouldn't be that each slave cost him a thousand dollars, he would wash his hands of the whole business.

***

A deathly silence fell over the area. It was well past midnight, and the moonlight shimmered on the vast stretch of cotton planted in the fields. As Jeddah looked over the fields, he thought about how beautiful the views were at this hour. Up above his head, the stars twinkled in all their glory.

He had much work to do at this hour, even though his weary body begged for rest. He would get little sleep tonight and come daybreak, it would be another grueling day of work. The men, women, and children who were forced to work these lands had their bodies pricked by the razor sharp thorns that hid in the cotton. The relentless sun beat down on them as they carried their heavily burdened sacks. The hot rays of the sun cooked them in the oppressive Louisiana heat. One felt the sweat as it crawled down the body, bringing with it a pleasant misery. The sweat brought a cooling effect to the wretched heat's torment.

Cotton was the lifeblood of this plantation. Their master believed that he could only survive through slavery. In truth, slavery did keep this plantation alive. The slaves here were treated no better than mules that brought the crop to harvest. Not only was the master a tyrant, but so was the overseer, Theodore Simon. He was merciless in dealing with any suspicion of defiance or even a whisper of a planned escape through the clandestine activities of the Underground Railroad.

Jeddah wondered what Theodore Simon, or even Andre Picou, would do if they ever found out Whispering Willows Plantation was a major player in the Underground Railroad, as was Jeddah. Jeddah considered it a personal triumph every time he slipped a slave by the two evil men. Tonight, six rescued slaves from plantations further south must be moved. The move would be risky, especially with Mr. Favre having a large party. However, Ms. Celeste believed that the best time to do a rescue this large would be during the party. Most of the plantation owners would be enjoying themselves at the party.

Jeddah feared for Ms. Celeste. No one had knowledge of her existence and tonight she planned to disguise herself so that she could enjoy the party with her one and only true love. No one could talk her out of joining the party, not even Mr. Favre himself. Jeddah said a prayer for her safety once more.

Apprehension grew deep inside of him as he slipped into the dark tunnel. Tonight was unusually quiet, too quiet. Even the coyotes, whose howl usually broke the silence of the night, remained silent.

As Jeddah made his way through the passages of Whispering Willows Plantation, he saw something that would change all of their lives. Acting quickly, he woke up the children's nanny, Olivia. "Plans have changed. We must gather the children and leave immediately. There is no time to explain."

Olivia gently woke the children, "Ya must be quiet. Go with Jeddah."

Marguerite was afraid of what had happened, but her mother warned her they might have to leave in the middle of the night, "What about Momma and Poppa?"

Olivia pushed her along, "Hush ya mouth child and go. No time to talk."

Fighting back the tears, the children followed Olivia and Jeddah, wondering where their momma and poppa were.

Chapter 3

Whispering Willows Plantation

Whispering Willows sat abandoned for five more years until the neighboring plantation seized the property. Andre Picou and his wife, Evangeline, moved into the massive estate after their home burned down, but Evangeline never found happiness at Whispering Willows. She continuously complained that the place was haunted. She stated that cries of anguish kept her up all hours of the night.

Several months after they returned to Cottonwood Plantation, a young mulatto woman came knocking on the door one night. She claimed to be Marguerite Favre, the eldest daughter of one Jean Paul and Celeste Favre. She told them a tragic story of how her parents were murdered at Whispering Willows the night of their Mardi Gras ball. Slaves took the three children, and provided them refuge from her parents' murderer. The slaves were close to the family and knew of her parents' forbidden love.

She continued with the story by adding that Jean Paul's slaves were given their papers at the time of purchase, and most stayed on out of respect for him. They saw how well he treated his beloved Celeste; Jean Paul's whole life was centered around Celeste. They worked hard to repay him for his kindness, and the family prospered because of it.

Marguerite confided that the slaves did not know what happened that fateful night. Her father was found shot in the front room, and her mother hanging from the front porch banister. There were whispers that Celeste found Jean Paul dancing with another man's white wife, so she shot him out of jealousy, and out of grief, she then hung herself.

Others whispered that Jean Paul killed Celeste in a jealous rage. Some claimed that men looked at her with envy in their eyes that night, wondering who this sensual creature was. Out of grief for killing his beloved, he shot himself. Marguerite knew someone murdered her parents and came home to find out who did this to her family.

Evangeline believed this young woman's story, and insisted that Andre return the house and land back to her. Evangeline hoped by doing so the ghosts would be appeased.

Evangeline's offer enraged Andre, but as he looked at Marguerite, he thought he could attain payment in other ways. She was, after all, a striking woman.

Chapter 4

Marguerite Favre

Marguerite's life was plagued with devastation and confusion. She loved her parents and dearly missed them. When her thoughts turned to memories of her life before, her blood ran cold. Tormented and twisted with grief, she was overcome with an insatiable loneliness.

The loss of her parents left her grieving and waking up in the middle of the night calling out for them. She lost track of the countless tears shed and the endless nights she tried to comfort her siblings. Nothing seemed to exist except for the emptiness that she felt. Marguerite vowed to return one day and find out who caused this tragedy in their lives.

As Marguerite aged, she looked more and more like her father. Her complexion was fairer than her siblings. The time had come to return to Point Creole and claim what was rightfully theirs. Surely someone there knew who killed her parents. As she left behind her siblings, she promised Olivia that she would send for them as soon as she could. First, she must make sure that it was safe for them to return.

Marguerite took great joy in being back in her family home and had been optimistic of sending for her siblings soon. She hoped to discover answers within these walls as to her parents' cruel death.

Marguerite enjoyed tending to the plantation and its gardens. With her gentle disposition, she coaxed the flowers to bloom and the birds to sing. The citizens of Point Creole slowly opened up to the young girl. She was transparently kind in her treatment of others and had a selfless demeanor. She was quiet and reserved, rarely making demands upon others.

Those who attended the ball that fateful night slowly revealed what they remembered. One night as Marguerite was preparing for bed, the scent of lilacs swept through the room. It reminded her of her mother; Celeste's favorite perfume smelled of lilacs. For just a moment, Marguerite swore that her mother was sitting on the bed next to her. Marguerite talked to her mother out loud, hoping she would show herself.

The next morning, Marguerite woke to find a worn picture of her father on her pillow and knew without a doubt that her mother put it there. As she looked at the photo, tears filled her eyes. Jean Paul Favre had been a stern, but loving father. He had an imposing stature and a deep, rich baritone voice. At the age of thirty-five, he showed signs of gray in his dark hair. Instead of making him look older, her mother commented on how it made him appear more distinguished.

Over these last few days, she learned from several citizens here in Point Creole that her father had been regarded as an influential businessman. He did a lot of business at the town cotton mill, and he also negotiated several contracts for sugar cane, indigo, and even tobacco for several plantations in Point Creole. He had a reputation for having one of the finest plantations in the south and numerous women vied for his attention. No one in town knew her dad had a family; he kept that fact well hidden from everyone.

As time passed, Marguerite turned this place into a profitable plantation once again. Once she proved to be the illegitimate heir of Jean Paul Favre, the banks turned her father's property over to her. She never realized just how rich they had been. Life had been simple growing up, and money never mattered.

Marguerite soon learned that Mr. Picou wasn't happy about her taking over the land. She learned that he had attempted to buy it from her daddy right before his murder. As unsettling as she found the man, she had little time to worry with him. The plantation took up all of her time. There was more involved in the making cane syrup than she realized. The sugar cane had to be crushed, shredded for its juice, and then there was the tedious job of boiling the naturally brown juice into syrup. To harvest the cane one must be careful to leave its roots intact so the plant didn't die. New crops were ready in as little as six months, which didn't allow much time for other activities.

One morning as the coffee brewed for breakfast, a knock on the door echoed throughout the house. Marguerite found herself alone in the house, as the workers were eager to finish the outside chores before the oppressive heat became too unbearable. She hurried to answer the insistent knocking herself. Much to her surprise, she found a man in his early twenties at the door. Marguerite had never seen a man before as handsome as he. He had wavy black hair that tumbled over his face, mesmerizing almond

eyes, and muscles upon muscles. His white teeth just
helped enhance the rich caramel color of his skin. There
was an exotic look about him that she found intriguing.
"Pardon for the intrusion ma'am, but the fellow down the
road said that you might be in need of a hired hand."

Marguerite stepped out onto the front porch and asked,
"Have you worked the fields before?"

"Yes, ma'am, I have."

"Well then, sir, what brings you this way?"

"Jobs are hard to come by in N'Awlins. I decided to see if
there was work on any of the plantations along the bayou.
It is hard for a man like me to find a job."

Marguerite nodded her head in understanding. Most took
her for creole, but some could tell her true ethnicity and
treated her with nothing but disdain, "Well Mr... I'm sorry. I
don't even know your name."

"Antoine, ma'am."

"Well, Antoine, there are cabins down by the bayou. You
can move into one. We will see how this works on a trial
basis."

"Much appreciated ma'am."

Unknown to either person, Andre Picou kept a close eye on
the two as they conducted their business on the porch.
Andre had believed when he killed Jean Paul Favre and his
lover that he would have the plantation. He did not count
on Marguerite coming into town and swaying the citizens

here with her personable demeanor. This young man seeking work was just what he needed to help soil her reputation. Soon, history would repeat itself, and two young lovers would die.

As the summer months passed, Marguerite found that Antoine was a beneficial hire. He helped to relieve some of her stress by working in the fields, and Marguerite had time to work in her beloved garden once again. The weeping willows blew gracefully in the wind, and the crepe myrtles were in full bloom. Antoine even helped with building a beautiful arbor at the entrance to the garden.

Andre was furious at how well things were going over at the Whispering Willows Plantation. His anger turned to an arrogant hostility that others noticed.

Late one night, Marguerite found herself in the garden as the full moon cast a blue hue on the grounds. Crickets serenaded her, fireflies danced and night creatures rustled about. A cool breeze gently lifted her hair. She wished her mother could be here with her right now. As she gazed towards the river, a steamboat traveled down the river to some undisclosed destination. She imagined traveling one day on a boat like that, but she knew in her heart that it would be a while before someone of her color was openly welcome in public.

A dark figure appeared near the garden entrance. At first, she thought it may be Antoine, but at the sight of Andre, she froze in fear. She couldn't imagine why he was lurking about this late at night. The aura around her turned frigid, and once again, she smelled the aroma of lilacs in the air. A sense of foreboding came over her as Andre moved in closer to her. Out of the shadows stepped Antoine, putting himself in between Andre and Marguerite. Without speaking, Andre picked up his gun and shot the man in the chest. Before Marguerite uttered a sound, he shot her. He dragged them both to the water's edge and rolled the bodies into the murky water of the bayou.

Once again, he must wait for his chance to take charge of this plantation. This time, however, it would appear as if the two lovers ran away in the middle of the night. His wife had their home, and for now, he would act as if Marguerite Favre asked that he tend to the plantation in her absence.

Chapter 5

Evangeline Picou

Andre's intense gaze cut deep into Evangeline, "So that is it then? You plan to leave me just like that?"

As he stood in front of the fireplace, the flames cast shadows around the room. Evangeline looked at her husband; this man in front of her was not the man she married. No, he was something sinister instead.

She watched as he raked a hand through his thick, wavy hair. She knew that any woman would find him devastatingly attractive. At one time, she did too. Now, though, she feared him.

Keeping her expression calm, she nodded, "Yes."

He turned his fierce glare on her as he worked his way around the room, "Let's talk this through my love. Surely we can work this out."

Her voice could not hide her panic, "There is nothing to work out Andre." The words come out sharper than she intended. She tried to break free of his glare as she wrung her hands uncomfortably. She struggled to regain her composure.

His eyes glittered in the firelight, "Everything I have done, I have done for you, you ungrateful wench. And you dare to leave me?"

She bit back her sharp reply. What he did, he did for greed.
It would enrage him if he found out she knew about
everything he had done. No, she was terrified of what he
would do to her if he discovered she knew his secrets.

Keeping her voice calm, she said, "I am going to go stay with
my parents."

His black eyebrows drew menacingly over his eyes. He
turned his ring, a habit he did when he worried.

Meeting his gaze squarely, she used her last card, "You will
never hurt me again Andre."

She watched as his expression changed. He knew she was
serious now. She felt a small victory as he winced, "How
many times must I tell you I am sorry? I lost control is all. I
promise it will never happen again. I swear to you that I
never meant to hurt you."

"But you did Andre. You did hurt me." She had never even
been slapped by her parents. Last night when she asked
him why he was out so late, he reared back and slapped her
across the face, hard.

There was a long moment of silence as his hands clenched
the fireplace. His knuckles turned white. She stepped back
in fear that he would strike her once again. She must get
out of here. She told him what she intended to, and now
she must leave.

She moved toward the door of the parlor, "Evangeline,
please don't go." His voice was so low that she almost
didn't hear him.

When he gripped her shoulders, she was paralyzed with fear. She did not even hear him move from his spot by the fireplace. He forced her to look him in the eyes, "Please my love. I promise I will never lay a hand on you again."

For a moment, she almost believed him; however, she wondered if love had him pleading with her to stay or her family's money? She often wondered if her father's money was the sole reason he married her. As she looked around the parlor, she realized just how much stock this man put in appearances. All around her were gaudy, ostentatious furnishings. There were rows and rows of expensive leather bound books, and a massive cherry desk with papers spread in disarray on top of it. There were gilt and bronze mirrors as well as various knick knacks. Even the marble fireplace was an elaborate piece of furniture. Several oil paintings in gilt frames adorned the room. Everything Andre did was to improve his social standing in life.

She informed him, "There is nothing that you can say that will change my mind. I plan to have my father's lawyer send the papers shortly."

"What about our son?"

"I am taking him with me."

Turning on her heel, she headed for the door. Her heart pounded hard in her chest. As she walked to the awaiting carriage, her crunching footsteps echoed in the silence of the night. For a moment, she thought she heard Andre's footsteps pounding on the gravel behind her.

She turned back to discover nothing behind her. She couldn't shake the notion that the night had eyes. She swore that an unseen presence watched her intently. Looking towards the trees, she saw a figure to the right of her. When she blinked, whatever was there had disappeared.

A delicious feeling of freedom overcame her as she made it to the carriage. These last few weeks were pure torture for her. She wanted to run when she first suspected what Andre was guilty of, but in order for her father to believe her, she needed proof to back her claim. She had to wait and bide her time to ensure that her true motivations were well concealed.

As she entered the carriage, she looked at her sleeping son. He was the main reason she was doing this. She wanted him to have a happy childhood.

She still had a nagging sense that she was being watched. When she glanced into the darkness of the night, she saw nothing. Tales of black magic and voodoo rituals whispered secretly in the slaves' quarters ran through her mind. Could those rumors be true? Was that what she heard?

In a matter of days, she would file the divorce proceedings, and be free. She pondered what her father would say when she told him what Andre had been up to.

As she adjusted the baby's blanket, Evangeline felt a sharp pain as the bullet penetrated her back. At first, she wasn't sure what hit her. She crumpled to the ground as if in slow motion. The searing heat felt as if a hot poker had been thrust into her. She couldn't move without dizzy agony.

She couldn't believe her life would end this way. She wasn't ready to die. She had so much to live for. In spite of her imminent death, she thought of home. If only she could see her parents one more time. She imagined herself in the magnificent façade of her childhood home with her parents waiting for her on the front porch. It would have been nice to die in the loving arms of her family. A strange, creeping numbness took over her body. She only knew a moment of fear before the darkness enveloped her. She closed her eyes in surrender.

***

The shot echoed through the night air. He wasn't worried. Those who worked for him would be too afraid to come and find out what the noise was. That silly woman thought she could leave him. How wrong she was. He stepped over the dead body and grabbed his son. He would say that she left without him.

Chapter 6

Cottonwood Plantation – 1962

He trembled with fear when he heard his father cursing as he made his way to the old barn. Trouble would soon follow, so he bolted up the rickety ladder and hid in the hay loft.

Evan Boudreaux staggered into the center of the barn in filthy overalls and a grimy shirt. He reeked of stale sweat and alcohol. "You better bring your ass out here now, hear me?" His voice, graveled by years of chain smoking and drinking moonshine, always struck terror in the small boy's heart. With Poppa this mad and drunk, the punishment would be invariably worse.

From up above, he watched his father stagger sideways and grabbed the wall for support. "Son, if you don't want the strap to your ass, you better show yourself." Too afraid to move, he kept as still as possible. He wished he could just disappear into the wall and never worry about being found.

He heard his poppa making his way up the stairs to the loft and knew he was done for. With a steady grip for a drunk man, he reached up and grabbed the boy, "I been told you were caught eavesdropping again. Your momma is in tears from embarrassment."

He cried out, "I'm sorry Poppa. I didn't mean no harm." The small, dark eyed boy knew he would suffer another whipping. His heart raced as his father drew back his arm. The strap cut through the air with a snap before it fell across his back. After venting his rage, his poppa threw the strap across the barn.

The boy swore that this was the last whipping he would get. He learned today from eavesdropping that there was a treasure in that creepy plantation nearby. He would spend his every free moment searching that plantation until he found the money that the old Mr. Andre Picou hid there.

The family here may believe they were rich enough without it, or maybe they were too afraid of going over there, but he wasn't. Fighting a dumb old ghost for a hidden treasure was better than being whooped to death by his drunken poppa. He would find that treasure and move far away from here.

Chapter 7

Present Day

The old plantation home looked silent and brooding against the turbulent sky. It resembled a gothic obsession hoarding dark and mysterious secrets. The grounds were large and unkempt, and the family cemetery was nothing but a crumbling ruin.

This had once been a splendid antebellum home with a spacious garden. Now, overgrown shrubbery concealed the home's foundation, and the plaster resembled old bones held together by decaying flesh. Once ornate columns graced the broad, sweeping veranda, but today, it looked old and brittle. Gothic turrets crowned the corner bay windows, and the sagging porch gave the impression of a sinister grin.

The branches of the oak trees resembled bony fingers waiting to grab anyone who passed. Ivy crawled along the ground, taking over once magnificent flower gardens and strangling the trees. The mansion's rambling structure concealed many large rooms and alcoves. What used to be the slave quarters at the rear of the property were now dilapidated ruins. There were several more sheds and workshops on the grounds that were dwarfed by the plantation's size.

If one closed their eyes, they could picture the grandeur of this place from times past. At one time, this antebellum house brimmed with life and produced bountiful harvests. Those days have long since passed. Nowadays, all that haunted this plantation were melancholic gloom and death.

Dylan Guillory taunted his friend, Jacob Johnson, "Come on, I dare you to go in J.J."

"No way, dude. Everybody knows that Gregory Ferris haunts the house. They say that he tortures his victims over and over again."

Both boys stood outside the old plantation that Gregory Ferris had used for his Haunted House. "It's not. That's what everyone wants us to believe, so we won't go in there. Besides, there is no such thing as ghosts."

"Well then you go inside. They say you can hear the screams of those he killed at night."

David let out a loud laugh, "I'm not the one who is scared of the house, you are!"

J.J. crossed his arms over his chest; a serial killer ghost was no laughing matter. "If you wanna go inside so bad, you do it then. My dad said it is haunted and I believe him."

"Aw dude, you believe all that superstitious crap?"

J.J. looked over at the forbidden plantation as it loomed eerily in the distance. The windows seemed to glow green suddenly, and he took a step back. A movement in one of the upstairs windows caught his attention. He squinted harder, looking for movement. A shadow moved in front of the window, but it disappeared in a flash. He shivered at the thought of a ghost watching them.

Dylan pushed him from behind, "Go in. I dare you."

J.J. was not going in that house. "No way! If you want someone to go in that house so bad, you have to do it."

Dylan antagonized his friend a little more, "What's the matter? You scared?"

"I'm not scared."

"Yes, you are. You are such a chicken shit."

A dark shadow moved to the first floor window causing J.J. to flinch involuntarily. Dylan saw J.J. jump back and asked, "What? What did you see?"

J.J. pointed to the window on the first floor, "Something moved in front of the window. At first it was on the second floor, but now it is on the first."

Dylan laughed at his friend, "It is probably just another person curious about the house. Maybe someone needed a free place to live."

J.J. saw the movement again and grabbed Dylan's arm, "Look! Look! There it is again."

Dylan looked just in time to see a dark shadow watching them, but this time it was on the second floor again, on the other side of the house. Neither boy could tell who or what it was, but they felt it watching them.

J.J. whispered, "It knows we are here. How is it getting around that big house so fast? Do you think we should call the cops and tell them someone is in the house?"

"Are you crazy? We aren't supposed to be out here anyway! They will lecture us about being here."

They heard a noise to their right, causing them to jump. "What was that?" J.J. asked.

"Relax dude. It was probably just a deer or something."

J.J. stuttered, "What if it is the ghost coming to get us?"

Laughing, Dylan said, "Maybe, it is the Rougarou coming to get us. He's probably looking for a snack."

J.J. swallowed hard and looked around to see what made the noise, "You don't think it's the Rougarou do you?"

The sound of a limb snapping in half and rustling in the bushes had both boys looking around. J.J. looked at his friend, "I think we should go now. I don't want to find out if it is the Rougarou or the ghost."

"Yeah, we need to get home anyway. I got homework to do." Dylan looked over at his friend and wondered if he was afraid too. There was no way he wanted to go home and do homework.

Neither boy felt the need to stay around the old plantation home any longer; besides, if they didn't get home soon, their parents would wonder what kept them. If they found out that they were near here, they would ground them.

Chapter 8

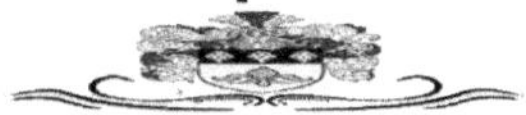

Henry Picou busied himself around the old dilapidated plantation. There was so much to do; the chores were endless here. This old plantation brought nothing but misfortune to his family. The house was quickly deteriorating, and the hardwood floors creaked with each movement he made. At one time, it had been the jewel of the once prosperous Picou family. Now his family's legacy consisted of this old house and a measly three acres. The rest had been sold off over the years.

Would their luck have been better if the old house had not been rebuilt after the original house burned down? If his great-great-great-grandmother had never disappeared, would their lives have been filled with love instead of grief? He heard the rumors about how rotten Andre Picou had been. Perhaps, it was a family trait.

After Evangeline left, Andre ruled with an iron fist. His treatment of the slaves was overly cruel. There were rumors that due to his unjust treatment the slaves cursed him. Henry believed a curse hung over his family as every attempt to run the once thriving cotton enterprise had failed. There were problems with equipment, slaves, and finances for years. Yes, this old plantation was a cursed birthright that had been passed from relative to relative over the century.

Andre Picou became senile as he aged and hid his treasures in these walls, as well as the walls of Whispering Willows.

Andre feared that the slaves or others would rob him blind; therefore, he hid everything of value.

Civil War soldiers tore the plantations apart looking for anything they could carry. When they moved to Whispering Willows Plantation, the ghosts retaliated and sent the intruders running in fear.

As he stepped out onto the rotting back porch, he stared out into the vast expanse of woods that separated his plantation from Whispering Willows. The land called him into the vast unknown.

As he walked towards the woods, the smell of wet earth hit him in the face. The sound of birds chirping lured one into a false sense of security. As a child, he had been afraid of venturing into these woods unarmed. He could just imagine the countless number of snakes hiding; waiting for the perfect time to slither up your leg and bite you. For a moment, something moved about in the woods. He peered through the dense woods, but it was difficult to make out anything.

A breeze blew through the trees, and for a second, he thought he heard a moan. Perhaps, it could be from the ghosts of those long since passed. For all he knew, it could have been the ghost of Evangeline Picou. He often felt the place was haunted. He wouldn't have put it past old Andre to kill her and hide her body somewhere on the property. Her parents always swore that she was leaving him and coming home to them. They never believed that she would leave her son. Could it be that Andre Picou's guilty spirit walked these halls?

As he turned back to head home, a sound caught his attention once again. The sound reminded him of someone stepping on a branch. Perhaps, an animal moved about. He had no desire to find out.

Rumors ran rampant about the Rougarou that roamed these woods. A few months ago, some men camping out in the woods swore something tormented them by throwing large rocks at their campsite. One of the larger trees near their site came crashing down as a loud piercing shriek echoed through the night air. It didn't take the men long to clear out of the woods and vow to never return.

A few other sightings were claimed recently of a large hairy creature terrorizing locals. As a kid, he swore something lived in the woods, and to this day, he was deathly afraid to go out there at night.

As he headed back home, he glanced over his shoulder to see if someone was following him. When he arrived home, he noticed that he'd left the back door open. He prayed nothing slithered in while he stepped away.

As he stepped into the house, the quiet seemed to surround him. The sound of his footsteps bounced off the walls. He did not like living in the house all on his own.

As he made his way deeper into the house, something seemed different. He couldn't quite place it. Perhaps, his imagination was playing tricks on him.

Chapter 9

As Caitlyn Reed walked into the kitchen, she heard the mail carrier dropping off the mail. She dreaded opening the mail lately. All that seemed to be in there were collection notices. Ever since it became public knowledge that she dated Gregory Ferris, she was avoided like the plague. She had to move now; she'd drained her savings after being released from her job, and no one wanted to hire her.

She may have to change her name and dye her hair in hopes of not being recognized. No one believed her when she said she had no idea about Gregory's sinister side; no one listened to her pleas of innocence. She had only dated Gregory a few times before his arrest. It didn't help that Gregory continued to reach out to her from prison, begging her to come see him. She ignored his requests, and it seemed that he had finally taken the hint because the calls and letters had ceased.

As she looked through the mail, she trashed the collection notices. However, one letter stood out. A knot tightened in her stomach. It was from William Anderson, an attorney, here in town. With everyone she owed money to, she knew someone would eventually sue her. She hoped it would be when she had the money to pay the debt.

She slowly opened the letter, fearing what it had to say and almost dropped the letter in disbelief. The lawyer wanted her to come to his office for the reading of Gregory Ferris's will.

She stared out the window as thoughts came rushing into her mind. Why would she be named in Gregory's will? Surely, his money would go to the families of his victims.

She poured a cup of coffee and paced. There was no time or date mentioned in the letter, which meant she must call and set up an appointment. She picked up the phone and dialed the number.   "My name is Caitlyn Reed. I just received a letter from Mr. William Anderson regarding a reading of Gregory Ferris's will."

The receptionist acknowledged the letter, "Yes ma'am. Mr. Anderson is anxious to get this matter closed as soon as possible. When are you able to come in?"

"I am pretty much free right now. Just let me know when he is available and I will be there."

"Mr. Anderson has an opening at one o'clock this afternoon if you can make it?"

Caitlyn looked at her watch. If she hurried with her shower, she should be able to make it there in plenty of time, "I can be there for one o'clock." The lawyer's office was several blocks away so it would be a longer walk than she liked. She wanted this behind her and to move on with her life. She wanted to move away from New Orleans as soon as possible.

By the time she made it the lawyer's office building, she had begun to sweat. The air conditioning in the lobby felt good against her heated skin. The building was one of the oldest in New Orleans; the lobby had marble floors, high ceilings, and exquisite crown moulding. By the time she made it to the fifth floor, where his office was located, she started to cool down from the heat outside. Her nerves were still strung tight, but she wanted to get this meeting over with.

The attorney's reception room was decorated similar to the lobby. There were marble floors in the reception area and gleaming wood floors in the rest of the office. The furnishings in here must have cost an arm and a leg. They appeared to be antiques from the same era as the building.

The receptionist looked up from her desk, "Ms. Reed?"

"Yes."

"Please have a seat. Mr. Anderson will be with you shortly."

After a few minutes, the receptionist got up from her desk, "Please follow me. Mr. Anderson will see you now."

The attorney was older than she thought, but still good looking. He had flawless olive skin; his dark hair perfectly styled, and his teeth looked as if they had just been polished. He had an aura of power and charm about him. "Ms. Reed, thank you for coming so promptly. I am not sure if you are aware that Mr. Ferris committed suicide recently."

Caitlyn let out a gasp. She didn't know Gregory that well, but she never suspected Gregory as a quitter. However, he did have his life crumble right in front of him. "No, I hadn't heard."

Caitlyn sat in a chair in front of the attorney's desk and waited to see what Gregory's death had to do with her. She looked around the office and noticed it was just as exquisite as the rest of the building. His large mahogany desk and black leather chair matched the furnishings of the outer office. Several exceptional oil paintings adorned the walls, and the back of his office looked over the Mississippi River.

As he opened a file, Caitlyn stated, "I am still confused as to why I am here."

"You were mentioned in Mr. Ferris's will."

"I'm sorry, but that doesn't make any sense to me. Didn't Gregory have a family and what about his close friends?" Caitlyn assumed that Thomas and Grace Billiot would at least be here if Gregory had a will.

"Mr. Ferris made no mention of anyone else in his will except for you. He left his entire estate to you."

Caitlyn found the room spinning from the news, "What? That makes no sense! I didn't know Gregory that well."

"Well, apparently, he thought the two of you had a special relationship. I have been Gregory's attorney since the beginning of his business openings. He came into my office not long after you met and changed his entire will. Not long before he took his life, he called me once more wanting to make sure that I had made the requested changes."

"This is too much to take in."

"There is a good bit of money as well as his mansion, cars, and the haunted houses."

A chill moved through Caitlyn as she thought about the haunted houses. What Gregory did there was unthinkable. "What about the lawsuits from the victims' families?"

"As they have come in, I offered each of them money to settle the matter. Each family has taken the money and signed releases. I have set aside money in another account just in case we have more lawsuits filed."

"What about the survivors? I want to make sure that something is done for them."

"I suggested that Gregory offer each of the survivors a sum of money and he readily accepted. They, in turn, took the money hoping to move on with their lives. I must tell you that the city has condemned the first haunted house and it is set to be demolished next week."

"What about the one in Point Creole?"

"It is still vacant. The crime scene clean up company came in and cleaned up the mess, but Gregory refused to have it put on the market."

Caitlyn couldn't explain it, but an overwhelming need to visit the plantation came over her. "So, I own the plantation as well?"

"Yes, you do, but I don't suggest you go there. I went once to make sure that the crime scene cleanup company did as instructed and the house just has an eerie feeling to it. The company had a hard time getting workers to stay there to clean. Several of the workers refused to enter the house stating that it was haunted."

Caitlyn had always believed in ghosts; it was a must living here in New Orleans. She had a feeling several souls were trapped in that house begging to be freed. Maybe fate called her to the plantation home.

As she left the attorney's office, she closed the door behind her and walked down the hall to the waiting room. She walked right past the receptionist without even acknowledging her. This was unreal. She never even noticed the man entering the attorney's office after her, as she was lost in her thoughts.

***

William Anderson watched as Caitlyn Reed left his office and cringed when he saw Antonio Ricci enter after her. He tried to sneak back into his office before the man saw him, but he was too late. William felt the man's firm grip on his shoulder.

William gave the man the most fictitious grin he could muster at the moment, "Antonio, it is always a pleasure to see you."

With his fists clenching by his side, Antonio growled, "Cut the crap. You've put me off long enough, and now I want my money."

William shifted from foot to foot, "I don't have all your money right now."

Antonio took his right fist and slammed it into his left hand as he invaded the attorney's personal space, "I warned you what would happen if I didn't get paid."

"I can have some money for you in the morning, but I am sure other arrangements can be made."

Antonio glared at the man, "If I accept this arrangement, I need to double what we bring in."

"But… but…"

Antonio held back breaking the sniveling idiot's jaw, "You have racked up quite a debt mon ami. I am not a bank; I want my money in ten days. It is either the money or trade."

"It turns out that the lady who inherited the place may move to Point Creole. She is considering renovating it."

Antonio jabbed his finger in the attorney's chest, "Not my problem. Fix it."

In a shaky voice, he replied, "It might take me a while to figure this out. I have a few things going on, and I need to convince her to sell the plantation."

"I don't want excuses. Pay up or you will be disposed of just like the rest of my problems."

The glare in Antonio's eyes told William he was serious about the threat.

Chapter 10

Scott Leger pulled into one of the few free parking spots in front of Rosie's Diner and climbed out of his truck. He wasn't in the mood to eat alone tonight. But he knew if he went to visit his parents, they would want to talk about his new job.

He still couldn't believe that he would be the one renovating Whispering Willows Plantation. There was so much to do that he feared it might potentially cost him some customers. He was the only local handyman, and while he knew he would never make a fortune doing what he did, he enjoyed working with his hands.

Right after high school, he enlisted in the US Coast Guard. After eight years there and contemplating whether or not to make it a career, he started missing home and working with his hands. So he came back and started his business.

As soon as he opened the door to the small diner, the smell of fried chicken greeted him. These familiar aromas reminded him of Sunday dinners at his grandmother's house. Growing up, his parents brought him and his siblings to his mother's parents' house where they ate a big meal. A typical Sunday meal there consisted of fried chicken, mashed potatoes, gravy, green beans fresh from the garden, fresh baked bread, and lemon meringue pie. When watermelons were in season, they had fresh watermelon and homemade vanilla ice cream. After eating the watermelon, he and his younger brother raced to see who made it to the chicken coop first with the watermelon rinds.

Scott sat at a booth in the back and waited for the waitress to come take his order. "Hi, hon. What can I get for you today?"

"Hey, Millie. I'll have a double bacon cheeseburger, fries, and a cold beer."

"Coming right up."

Just as Scott prepared to bite into his burger, Mr. Eli Fontenot sat across from him in the tiny booth. "Sir, how are you?" Scott asked pleasantly.

"I can't complain much. I hear you are renovating Whispering Willows."

Scott took a swig of beer and let it roll down his throat before replying, "Yes, sir, I am." Scott didn't even bother to ask him how he knew. You couldn't keep a secret in this place.

"I also hear a young lady owns the house now."

Scott shrugged his shoulders, "To be honest with you, I don't know. I have only talked to her on the phone. The Chamber of Commerce gave her my number when she asked who would be the best person to help repair any damage to the house." Taking another swallow of the cold beer he explained, "She said she inherited the place and wanted to know what kind of damage there was."

"That place has been empty for a long time."

Scott nodded his head in agreement, "Yes, sir, I know."

"That house is liable to be in bad shape. No telling what that man did to it."

Something in his gaze unsettled Scott, "I guess I will find out soon enough."

"You know that house is haunted."

"Yes, sir, I have heard that. I am sure if I leave them alone, they will leave me alone."

"Good luck boy; if you need any help, give me a call. My pa worked over at the Cottonwood Plantation, and I would sneak over to Whispering Willows whenever I could. I have always wanted to get in that house and see a ghost."

Scott sure hoped that the lady didn't plan to live out there all alone. It could be a harrowing experience for her. Hell, even the locals were scared half to death to go out there.

Eli Fontenot looked over at Scott, "Yep, if I were that woman, I sure wouldn't stay out there. I would sell that place and move on. A lady shouldn't live out there all alone."

Scott looked over at the man, "We don't know for sure if she will be alone. She may have a boyfriend or husband coming out with her."

"Yeah, well, I wouldn't want to spend the whole night out there. The ghosts probably don't want to share the house with someone new, especially not after what that man did."

After Eli Fontenot said his piece, he walked back to his table and Scott drew his brows together. He wondered why Eli

Fontenot was so concerned about the new resident of Whispering Willows. Perhaps he was concerned about her safety, but Scott's gut told him that there was more to it.

Chapter 11

As Caitlyn headed to Point Creole, trepidation moved through her body. This last week had been surreal; she went from barely being able to come up with gas money to never having to worry with money again. Still, after seeing Gregory's house, she couldn't find enough strength to move into it. It would remain vacant until she made some important decisions. She did go through his car collection to find one that she could drive comfortably to Point Creole. She decided on his Range Rover, as the road to the plantation house would more than likely be overgrown. Point Creole was a small Cajun town located along Bayou Teche in Southeast Louisiana. Until Gregory's arrival, there was a sense of peace in the area. The people here soon learned that even evil could move into their town though.

Caitlyn instantly fell in love with this charming town. She liked how this small town took pride in its heritage. Some of the original buildings and plantation homes dating back two centuries still stood. It felt as if you were stepping back in time when you entered some of the antique stores and businesses. There was a relaxed, unhurried feel about the town. As she looked around, she could imagine wealthy merchants and aristocratic Southerners from antebellum homes mingling with the Acadians who settled in this area. There were huge oak and magnolia trees that more than likely dated back to the late 1800's, if not earlier.

She had dipped into the funds Gregory left her and had a travel trailer moved out to the property. Caitlyn had no desire to move into the plantation house, and the travel trailer would be big enough for her to live in. Besides, this would be an adventure for her.

Once the house was freed of its spirits, she could sell the travel trailer and the house before moving on with her life. Freeing the spirits was her way of helping right the wrongs Gregory committed.

It was lunch time by the time Caitlyn drove into town. She figured she might as well get something to eat before heading to the plantation. There were several Creole restaurants to choose from. She decided to try one of the newer restaurants, Beazell's II. She had been to Beazell's On The Bayou in New Orleans and if the food was as good as the parent restaurant, she couldn't go wrong eating here.

The entrance to the restaurant incorporated the town's rich history of plantation homes and created a welcoming atmosphere. On each side of the entrance were planters made from the sugar mill pots. As soon as Caitlyn entered the restaurant, she could tell she made the right decision. This place appeared to be popular with the locals and the tourists. She loved how the decorator brought the outside swamps of Louisiana inside the restaurant.

She waited less than five minutes to be seated and only had to peruse the menu a short time before knowing what she wanted. "I will have a Beazell's Bloody Mary and the crab cakes, please."

As the waitress took the menu, she replied, "Yes, ma'am, coming right up."

After having a satisfying lunch, and ordering a bowl of gumbo to go, she headed to the plantation. As she drove down the meandering tree lined road that led to the plantation, she found her foot hitting the brake at the entrance. The home seemed to rise like an ethereal mirage. It was framed between two rows of ancient oak trees. From here, the branches looked like grotesque arms reaching out to grab those that dared to enter the house. Gnarled roots reached up from the ground, as if bodies were making their way out of unmarked graves. The home looked hauntingly sad as if pleading for someone to rescue it from its misery. It broke her heart to see something such beauty and with so much history go to waste.

Looking at the house sent a chill down her spine. Just ahead of her, she swore a shroud of darkness hung over the house. A greenish haze came from the windows of the plantation home. It reminded her of swamp gas, but that was impossible for it to be coming from inside of the house. The Bayou Teche ran behind the house; she wondered what deep dark secrets were hidden in its murky depths.

From here, she saw what remained of the old iron fence and gate, which seemed to have an intricate detail of roses and leaves. At one time, the gate probably stretched across the road. The plantation appeared to be secluded in its own private world, tucked away from the rest of the world.

Muttering to herself, she said, "The only thing missing now is the lightning." At that moment, a streak of lightning zigzagged across the darkening sky.

At the restaurant, she overheard several locals discussing the plantation. They believed that even before Gregory bought the old home it was haunted. That it was surrounded by fear and mystery as well as ghosts.

She could see what Gregory found so alluring about this place. The sheer size of the house rendered it terrifying. The dark, dilapidated corridors, old rusted pipes, and flaking paint helped to enhance the haunted look. And Gregory did nothing to improve the exterior's look.

She hoped that there was at least electricity. She called last week to make sure that it would be turned on in time for her arrival and found out that the attorney had kept the utilities running here. A local contractor planned to meet her this afternoon to go over everything that needed to be done. She has researched séances and ways to set earthbound ghosts free. She had a backseat full of groceries she bought in New Orleans along with several books that she believed would be useful in her quest.

The house was monstrous. Looking over the home, there was a bit of Greek inspired architecture. It stood over three stories tall and had a basement. There was a wide wraparound porch with French doors that lead into the house. The black shutters framing the windows needed painting; however, it did look as if all the shutters were still here, albeit haphazardly hung.

Digging in her purse for the set of keys the lawyer gave her, she headed for the house. She had no idea which key opened the front door, but she assumed it would be the largest key. As the thunder rumbled across the sky, she slipped the first key into the lock. Her assumption was wrong, but by the fifth key, she opened the front door just as large raindrops pelted the ground. As soon as she opened the door, the fetid odor inside hit her. A tornado of dust rushed through the open door, almost knocking her down. Waving her hand in front of her, she coughed and sneezed as the dust caught in her nose. She wrinkled her nose at the smell and decided it would be best to keep the door open. Even though the crime scene cleanup company managed to do a fairly thorough job of removing of the biological waste, there was still a strong smell of death and decay in the old house.

A cold breeze swept over her as she made her way into the house, causing her to wrap her arms around herself. The house was eerily quiet; the only noise came from the raging storm outside. Giant cobwebs cascaded down from the ceiling and clung to everything they touched. Some of the plaster from the walls and ceiling had fallen, littering the floor with a powdery dust.

Walking through the house, she found that it had an essence about it, as though it was engulfed in evil. Unsure if it was her imagination or not, she suddenly felt someone walk up behind her. She glanced over her shoulder and saw nothing. She figured her mind must be playing tricks on her.

As she continued to walk through the house, she felt as if she stepped back in time. The hardwood floors have lost their luster, but she could tell how grand this house must have been at one time. In the foyer, pictures and pieces of furniture were strewn about. Looking around, she noticed that Gregory left most of the furnishings and decorations where they were, and built the haunted house around the décor. The house still boasted golden, gilt-edged wainscoting, velvet wallpaper, crystal chandeliers, and ornate furniture. Any antique dealer would love to get their hands on these wondrous possessions.

In the center of the foyer was a grand staircase that needed to be checked for stability. A crystal chandelier still hung from the ceiling just as it once had welcomed guests into the brilliance of the house. At one time, this had been a grand foyer. Along one of the walls was a huge fireplace with a finely carved mantle. Intricate woodwork could be seen in every direction around the room. On either side of the fireplace were massive bookshelves that at one time must have contained volumes and volumes of books.

At one time this had been a flourishing plantation. Slaves toiled in the cotton and sugar cane fields. They had grown and picked crops that were loaded onto barges traveling the bayous to make it eventually to the city of New Orleans where the cargo would then be sold. There was a dock on the plantation where barges were loaded directly from the fields.

The family who once owned this property had been wealthy and influential. She pondered why the plantation was abandoned and left for Gregory to purchase for his evil intentions.

Her mind raced with everything that needed to be done here. She envisioned how beautiful the place could be with a little tender loving care. It just needed someone to give it the love it so richly deserved.

As she surveyed the downstairs, a dark blur bolted across the living room. A startled shriek escaped her as the dark shadow disappeared. She put her hand over her heart as she struggled to catch her breath. As she regained her composure, she heard a knock at the door. As she headed to the door, she found a man of average size standing in front of her. He appeared to be in his early thirties, had a deep tan complexion, wide cheekbones, and the most mesmerizing blue eyes. Just looking at him, she felt the power pulsing from him. Something about him made her heart race and skin tingle. She felt an overwhelming urge to touch his hard muscles and see if they were as tight as they looked. She found herself longing to run her fingers through his hair and kiss those luscious lips of his. Confused by her feelings, she wondered if it was a good idea to be working with a man like this. The two of them working together could turn out to be dangerous.

She reached out her hand, "You must be Scott Leger."

He accepted her outstretched hand, enveloping her in his warmth. He noticed how well her shapely body filled out her jeans. Her breasts appeared to be the perfect fit for his large hands. He had to remind himself that she was not part of the job. He was hired to do a job on the plantation and nothing more. It would be hard to keep his hands to himself though. This woman standing in front of him was exquisite and built for pleasing a man. "I take it you aren't afraid of the ghosts."

She laughed at his comment, "Ghosts can't hurt you. I must say the same about you though. I had a hard time finding someone willing to help me fix this place up."

"Most of the locals believe this old house is haunted." Just listening to this man's sexy voice made her breath catch and knees weaken. Oh boy, she may be in trouble if she worked with him day in and day out. "So exactly why did you come here?"

"I want to help the souls of those that Gregory Ferris trapped here. I plan on helping them find peace so they can move on."

He almost laughed at the woman's nonsense, "You believe this house is haunted?"

"I intend to find out. I heard rumors that there had been some strange happenings around here even before Gregory moved in."

***

After Scott had completed his inspection of the house, he found Caitlyn standing out on the porch. "It looks as if the crime scene cleanup company did a reasonably good job removing what they could, but this place still needs some work. There are some structural issues on the porch that need to be addressed right away. You have running water in the bathroom, but there are some electrical issues that I will need to repair. This house is no where near professional standards, but you should be able to sleep here if you want."

Caitlyn shook her head and pointed to the trailer sitting near the house, "You see that trailer right there? That is where I will be sleeping. They were supposed to hook it up to the electricity here in the house, but would you make sure that they did it correctly, please. Once there is an opening in town, I will more than likely move there, but I don't see me sleeping in this house. I will see if this house is haunted, make sure that it is cleaned up, and donate it to the historical society here in Point Creole so that they can use it for tours, etc."

"You mean you plan on spending all this money to fix it up and just donate it?"

"I find it very discomforting when I think about what Gregory did here. I want to help those poor souls that may be haunting these grounds before I sell the property. I still have not made a decision on what I will do with this place once it is completed though."

***

Later that evening, as Caitlyn walked around, she realized that she wouldn't be spending much time in this house after dark. The house still smelled of decay, dust covered much of the interior, and a good cleaning was needed. Maybe while here, some of the trapped souls would reach out to her. She has never tried to contact a ghost. She wasn't sure if this would work, but she could try.

Before leaving New Orleans, she visited one of the local voodoo shops and bought everything to help her free these lost souls. The shopkeeper even gave her sage to burn in the house as well as salt and white candles so she could properly cleanse each room. He also gave her his business card in case she needed any help with the spirits at a later time.

She hoped she could do this. She had a grandmother who claimed to be a traiteur and she hoped she has inherited some of her grandmother's powers and just didn't know it yet. She also bought an Ouija Board and everything to do a séance.

As Scott made a list of everything he needed to do, Caitlyn explored the house. She eyed a claw foot tub in one of the bathrooms and imagined running a hot bath with scented oil and bubbles to relieve all the aches from the day's activities. That would have to wait though. For now, she had to make do with the small shower in the trailer.

For a moment, Caitlyn thought she saw a reflection in the mirror. A hazy, indistinct image began to form, but then disappeared. She shook her head; it was just her imagination.

She continued to move through the house and opened windows to help air out the old house. Sunlight streamed in through tattered curtains that weaved into dancing phantom shadows around the rooms.

The sound of plodding footsteps caught Caitlyn's attention. She listened intently, trying to figure out where Scott was working as to not scare him as she continued to open the windows. Suddenly the footsteps ceased.

Moving on, she listened as the noises from the bayou filled the small bedroom. She wanted to bring happiness to this house once more. It could be such a beautiful home, and the view from this window was gorgeous. She could imagine waking up in this room and looking out on the bayou. She stepped out onto the balcony and smelled the sweet air. She noticed Scott over by the trailer checking the connections and wondered how he moved about the house so fast.

As she walked into another room, the branches of an oak tree brushed up against the window. She jotted down a note to have Scott cut back the limbs of the tree. She couldn't explain it, but it was not as cheery as the previous room. This particular room was cold and unsettling. She jotted down another note to remind herself to cleanse this room.

Suddenly, the air in the room became thick and oppressive. Footsteps sounded through the house again. The room turned frigid as the smell of cigar smoke permeated the air. The footsteps came closer and closer as they echoed throughout the entire house. The room fell deathly quiet and all she heard was the sound of her breathing.

The bedroom door slammed shut and shook the small room. Her eyes grew wide with terror, she yelled, "Who's there?"

Her rapid breath turned into a misty vapor as the room was now ice cold. She gathered enough nerve to walk over to the door and tried to open it. Even the door knob was freezing. The door creaked loudly as she opened the door, peering down the hall. Nothing but dust particles floated in the air. She speculated if she even knew what she was getting herself into.

From the hall, Caitlyn heard the front door open, "Scott, were you in here earlier?"

He called out, "No, I wanted to make sure you were all set to sleep in the trailer tonight. Are you sure you want to spend the night out here by yourself?"

At this moment, Caitlyn doubted all of her current decisions. "To be honest with you, I am starting to wonder if this was a smart move. Unfortunately, I don't have a choice. There are no rooms available in town, so this is my only option."

"What happened to have you doubting your decision?"

"I swear I heard footsteps echoing throughout the house and then a door slammed shut."

Scott looked around, "Well, you do have all the windows open. That could explain why the door blew shut. The wind is picking up out there." He scratched his head as he thought, "Look, if you are having doubts about staying here by yourself, I can stay with you."

His offer was tempting, but she responded, "I can't put you through that trouble."

"It isn't putting me out. I will be spending most of my time out here as it is. Besides, with me staying here, I can find out what needs the most work."

"Surely, you have a wife who wants you at home?"

He let out a loud laugh, "There is no wife or family waiting at home for me."

Caitlyn informed him, "I haven't checked the rooms to see if they are even livable, but for now if you want, we can share the trailer. It is big enough, but I do have to warn you that I don't sleep well at night."

"That's okay; I am an early bird. I plan to get everything set up quickly so you can sleep in the house. There is no reason to sleep in the trailer. If you are worried about my intentions, they are honorable."

Caitlyn looked up and down his body. *His intentions may be honorable, but she wasn't sure if she could trust herself around him.* "It is just my overactive imagination at work. You're probably right, and the wind blew the door closed. Maybe I let everyone in the restaurant scare me more than I realized."

"I don't believe in ghosts or an afterlife. Once we die, our souls are delivered to purgatory where we wait to enter heaven. Kind of like they say, ashes to ashes and dust to dust."

"I guess having lived in New Orleans for as long as I did I came to believe in ghosts and the supernatural."

***

Caitlyn stepped onto the front porch for some fresh air. As she looked over the grounds, she felt overwhelmed by everything there was to do here. Maybe, she should put the place up for sale as is and take the first offer that came to her. No one in this town had good feelings about this place and from what she learned today; those feelings were in place long before Gregory bought it.

Deep in thought, she made her way to the bayou. A shadow moved in behind her that caught her attention.

When she turned around, she was amazed at the sight before her. For just a moment, she saw how majestic this plantation had looked some two hundred years ago. That very image gave her the desire to restore this old place once again to its elegant status. If she closed her eyes, she saw the lush gardens buried under the kudzu and ivy vines. She could just imagine the sugar cane fields alive with workers busy working the fields.

No, she refused to allow this place to be demolished. She would make sure that this home was brought back to its former status.

A movement beside one of the oak trees caught her attention. For a fleeting moment, she thought she saw a man watching her. Giddy with excitement, she wondered if she'd seen her first ghost. She stopped and thought for just a moment and realized that it could have been a trick of light.

As she looked over the water, she noticed a sheen. There was a residue lying on top of the water and a couple dead fish floated on the water's surface. She heard that if there wasn't enough oxygen in the water that fish floated to the surface, but the weather hasn't been bad enough to cause something like this. Maybe, an alligator poacher hoped to lure one of the reptiles to the surface with a favorite snack, rotting fish. Just the thought of one of those creatures this close to the house sent shivers down her body.

She recalled a warning at the diner not to drink the town's water and wondered if they feared it was contaminated.

***

He watched the plantation from the bayou; shifting his weight from one foot to the other and ignored the cracking in his knees. He stretched his back as he tried to relieve some of the aching.

He let out a deep breath; he didn't even realize he had been holding his breath. He must be more nervous than he realized.

He then let out a silent curse. The rumors were right; someone had moved into the plantation, and it looked as if she hired a local handyman in town to help her renovate the place.

He must convince her that the house was haunted. He had searched that house for too damn long to give up now. He couldn't afford for this woman to stay out here and he sure as hell couldn't have the two of them snooping around. There was too much at stake.

***

Her eyes snapped open as she looked around. She was still trapped in the basement. She shuddered in fear as she realized she was still in this ghostly body of hers. She was merely a wisp of air; her soul naked and cowering.

Taking a deep breath, she could taste the dankness of the air. The horrible memories of what happened flooded back. If she stayed here in the darkness, maybe, he wouldn't notice her.

As a shadow passed in front of her, she knew he was back. She would be forced to relive her nightmare once again.

She waited quietly and then the awful flickering began, but this time, it was much worse.

Chapter 12

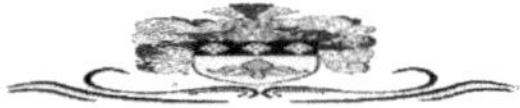

While Scott took a shower, Caitlyn slipped outside to look at the bayou by the moonlight. The glow from the moon shimmered across the water. A light breeze flirted with the long grass and dead leaves. Caitlyn listened to the gentle sloshing of the water. It would be a romantic night if it weren't so sticky with humidity.

Sitting beneath the canopy of trees, she noticed how isolated this area was. They were cut off here in this small corner of the world. It could be reassuring, but also disarming.

She studied the black water of the bayou and wondered what secrets it hid. She looked back at the plantation and suddenly felt overwhelmed. Would she be able to handle the house? She assumed it would be a few months of work, but after touring the house today, she wondered if that was even plausible with the amount of work to be done.

A misty glow formed over the dark water. Was this a strange fog or just a trick of the moonlight? The mysterious fog slowly moved across the bayou as Caitlyn watched. She was mesmerized as she watched its progression. By the time it made it to the shore, the fog had taken shape. The apparition glided across the lawn. The spirit was blurred and out of focus, but definitely a woman.

Instead of fear, Caitlyn was struck with curiosity. The spirit seemed to be unaware of Caitlyn's presence. This poor apparition was caught in some kind of loop and repeated this nightly journey without disruption.

As the woman made her way closer to Caitlyn, the face was discernible, but her eyes caught her attention. They looked haunted. "What happened to you?" Caitlyn asked, "Are you one of Gregory's poor souls?"

Instead of answering, the spirit just lifted her hands and pointed off into the distance. Caitlyn wondered what was in that direction, unable to see what she may be pointing to.

The ghost stared at Caitlyn and started talking, but her words were inaudible. "I am sorry, but I can't understand you."

Eerily, the ghost's mouth continued moving. Once again, the spirit pointed to the far off distance as if hoping Caitlyn would understand what she meant. As quickly as she appeared, she disappeared, fading into the night air. Caitlyn was left alone and wondering what the ghost tried to say and what she had pointed to.

When she entered the trailer, everything was quiet. The water from the shower no longer ran, and Scott was nowhere in sight. She tiptoed to his room door and heard nothing but silence. He must be sound asleep. She looked at her watch and realized that she had been outside longer than she planned.

She headed to the shower to wash off the dust and grime of the day. She had felt lost lately and perhaps, this project would give her a sense of what direction she wanted her life to go in.

As she maneuvered around the tiny shower, she wondered if this was what camping would be like. Her mom needed the luxuries of everyday life around her, and her dad never wanted to venture far from home. This was the first adventurous thing she had ever done.

Later, as she lay curled up in bed, her mind drifted to the plantation once again. It was a shame to see what Gregory did to the house. Underneath the remodeling he'd done to create the haunted house, this place still remained beautiful. She wished she could have seen it in its original grandeur; it must have been a sight to see.

***

Caitlyn woke up later than she wanted and let out a groan when she saw that it was almost eight o'clock. She wasn't making a good impression; Scott probably thought she was one of those women who needed her beauty sleep. She honestly hoped to be up bright and early this morning to get started on the house.

As she walked into the foyer, she heard Scott busy pounding away with his hammer. She had brought coffee, cream, and sugar into the kitchen so she could go search for Scott. The kitchen was a large expansive room that needed to be thoroughly cleaned. A layer of dust covered everything. Maybe bringing coffee into the house wasn't the smartest move just yet, but if she wanted to get any work done she needed the caffeine.

Juggling the items, she took a rag from the pile and dusted off a countertop. It may not be clean with regards to the sanitary conditions, but at least there wasn't an inch of dust on the counter anymore. This would be one of the first rooms she cleaned, especially if she wanted to cook in here. The tiny kitchen in the trailer was too confining to cook any substantial meals. This kitchen could be transformed into a gourmet chef's dream kitchen.

As she finished setting the coffee on the counter, she heard footsteps. By the sound of it, Scott was coming downstairs. She called out, "Coffee is ready."

Not hearing a response, she peered into the foyer to see that it was empty. She swore she heard someone coming downstairs though. Shrugging her shoulder, she made her way upstairs to find Scott. Halfway up, she heard footsteps on the stairs once again. This time, they sounded as if they were right behind her.

The hair on the back of her neck rose as she felt a cold breath on her shoulder. Swallowing hard, she looked back and a shiver ran through her. No one was there. Not wanting to waste any more time, she began walking upstairs once more. Suddenly, an icy cold grip reached out and grabbed her ankle. Her legs refused to move and cold air encircled her to the point of almost smothering her in its icy grip.

Her heart pounded as adrenaline rushed through her veins. She fought to free herself as whatever had her tried to pull her back down the stairs. She called out to the unknown force, "Let me go!"

She stumbled backward when strong arms grabbed her. As she regained her balance, she looked up to see Scott behind her. "What is going on?"

Shaking her head, she tried to explain, "I'm not sure. All of a sudden, it felt like someone wanted me to stay downstairs. I thought you were upstairs and was coming to tell you I had coffee in the kitchen."

"I'm working in the front parlor this morning. I heard footsteps so I came to see if you were awake."

As they headed back into the kitchen, she informed him, "I stayed up later than I intended. Normally, I am up at the crack of dawn."

Out of nowhere, a noise sounded from behind them and they both glanced backwards. Caitlyn knew for certain that the house was haunted now.

Scott looked over at her, "Should we go see what that was?"

Shaking her head, "No, it was probably just the house waking up. Let's go get some coffee."

Stifling a yawn, he replied, "Coffee does sound good."

"I wasn't sure how you took your coffee so I brought cream and sugar."

"As long as it is strong and hot, I am good."

Laughing, she said, "I hope that it is still hot."

By the time they made it to the kitchen, the coffee was lukewarm at its best. Over the coffee she'd made, they planned out their morning.

Interrupting Caitlyn's train of thought, Scott informed her, "Surprisingly, the electrical system in this old house isn't that bad. There are just a few minor tweaks needed here and there, but at least you don't have to rewire the entire house."

As Caitlyn listened to Scott talk about what needed tending to, the list seemed to be unending. Several of the columns needed replacing, and some just repaired. The porch needed to be replaced in some sections, as did the shutters on the windows. The wood floors needed to be stabilized in some places, and the floors had to be sanded, stained, and sealed. Then there was the plumbing and plaster work that had to be addressed. Scott looked her directly in the eyes, "The only good thing going for you is that the foundation is in good condition, as are the walls."

***

That afternoon, as Caitlyn cleaned the kitchen, she ignored the slamming cabinet doors. She gathered the ghosts wanted to make their presence known. Could it be that they weren't happy she was remodeling the house or something else all together?

She stayed busy in the kitchen for several hours when she heard a car coming down the driveway. She stepped out onto the porch and watched as an SUV stopped in front of the house. Once the dust settled around the vehicle, an imposing man stepped out of it. The way he carried himself had Caitlyn suspecting the man had never worked a day in his life.

***

Harlan Guillory looked at Whispering Willows Plantation with pure envy. The house should be his. If only the damn bank had loaned him the money to buy it before that maniac Gregory Ferris got his hands on it. This place would be perfect for a bed and breakfast. So many people out there wanted to stay in a haunted plantation and that could make him a fortune.

He had hoped that the ghosts would frighten the new owner away so he could buy it for cheap. Perhaps he needed to help the ghosts along in that matter. The last time he was in the place, he noticed the antiques would fetch a pretty penny. He hoped that the demented man didn't destroy them when he built his haunted house. That would be a shame.

He must convince this woman to leave. The Rougarou legend would have even more people wanting to stay out here hoping to catch sight of him. He could charge triple what rooms generally went for in this area.

***

The man moved with determination and purpose to the front porch. The glare he gave her packed a powerful punch of discontent. Caitlyn never backed down from a challenge and met the man's glassy stare head on. A scowl was plastered on his face as he looked at her accusingly. Caitlyn wondered what she'd done to piss this man off.

In a very harsh tone, he stated, "Young lady, I hear that you are now the owner of this house."

"Yes sir, this is my house."

"Well, my name is Harlan Guillory and I am president of the Historical Society here in Point Creole. I heard that you planned to fix up this plantation. I want to know what your plans are for this place; we won't have you defacing this property any more than it already is. Your boyfriend turned this place into a mockery with what he did."

Trying to smooth his ruffled feathers, "I am sorry for what Gregory did here. I plan to restore it to its natural beauty. From there, I haven't decided what I plan on doing with the property."

Scoffing at her, he replied, "You would be better off just leaving this place and forgetting that you ever saw it. Only bad things happen to those that stay here."

Shaking her head, she said firmly, "I can't do that. I want to return this place back to its original grandeur."

Pointing his finger at her, he said, "Listen here young lady, you better take heed to my warnings. Strange things happen in this house; anyone who enters this house is cursed. Even your boyfriend is dead. Is that what you want for yourself too?"

"Gregory took his life and he was not my boyfriend. Killing himself was a tragic end to his life, but it had nothing to do with the house. He probably didn't want to spend his life in prison."

Harlan shook his head, "I am telling you that the house is cursed. The house killed him."

Knowing that she wouldn't be able to convince him otherwise, she let him ramble on. She wouldn't win this argument.

With venom oozing from his eyes, he warned her, "I have my eyes on you. I will be watching your every step."

As the man stomped away to his car, a chill washed over Caitlyn. She swore someone was watching her. She cautiously looked around, praying she didn't see anyone. Her breath caught with a gasp. In the trees near the bayou, a man stared back at her. With him hiding in the shadows, it was difficult to make out his appearance. He stood motionless with his arms at his sides and had a disheveled appearance.

Scott walked out of the house, "What was all that commotion?"

"I will tell you about that later." Pointing her finger to the woods. "Look, there is a man staring at us in the woods."

"Where?"

"There, behind the large oak trees at the bayou's edge."

As soon as the man noticed Scott, he took off. Scott sprinted off towards the bayou and Caitlyn followed him as quickly as possible. It took her three steps to his one, but she couldn't let him chase after some man in the woods by himself. Maybe, it would have been better if she had just kept her mouth shut.

Looking back, Scott ordered, "Stay back. You don't know if this man is armed."

As if she would follow that order, she shouted back at him, "Neither do you."

As they made their way over to the bayou, there was no sign of the man. Looking around, Caitlyn asked, "Which way do you think he went?"

"I'm not sure where he went. It is as if he disappeared into thin air."

Caitlyn noticed how quiet it was; even the birds were silent. With it being this quiet, they should hear the man running, but there was no noise.

As if he knew what Caitlyn was going to suggest Scott said, "Don't even say that it may be a ghost. Whoever it was more than likely had a boat nearby and took off as soon as he could."

Listening once more, Caitlyn responded, "I don't hear an engine though. Do you?"

Shaking his head, he started back to the plantation, "Maybe, it was just a trick of light, and there was no one there."

Not wanting to lose this argument, Caitlyn said, "I know I saw someone, and you saw him too."

Holding his hands up in surrender, he laughed, "You're not going to let this go are you?"

Shaking her head, she firmly replied, "No!"

"Yes, I did see something, but maybe it was a deer. It was hard to make out the shape." Laughing as he tried to break the tension in the air, he jested, "Hell, maybe we just saw the infamous Rougarou."

Now he'd piqued her curiosity, she asked, "What is a Rougarou?"

"It is an old folktale here. The Rougarou is said to prowl the swamps around Louisiana. It is rumored to be a creature with a human body and the head of a wolf or dog. My grandfather told me the Rougarou lived in the bayou and came to get you if you misbehaved."

"Great, just what I need - something else to worry about. As if a serial killer ghost isn't bad enough."

Looking at her apologetically, Scott said, "I'm sorry. I didn't mean to scare you more than you are right now. I was trying to lighten the mood; I honestly have no idea who was out here. It may have been a local, curious about what was going on, or even a fisherman. You have to keep in mind that this plantation has been vacant for a while. Word spreads like wildfire around here, and I am sure people will be curious as to what is going on here."

"I suppose you are right. I already had one visit this morning."

Scott looked at her sympathetically, "Who came by this morning?"

"A man in an SUV stopped by claiming to be the head of the Historical Society. He was adamant that the house was cursed and that I should leave."

Scott responded, "That was more than likely Harlan Guillory. He didn't want Gregory Ferris to buy the plantation in the first place. Rumor has it he had tried to purchase the plantation for a while, but could never get a loan. I guess the bank didn't want to lend anyone money to buy this house."

Intrigued Caitlyn said, "I wonder why?"

"I guess it has something to do with the condition of the house. They were probably afraid that the buyer would find out how much it would cost to repair this house and abandon it once again. It happened several times in the past, which is why it was up for foreclosure. When Gregory Ferris offered them cash, they greedily accepted his offer. Even though he paid less than what Harlan offered, it was a huge headache off of their shoulders. They said that as soon as Harlan found out he was fuming mad. He even stormed into the bank and withdrew his money. He still refuses to do business with them."

Caitlyn let out a deep sigh, "So, basically, I have pissed off the wrong man. He will more than likely make my life miserable."

"He may try, but he won't have a leg to stand on. As far as I know, this house was never registered with the Historical Society."

Caitlyn nodded in agreement, "That is one of the first things that I checked. I had a feeling for Gregory to turn it into a haunted house that the plantation was not registered with them."

"To be honest with you, the whole town was skeptical about the haunted house, but they also knew that it would bring in tourists."

Looking back to the bayou, Caitlyn asked, "What do you say we take a break and go into town to get something to eat?"

Caitlyn left out the fact that she had no desire to work in the house after dark. She wondered if she would ever build up the nerve to work in the house late at night, especially alone.

As they headed to the trailer to clean up, Caitlyn looked back once more. She let out a sigh of relief when she didn't see anyone. Unfortunately, that relief was short lived. While pulling away from the house, she noticed the man standing in the same spot watching them. A shudder of fear moved through her body, but instead of telling Scott, she kept her mouth shut. Why was he watching the plantation or could he be watching her?

On the drive into town, her mind wandered back to her experience on the stairs. So much happened to her today; she started off with a ghostly encounter and then being watched by the man in the woods.

Who could the man be and why watch her from the shadows? If he was curious, it seemed he would have done just like Harlan Guillory and flat out asked her what she was up to. Instead, he hid in the shadows and watched. The place was eerie enough and then to think of someone watching her gave her the creeps.

Could it have been a ghost? After all, he seemed to vanish into thin air.

As they pulled up to the front of the house after dinner, Caitlyn surveyed the area once more, searching the darkness for the mysterious figure. Was he still out there watching their every movement? Did he plan to wait until they were asleep to make his move?

The following morning Caitlyn woke up bright and early. Needing to get out of her cramped confines, she poured a cup of coffee and stepped out of the trailer.

She watched as the sun rose over the bayou, casting shades of pink, orange, and yellow over the area. She breathed in the air, catching the rich scent of pine and damp earth. The warm sun hitting her face felt welcoming.

The scenery lifted her mood and took her mind off of the problems she had yesterday. She tossed and turned most of the night wondering if she had bitten off more than she could chew. Her mother used to tell her that her eyes were bigger than her stomach and perhaps this time she was right.

Anxious to look through the treasures in the attic, she walked upstairs. As soon as she opened the door to the attic, it looked as if someone was recently in the room. Dust floated in the air, and she saw that there were large footprints in the dust on the floor; footprints that were too large for a woman or child.

The realization made it hard to breathe as terror swept through her body. She grabbed onto the railing of the stairs as she forced herself to calm down. A ghost wouldn't leave footprints. Sure, she heard footsteps, but so far, the ghosts she saw in the house almost glided and didn't actually walk.

For a moment, she considered finding Scott, but then had second thoughts. When she came back with Scott, the person would be gone.

She carefully looked around the room, the whole time her heart pounded in her ears. She searched every nook and cranny, only to find no evidence of anyone hiding in the attic. Shrugging her shoulders, she decided it had to have been a ghost.

Finding the footprints in the attic had Caitlyn second guessing her decision to explore up here this morning. Instead, she headed back into the kitchen and grabbed a bucket along with the cleaner. She may as well clean one of the guest bathrooms upstairs. The hard task of cleaning years of grime from the bathtub, sink, floor, and commode was not fun. Slowly but surely, one of the bathrooms became clean. The beauty of it caught her by complete surprise. Little renovation needed to be done to this bathroom. The floors were beautiful twelve inch rich ivory with thin beige ribbons of Carrera marble tiles. The shower and tub combo had the same marble tiles for the wall. The commode needed replacing, but the pedestal sink was in fantastic condition. The frame around the mirror was an ornate piece of work. Even the wainscoting in this bathroom held up well over time.

Anxious to see if any of the other bathrooms were in the same condition, she continued cleaning. As she scrubbed the walls of the tub, she felt someone watching her every move. She turned her head and saw the bloody stump of a young woman standing in the corner of the bathroom.

She swallowed down the lump of fear caught in her throat. The disfigured woman slowly used her hands to pull herself closer to Caitlyn, and she left a bloody trail behind her. Caitlyn stood and bit back a scream as she saw a figure appear in the mirror; it was the reflection of Gregory. He had a sinister smile on his face as he watched the woman move toward Caitlyn.

Unable to stop herself, she screamed in hysteria, jumping backwards to get out of the way of the woman. She used her hands for support to keep herself from falling into the tub. In the next instant, Gregory's reflection and the dismembered woman disappeared. However, the smell of blood remained heavy in the air, even though there were no signs of blood on the floor.

Caitlyn stood there shaking for a few seconds when Scott came rushing into the bathroom. "Are you all right? I heard you screaming all the way downstairs."

Stuttering she said, "I... I... I'm sorry. A roach jumped out from the drain in the tub and scared me half to death." Caitlyn tried to play it off as best as she could, hoping he wouldn't see what was really in her mind.

Scott looked at her with skepticism, "A roach huh?"

Caitlyn acted as if just thinking of the roach sent a shiver up her body, "Well, it was a big one, and I didn't expect it."

"If you say so. If you need anything, just give me a holler."

Nodding her head, Caitlyn sat on the commode while she tried to get ahold of her emotions. She could feel the fear emanating from the young girl. At first, it had been sheer confusion as to why she was here, but when she saw the reflection of Gregory in the mirror, that confusion turned to terror.

After a few minutes, the fear of what she'd witnessed subsided and she finished cleaning the bathroom in record time.

Once she finished, she decided that she'd had enough excitement for a while. She called out to Scott, "I am going to take a break, fix a snack, and grab a drink if you want anything."

Scott called out from upstairs, "I will be there in a minute."

As they ate the club sandwiches that Caitlyn prepared, she looked around the kitchen. She was still unsure what she wanted to do with it. She knew that she wanted to keep the butler's pantry as it was an integral part of the plantation's history.

This room may be one of their hardest challenges. It needed new appliances and cabinets. Maybe, she would take time off to look at appliances and tile. A few of the ceiling tiles needed replacing as well. She might have a hard time finding replacement tiles. The old hardware store in town may be able to help her locate them.

***

He plunged deeper into the underbrush as he made his way
to his hiding spot. Briars grabbed at his jeans as a bolt of
lightning streaked overhead. He prayed that the rain held
off for a little longer. As the smell of decaying leaves hit his
nose, he wrinkled it. The deeper he moved into the swamp,
the spongier the ground became. He had to move carefully
to avoid slipping and falling in the foul smelling muck. He
let out a curse as a clump of sodden moss smacked him
straight in the face.

A loud clap of thunder boomed in the night. He peered up
at the black sky fearing that the rain would break free from
its confines at any moment. Up ahead, he spotted a pair of
red eyes and he prayed it was a nutria rat and not an
alligator. A low growl came from the bushes, and he shined
his light in its direction. Nothing moved; yet, he remained
motionless, not even taking the chance to breath.
Suddenly, the trees seemed to close in around him as he
waited to see what lurked in the bushes. He slowly exhaled
the breath he held as the alligator dropped into the bayou.
That was a little too close for comfort. He cursed himself
for coming into the swamp unarmed; he knew better. He
let out a muttered curse as he confirmed that she was still
in the plantation. He needed that woman and her new
friend out of there. It would be more beneficial to him if
she was out of Point Creole all together. He had hoped
hearing footsteps in the house would be enough to send her
running. So far, she brushed it off as ghosts and stayed. He
would have to step up his efforts if he wanted her out of
there. If they found out his secret, there would be hell to

pay. Just the fear of her finding out what was hidden there sent his blood pressure boiling.

Chapter 13

She rose from the bayou and drifted across the swamp like a mournful song of lost love; her long white gown trailed behind her. Fingers of fog snaked their way between the trees and reached out before her as tall blades of grass bowed to her natural beauty. Dawn stretched itself along the horizon; the sun eager to bring forth the light and as the ghost moved to the sad tune, the notes eerily carried her upon the breeze. She seemed to be part of a dream, elusive, and just out of reach.

Caitlyn watched as she danced across the grounds; her bare feet rose above the ground and her hair fluttered in the breeze. She moved closer to the plantation, humming a tune that carried in the night air. The faint and haunting tune gently escaped the tightness of her pale lips. She looked back to the bayou with a longing on her face as if searching for someone.

When she turned back to face the plantation, there was an expression of pure grief. She held her arms out in front of her as if waiting for a long lost lover, closed her eyes, and let out a low moan.

The rising sun neared the distant horizon as soft pink and orange hues streaked the dark sky. The moon bright and full above paled in comparison to the growing illumination. As soon as the sun made its way over the horizon, she was gone.

Caitlyn looked around once more hoping to see the ghost. Maybe, she imagined the woman rising from the bayou. She pinched herself to make sure that she was awake and not dreaming.

She walked along the bayou to find any evidence of the woman's footprints. A shiver ran down her spine as a frigid breeze blew across the bayou. This was where the woman rose from the bayou's depths.

A haunting tune had awakened Caitlyn from a restless sleep. Curious to see where it came from, she went outside. That was when Caitlyn saw the woman rising from the murky bayou's depths.

There was no pause or hesitation in the young woman's movements as she drifted onto the land. It was as if something called out to her, almost beckoning her to its cold embrace. Caitlyn stared out across the bayou wondering what secrets were forever trapped beneath its murky waters.

As Caitlyn made her way back to the plantation, she wondered who the ghostly woman was. For a moment, Caitlyn just stared at the plantation. The darkened windows held a sense of foreboding and gloom within those walls.

***

He watched her every move, using the trees as his cover, and being careful where he stepped. He couldn't make a sound and alert her to his presence.

He was pleased to see her alone. A soft breeze from the bayou carried her sweet scent over to him. As he moved closer to her, a twig snapped behind him and he pressed deeper into the shadows. With his heart racing, he peered from the shadows to see if anyone followed him.

***

A branch cracked from somewhere behind her. She turned around and peered deeper into the darkness. The eerie sound of the wind blowing through the trees was unsettling tonight. She shivered and became aware of her isolation.

She should know better than coming out here alone. The hair on the back of her neck stood on end, and her skin had goosebumps running up and down her body. She swore someone was watching her. She fixed her gaze on where she heard the noise, but there was no movement that caught her attention. Perhaps, it was just a bird or some other creature scurrying about.

She hurried back to the house, not wanting to think about the ghost.

***

Caitlyn tossed and turned for a while before sleep wrapped her in its warm embrace. The sound of a hammer woke her. Her head throbbed from tossing and turning most of the early morning hours. She pulled the pillow over her head and burrowed deeper into the mattress. The air around her became frigid. Not in the mood to deal with another ghost, she threw back the covers and got out of bed.

She walked out of the trailer to find Scott busy working on the front porch of the plantation. "Morning, sleepyhead. I hope I didn't wake you."

"I guess it is past time for me to wake up. I had a visit early this morning from a ghost who must live on the bayou. Surprisingly, I haven't seen too many of Gregory's victims yet. I wonder why that is?"

"Maybe, they moved on after his death; that is if there is such a thing as ghosts."

She let out a laugh, "If you had been with me this morning, you would have become a true believer. The woman appeared to be from the late eighteen hundreds from the way she dressed. She hummed such a sad tune. It looked as if she was searching the grounds for a lost love." She shook her head to break her out of her reverie, "I guess I better get us breakfast cooked and start cleaning."

Scott looked down at his watch, "Don't you mean lunch?"

She let out a small gasp, "Did I sleep that late?"

"Relax, I am only teasing you. It is going on nine."

As she made her way down the steps, she lost her balance. Acting quickly, Scott caught her by the waist and pulled her to him. The look he gave her could melt a glacier, and the silence thickened as his unrelenting stare missed nothing in her eyes. Powerless to fight the need rising inside of her, she wrapped her arms around his neck and pulled him to her. His chest was rock hard and welcoming. Looking into his eyes, she whispered, "We shouldn't be doing this."

Shaking his head, he replied, "No, you are right. This could complicate matters."

Caitlyn told him, "I don't want this."

Scott smiled at her, "Neither do I."

They were both lying to each other; she saw the desire in his eyes. Her eyes showed the same passion; there was a glow that matched the fire burning inside of her. The flame rapidly spread through her body, making her want him more than she'd ever wanted a man.

His arms curved around her back, clutching her as if he never wanted her to leave his arms. She didn't want him to let her go, not until he doused the flame inside of her.

He whispered in her ear, "If you don't want this, then you have to stop me." He touched her lips with his. With a desperate moan, she greedily accepted his kiss. He tasted as if he was made for sin.

His gentle seduction sent her pulse racing. Not wanting the kiss to end, she ran her hands through his hair and deepened the kiss.

As they ended the kiss, Caitlyn looked deep into Scott's eyes and saw the passion he felt for her. It turned her blood to hot lava. As he pulled her closer; she felt his erection pressing into her body, his hardness pushed into her softness. Every nerve in her responded to his touch. For the first time in a long time, she contemplated a romantic relationship. Swallowing hard, she said, "I guess I should get in the kitchen and cook us something to eat before we starve to death."

He let his hands drop from her waist, and she instantly missed their warmth, "And I guess I should finish this porch before it collapses." Looking into her eyes, he warned her,

"You do know that people will talk about us. This is a small town and people tend to gossip."

She smiled up at him, "Let them talk. I don't care what people have to say. Anyway, I am sure most of the people are talking about how you are such a gentleman to sleep in a haunted house with a crazy woman who dated a serial killer."

He let out a laugh, "I don't think they are calling me a gentleman by any means."

"Well, then they are calling us both crazy."

As Caitlyn headed inside the house, she looked back at Scott once more. She wondered what he would do if she turned around and jumped into his arms. Instead, she made her way to the kitchen to whip them up something to eat. Maybe cooking would take her mind off her out of control libido.

While pulling eggs and buttermilk out of the fridge for pancakes, the lights flickered. She suddenly felt overwhelmed with a sense of nervousness. Why would the electricity flicker now when there wasn't a cloud in the sky?

A blast of cold air puckered her skin as she preheated the griddle. She heard a noise coming from the basement and rubbed her arms at the thought of venturing down those stairs. She slowly opened the door and saw nothing but darkness. She flicked the light switch, but nothing happened. The light bulb must have blown; they had a lot of trouble with the light bulbs blowing lately.

A voice rose from the basement, "Help me."

A shiver ran down her spine. Did she just hear a ghost asking for help?

Suddenly, a howl echoed from somewhere in the basement. That was not just the mere wind. Its tone changed and turned to a shrill pitch that hurt Caitlyn's ears. She covered her ears just as the air in front of her began to sway. The darkness pulsated with life around her, and the air became icy cold against her skin.

At the bottom of the stairs, a hazy vapor took form. The shape changed from a swirling outline of smoke and light to that of a young, but haggard, woman. Her dark brown hair appeared stringy, and her face contorted into a mask of pain. As the woman dragged herself up the stairs, her complexion transformed into black, decomposing flesh. Her hair fell in clumps; the dank smell of death filled the air.

Caitlyn was paralyzed in fear as the young woman pointed a blackened skeletal finger at her, "Leave this place. Do not come down here. He means for you to join us; he wants you to join him for eternity. You must get away from here!"

Caitlyn tried to back away from the doorway, but her legs wouldn't move. She began to feel woozy and dizzy. A black mist enveloped Caitlyn, pulsing with evil. A noise emitted from deep inside the house; it was as if a thousand discordant voices cried out in pain.

Scott heard the cries of anguish and came rushing in just in time to see Caitlyn fall down the stairs. He rushed to grab her before she fell and was startled to find her ice cold.

"Are you all right?"

Caitlyn looked up at him with confusion in her eyes, "Yeah, I thought I heard a noise in the basement, and must have lost my footing."

Scott looked at her skeptically, "Why don't I go check it out for you?"

Shaking her head, she said, "No, that's okay. Besides, I've been anxious to explore the attic."

After they ate breakfast and she cleaned the dishes, they walked upstairs to the attic. As they rummaged through the attic, he looked around, "Look at all this stuff. I'm surprised there is still this much stuff here."

"I have a feeling Gregory never bothered with anything up here. It looks as if the items were stored up here for years and no one looked to see what was up here. Instead, they just piled more stuff in the space."

"Where do you even start?"

Caitlyn looked around, "I'm not even sure, but I did see an old trunk that seemed to be almost buried in the corner back there."

As they dragged the trunk out of its hiding place, they stirred up dust, "Whew, it's probably been years since anyone has been up in here."

Caitlyn fanned the dust from her face, "As long as we don't find any bodies, I will be fine."

She gasped in delight as they opened the trunk. There were old clothes and letters inside the trunk as well as old photographs. Near the bottom of the trunk was what appeared to be an old leather satchel.

Caitlyn looked at the dates on the letters to see that they were all dated around the turn of the century. There were also several old newspaper clippings, ledgers, and invoices. Caitlyn became giddy with excitement when she found two journals, one written by a Jean Paul Favre and one simply with the initial "C" etched on it. "I wonder if these could be diaries of their lives. I can't wait to read them."

Scott looked around the room, "Did you want to see what else is hidden here or do you want to check out the journals?"

"Let's see if there are any more treasures hidden up here while we can."

They found a smaller trunk with a lock on it. It took Scott a few minutes before he could jimmy the lock open. Scott excitedly exclaimed, "These are journals showing that the property was indeed part of the Underground Railroad. It looks as if old Jean Paul kept meticulous records on each and every slave that passed through here. He documented the names of the runaway slaves he helped."

Caitlyn looked over his shoulder and pointed out in excitement, "Look, he even wrote down which plantation the slaves came from. This may prove helpful for anyone who wants to find their roots. It will be a great collector's item."

A comfortable silence fell between them as they continued to go through the remaining pages. This was so exciting for

Caitlyn; of course, when she learned about the Underground Railroad in school it seemed so far away and long ago. To Caitlyn, it had always been a fairy tale. It never felt real until now.

Scott flipped through the journal hoping to find out more information. He closed the journal in disappointment, "I had hoped that he would have mentioned other stops on the Underground Railroad, but he didn't. Several other towns in Louisiana were part of the Underground Railroad, including Morgan City, which isn't too far from here."

Caitlyn reminded him, "Yeah, but they had to keep it a secret where the next stop would be."

Scott picked up another ledger and realized that this one was used for cargo that came in and out of the plantation. As Caitlyn looked at the dates, she went back to the ledger with the slave names. She showed Scott, "Look some of the deliveries coincide with the dates of the slaves' arrival and departure. Sometimes the slaves would hide in the cotton going north."

As Caitlyn picked up the journal, disappointment ran through her, "It seems to be written in French. I will have to find someone who can help us translate it." Scott paused for just a moment, "Most of the older people know how to speak the language, but when it comes to reading, they have a hard time. You may have a hard time finding someone that can translate Jean Paul Favre's style of writing."

Excitement built inside of Caitlyn. There was definitely a mystery to this house, and she hoped to solve it. She came to free the souls of Gregory's victims trapped here, but it had now turned into something so much more. She must find out the history of this house and the people who lived here. There had to be something from the past that would help with the events in the present.

Caitlyn glanced over at Scott to check him out. He looked unbelievably sexy this morning and smelled even better. He wore a pair of blue jeans that appeared to be made for his body and a T-shirt that showed off his muscular chest and arms. She tried to shake off the fog of lust that took over her mind.

Scott looked over at her suddenly and asked, "Is something wrong?"

She swallowed the knot in her throat, "It's just that... Well... I was distracted by how studious you look."

Scott let out a sexy little laugh, "You know what Caitlyn?" Her breath caught as he leaned in closer to her and whispered, "So do you."

Her heart was stammering now and she drew in a deep breath, catching a heady scent of Scott's rich maleness. Scott closed the small gap between them and pressed his mouth to hers. She parted her lips and met his tentative kiss. As the kiss ended, Caitlyn already missed his lips on hers.

Scott hated ending the kiss. Hunger clawed at him; he wanted to feast, to taste every inch of her. Not wanting this feeling to end, he took her in his arms and pulled her closer. Heat skimmed along her nerves as his hands slid up and down her body. Any objection she may have had floated away with his kisses. Later, she may be sorry, but for now, she couldn't resist him.

She let out a low, throaty moan as he nibbled on her neck. Warmth filled her deep inside, flaming up higher and higher. His lips took hers once more and passion ignited in her body. As his hands moved up and down her spine, her body melted into his. Her body became a vessel for passion; she vibrated with need and her blood simmered with desire.

As his hands slid over her breasts, her legs turned to liquid. Her breath caught as his hands slipped underneath her shirt. He cupped her breasts and squeezed softly. As his fingers teased her nipples, she shivered with delight. His touch felt so good that she wanted it to go on forever.

Chapter 14

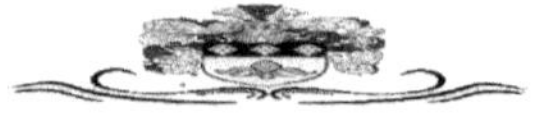

Lindsey Miller curled up in the recliner and made herself comfortable. The man seemed nice enough when he approached her. He was another do-gooder who believed he could make her see the light, and she had no problems with taking his charity. By the time he realized that he couldn't change her, she would be long gone, but until then, she planned on milking this for as long as she could.

This guy was nicer than others who offered to put a roof over her head for a night. At first, she took him for another nervous john, but soon after climbing into his car, she realized he honestly thought he could help her. She almost laughed in front of him at the thought, but stopped herself at the last minute.

She assumed he lived nearby, but it took a while to get to his house. That put a kink in her plans for the evening. It would take longer to get back to the city. Hopefully, she would get lucky and hitch a ride with someone.

She sipped the water he gave her, wishing it was beer instead. The shrimp po'boy he promised convinced her to go with him. She couldn't remember her last hot meal; most of her food came from what people threw away from uneaten meals. It surprised her how much food people wasted, but she quickly learned not to be picky or she would starve to death.

She turned on the TV and flipped through the channels. It had been a while since she stayed in a place where she could watch TV. When she was younger, she had big dreams. She dreamed of being a famous movie star, making lots of money. She had a hard time in school and even more difficult time memorizing lines. No matter how many auditions she went to, she would always flop. No one wanted to hire someone who couldn't memorize even a simple line. Her modeling career didn't pan out either. Most photographers found her boobs too big, and the ones that offered her money were interested in nudes.

That was how she became involved in this business. Nude photo shoots soon led to her accepting money for sex. From there, she became hooked on drugs, which resulted in the need for more money to buy those drugs. It became a vicious cycle that caused her dreams to come crashing down.

Some days she wished she could go back home. She would tell her parents how sorry she was and that she now understood their reasoning behind the rules and discipline. Had her parents even missed her or were they glad to be rid of her?

The room became hazy, and she found herself falling asleep on the couch. She tried to ask the man, who looked more like a woman, where her room was, but instead, her words were slurred and hard to understand.

He must have understood her, "Are you ready to go to bed?"

She could only find the strength to nod her head in agreement. He helped her to her feet, and she stumbled through the house leaning on him more and more for support. He was stronger than he looked.

She tried to focus on the furnishings in the room. If only she could stop the room from spinning, but it was easier to close her eyes. Instead of placing her on a bed, she felt cold vinyl hitting the bare skin on her legs. She was too weak to fight him as he restrained her wrists and ankles to the chair. Her heart pounded in her chest as fear washed over her, causing her head to spin even faster.

As she lost consciousness, she felt her clothes being cut off. She was fearful of what he would do to her. Even in the line of business she was in, she had never been raped.

He arranged his tools on the cart. His mother had her salon here, and now it was his. The room had all the tools he needed for his work. He was most proud of his recent find, coolers from a local flower shop. The lady didn't even ask him why he needed them.

Unable to help himself, he ran his hands through the girl's hair. It was lustrous, shiny, and silky to the touch. He bent down and inhaled the apple infused shampoo she used. He had chosen a better shampoo for her, one that would make her hair perfect. Soon, she wouldn't be able to look at him with that condemning, haughty look. She couldn't tempt him with her sinfully alluring long hair.

In the cooler, he had each of his masterpieces stored. His mother never allowed him to style hair, but since her death, he could do as he desired. He never wanted to hurt anyone. If only he could live his life as he wanted to, he wouldn't have to do this. His life didn't turn out the way he wanted it to.

He splurged recently on an internet purchase. He found the perfect mannequin heads and bought the lot. He could make them up and include his wig. He couldn't wait to find the perfect hair for each of them. Each day, he took out the mannequin heads and styled the hair as he saw fit.

The other day at the supermarket, he found his newest client. He found her hair perfect, although her face was flawed. He wanted her lustrous shoulder length and wavy hair. He tingled with anticipation at the thought of styling her hair, and he became anxious to run his hands in the silkiness of it. She sat before him with duct tape sealing her mouth closed and zip strips restraining her arms and legs to the chair. She reeked of fear; its sharp, tangy scent had a powerful effect on him. The terror was clearly evident in her eyes.

"I can't tell you how thrilled I am to be given this opportunity." He picked up a lock of her hair and let it fall from his fingers.

Her eyes widened in fear as tears streamed down her cheeks. "This shop belonged to my mother, but it is mine now. Mother didn't like me helping her in here. She kept telling me that she wanted me to make more out of my life. I think it had a lot to do with my dad; he didn't think being a hair dresser was manly."

She felt nausea rumble in the pit of her stomach. He looked over her body; he was usually only interested in their face and hair, but he couldn't resist watching her breasts rise and fall with each breath she took.

She trembled with fear as he picked up one of his surgical instruments. Grateful that the drugs he gave her kicked in and she slipped into the darkness that had lured her from the beginning.

As he began the delicate work, her sightless emerald green eyes stared up at him, accusingly. Unable to work with her looking at him, he closed her eyes and finished what he started.

***

As he brought her body to the bayou, a noise echoed through the trees. An early morning fisherman must be on his way to beat the impending heat and humidity of another scorching summer day.

He heard the motor of the truck moving closer. Sweat broke out on his forehead as he listened to the truck approach.

Knowing he didn't have the time to bring her further, he dropped her and slipped into the nearby woods. He emerged into a clearing where his parked truck sat waiting.

Chapter 15

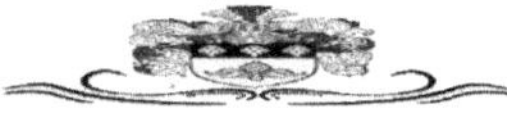

Summer gripped Point Creole by the throat and slowly strangled it with a vicious grip. One could fault the heat and curse the humidity, but Detective Tony Bertrand knew that the weather wasn't to blame for the suffocating pall. Evil once again settled over the city and spread its tentacles of misery as far as it could reach.

He hoped that they could keep this latest murder under tight wraps for as long as possible. Once it became known that another murder occurred, all hell would break loose once again.

Bertrand guided his truck along the flooded highway and parked behind the police cruiser. That's when he saw the crime scene was already cordoned off.

He settled his hat on his head and walked towards the boat landing where the remains of a woman were discovered. Bertrand carried his height with a forceful stride that made his stature seem even more intimidating. Women had always found him irresistible, but he had yet to find one who captured his attention.

He winced at the expression of dread on the young, rookie cop's face. "I take it you were first on the scene?" Bertrand asked.

"Yes, sir. A boater called it in. He went to launch his boat and found her. The scene is right out of a slasher movie, sir."

Looking at the young officer, Bertrand told him, "Make sure that those nosy reporters stay back."

"Yes, sir."

The rain didn't help either; it may have washed away most of their trace evidence, but it couldn't wash away the evil that had selected this town to stain with blood once again. Unfortunately, the smell of blood was still heavy in the air.

Bertrand noticed that forensics was already on the scene and busy taking photographs of the remains, along with the crime scene. His partner, Detective Morvant, walked the scene looking for evidence left behind by the killer. They had worked many scenes over the years, and he was superb at what he did.

Morvant and Bertrand were as different as night and day, but somehow, they made great partners. Morvant was a little green and saw everything in black and white. He was not jaded enough to see the various shades of gray. It wouldn't be long though before seeing the violence this world had to offer would change his mind about mankind.

He approached the coroner, Dr. LeBlanc, hunched over what remained of the victim. Things were returning to normal in Point Creole and now this. Bertrand sure hoped that they weren't dealing with another killer.

"What do we have Doc?" Bertrand asked, almost worried about the response.

"I don't think you want this leaking out. The killer knew exactly what he wanted from our victim. I've never seen anything like it."

"I heard it was bad."

Dr. LeBlanc replied, "Oh, it's one for the record books. He removed her face and scalped her with sheer perfection. He waited for her to bleed out beforehand. The young woman was gutted just like a hunted animal."

As Morvant finished his appraisal of the crime scene, he walked over to the body to join Doc and his partner. Morvant found it difficult to keep his lunch down; he felt even more queasy when he looked at the victim. This was one of the worst cases he'd ever worked, and he had worked some pretty severe cases in the past.

Looking down at this body caused Bertrand's stomach to churn. Bertrand felt a chill reach his soul. Someone had peeled away her face and hair with surgical precision. "Douce mère de Mary de Dieu." As he looked at the body once more, an anxious feeling gnawed at him, deep in the pit of his stomach. He noticed ligature marks on her wrists and ankles. "How long has she been dead?"

As Dr. LeBlanc finished securing paper bags on each of the woman's hands, he answered, "Full rigor hasn't set in yet. Liver temp indicates about four hours. With this heat, it could be longer though. I will know more when I get her on the table." As he covered the body, he replied, "Right now, very few people know the details about the body. We should keep this quiet for as long as possible."

"Mais oui, this will create a panic throughout the town."

Bertrand noticed Morvant had difficulty looking at the body. Morvant nodded his head in agreement, "Mais, this needs to be kept quiet."

Dr. LeBlanc looked at the victim, "I will perform the autopsy myself so that we know the details are contained."

Looking at the corpse sent chills down Bertrand's spine. "Were there any signs of rape?"

"Nope. None that I can tell. I have an intuitive feeling this killer was interested in one thing and one thing only--her face and scalp. I wish I could say why."

Bertrand surveyed the crime scene. Even if the rain washed away most of it, there would still be some blood at the scene, "This wasn't the kill site. There is no blood and with this rain I doubt forensics will find any trace evidence."

Bertrand asked Dr. LeBlanc, "Did you find any trace evidence on the body?"

"A few fibers were found, but nothing remarkable or distinctive. I will have those rushed to forensics for you. There were no hairs, bite marks, nor any defensive wounds noted on the body either. Exsanguination is the cause of death."

Bertrand guessed the woman was at least lucky she had been dead before he massacred her face. Anger built up inside of him, but he forced it back down; he couldn't let anger cloud his judgment. They were searching for a serial killer, and other women's lives may hang in the balance. He wanted no mistakes in this investigation. Bertrand suspected that this was the work of someone who had killed before and would kill again.

Bertrand and Morvant walked over to the witness. The man's face was pale and his hands were shaky, but that was only natural after witnessing something as grotesque as he had. Unfortunately, he didn't see anything that helped them identify the killer.

***

Bertrand and Morvant made it to the morgue a few minutes before the autopsy was scheduled to begin. Upon entering, they both noticed the drop in temperature. The chill seemed to hang onto every breath they took just as death clung onto the victim.

Morvant confided in his partner, "This place still gives me the creeps."

Bertrand just nodded as he adjusted to the surrounding smells. Before entering the autopsy room, they peered through the viewing window to make sure that Dr. LeBlanc was ready for them. Inside the room, the latest victim, or what remained of her, was laid out with a white sheet pulled up to where her chin was supposed to be.

A visible shudder moved through Dr. LeBlanc as he set out his instruments. As he pushed the sheet down to start the autopsy, it was all Morvant could do to keep from losing his lunch on the autopsy room floor. Working the crime scene had been bad, but it was much worse looking at the grotesque mutilation of the body under the harsh lights of an autopsy.

Morvant just shook his head and asked while walking into the autopsy room, "What kind of monster can do this to another human being?"

Bertrand looked over at him grimly, "Another human being unfortunately."

Dr. LeBlanc informed the detectives, "This young lady was in relatively good health. We will have to wait until the tox screens come back, but it is safe to say that he sedated her and used one swift incision to eviscerate her. He is good; he knew where to cut so that she bled out fast. You are looking for someone that has smaller, more delicate hands because of the precision used in the removal of her face and hair." Handing Bertrand a scalpel Dr. LeBlanc said, "Here, hold this and see how easy it is for you to hold."

With a little bit of maneuvering, Bertrand found a comfortable grip on the scalpel. Dr. LeBlanc stepped into his office and brought out an apple, "Now, try to peel this apple with the same precision he used to remove her face."

After several attempts, Bertrand threw the scalpel and apple in the sink, "I give up. Your point is taken. Bigger hands just make it harder to cut with that much precision."

Dr. LeBlanc replied, "I wouldn't rule it out, but I believe you are dealing with a small man or even a woman. That could explain the sedation. A larger man would have manhandled a woman, but this killer may need an upper hand."

The two detectives told the good doctor goodbye and left him to his work. He would attempt to put her back together as best as he could, but there wasn't anything for the family to identify. They would have to wait for a match from fingerprints or dental records to confirm their victim's identity.

So far, they had kept the gruesome details out of the paper. Thankfully, the person who discovered this body was too shaken up to repeat anything about the case, but it wouldn't be long before something was leaked to the press. When that happened, the shit would hit the fan.

Right now, they had to wait until the killer made a mistake. Bertrand looked over at Morvant, "How many more women must die before he makes a mistake and leaves us a clue?"

***

Bertrand thought he knew what hell was, but that had been before he told Lindsey Miller's parents about their daughter's death. It had been pure hell to watch the light of hope dying in their eyes. They'd hoped their daughter would come back home and apologize for running away. Instead, she came home to be laid to rest.

It was devastating to watch Mrs. Miller crumple to the ground in tears; her face ravaged with grief. It took all of his strength to accept Mr. Miller's outstretched hand as he thanked him for letting them know what happened to their daughter.

Bertrand had made notifications before, but it never got any easier. Every time, it was a punch in the stomach, almost as if somebody had ripped out his own heart.

He let out a shaky breath and blinked his tired eyes as he tried to concentrate on the computer screen in front of him.

He'd just finished entering the information in VICAP and prayed that he received a hit where this killer had struck before. This was not the first kill; he had been too precise with his killing for a newbie.

***

The next morning, Bertrand let out a deep sigh as he gazed at the computer screen. He still couldn't believe he'd struck out. There were no murders reported anywhere in the country that resembled the way his victim was mutilated and killed. He found plenty of serial killers that collected fingers, locks of hair and personal items, but from what he could tell, this MO did not exist.

He looked at Morvant as he made his way to his desk, "I find it hard to believe that this killer didn't show up on any of the sites. This guy didn't just start killing with this much precision."

Morvant shrugged his shoulders, "Who knows? Perhaps, he hid the bodies before now."

Bertrand rubbed his temples. He felt a monster of a migraine coming on.

***

He had closed the curtains to the windows before he pulled out his treasure. He carried the mannequin's head over to his work station and brushed its hair. Once her hair was perfect, he brought her back to his collection.

A grin formed on his face as he looked at his prizes. He had never felt this much pride. His first efforts were unsuccessful; he quickly discovered that he needed more than the hair. There was something about removing the whole face that he found satisfying.

Surprisingly, he learned most of what he needed to know at his public library and the internet. Of course, the research he found didn't show you how to remove a human face. But there was a great deal of information on taxidermy and tanning skin that proved to be useful for what he had in mind. He also found several articles on scalping alone.

He had enjoyed practicing on the dead. He could take his time before sending them for cremation. He carefully peeled away the skin and hair, perfecting his skills. He lost count of the number of deceased he performed his procedures on, but it didn't bring him the satisfaction he desired. So far, no one had yet to discover his trial runs as the bodies were sent straight to cremation.

Chapter 16

He'd heard that a new owner lived at the old plantation home now. He must find out for himself if that was true. The air was still thick with humidity as the sinister waters of the bayou lapped lazily at its banks. He hid in the murky abyss of the shadows, watching and waiting. Eerie oak and cypress trees cast out their shadows while protecting his hideout from exposure, even in the bright moonlight. His breath caught as he saw a vibrant, beautiful, young woman in tight jeans and a T-shirt walk out on the sagging porch. Her figure was silhouetted against the morning light coming up over the bayou. Her outfit showed off her curves to sheer perfection. Her hair cascaded down her back and framed her sensual face. She had a long delicate neck, aristocratic cheekbones, and a full mouth. He envisioned her with a pair of vivacious eyes that showed her every expression. She appeared to be no more than twenty-six or so.

She placed one hand on her hip and the other hand shielded her eyes to peer into the distance. Her ample breasts rose up and down with each breath she took. She appeared to be looking for someone, trying to see as far as she could. Behind him, he heard someone fast approaching. Not wanting to be detected, he moved deeper into the woods.

***

Caitlyn watched as Scott pulled up, "I didn't want to head out until you arrived. I need to go into town for a few supplies."

As he walked up the stairs to the front porch, he said, "You could have told me. I would have picked up anything you needed."

"I know that, but I want to do some more research on this family. I tried searching the internet, but there just isn't much available about this particular house."

Scott thought about who may know something about this house, "There is an antique shop in town you may want to visit. The owners, Evan and Marie Boudreaux, have lived here all their lives. Their family is from here so they may know some of the history around here and can tell you what happened."

"Thanks. I will stop by there."

As Scott headed off to work on the house, Caitlyn headed into town. Her first stop may as well be the antique shop. From there, she would visit the library, and before leaving town, she would pick them up something to eat for supper.

The Boudreaux's antique shop was easy to find. It was an old vintage wooden building with very few windows. She parked the Range Rover in front of the store and walked into the dimly lit shop. Her attention was immediately drawn to the shelves filled with various antique housewares, tools, and assorted knick knacks. An elderly man must have heard the bell ring at the door and came to see if he could offer her any help. He greeted her with a broad smile on his face, "Bonjour, is there something I can help you with?"

Caitlyn gave him a warm smile, "Scott Leger suggested I come visit your shop. I just moved into Whispering Willows."

His grin quickly faded, "Mon Dieu! Mais, that house has a bad reputation. Le fait de tuer un individu illegalement. There have been many murders committed there. There are even rumors of a phantom. Il est hantee. No one from this town will go near that old house; it is believed to be haunted."

"Do you know who they believe haunts the grounds?"

"Mais non, no one knows what happened there. It is nothing more than rumors. The previous owners disappeared in the middle of the night and were never heard from again. Evil lurks in the mists of the bayou waiting to harm anyone in its path."

A cold shiver ran through Caitlyn as she heard the warning. She asked, "The house was just abandoned?"

The shopkeeper nodded his head in acknowledgment, "Mais oui. They left with the clothes on their backs. Nothing but misfortune and bad luck have happened to those who live in that house. If I were you, I would leave that house and forget that you ever saw it."

***

At the library, Caitlyn found more information on the house. The house was built by a Jean Paul Favre, who settled here after being exiled from Nova Scotia. There were notations about the Acadians being loaded onto the small ships, similar to cattle. Caitlyn's heart cried out in anguish for what those poor souls went through. Records of those forced onto the ships had been poorly kept, but from what she could tell, many of them died from hunger and sickness. Nothing was done to ensure that they had food, proper clothing, or any other necessary provisions. It was as if no one cared about these poor souls being exiled from their homes, not even the French.

A later notation mentioned that one of Jean Paul and Celeste's illegitimate children came to claim her inheritance a few years after her parents' tragic deaths. This Marguerite Favre must have had some pretty convincing evidence because she was awarded her rightful inheritance and the land.

From what other information Caitlyn found, Marguerite ran off with a stranger in the middle of the night a few years later. After fighting so hard for her inheritance, she left the plantation in the charge of one Andre Picou.

Over the years as the plantation fell into disrepair, the land and plantation were sold and resold. It has had numerous owners; each of them attempted to modernize and restore the old home before moving on for unknown reasons.

Caitlyn was getting ready to dig further into the record books when she heard a noise in front of her. It was the young librarian who quietly said, "I'm sorry, but we will be closing soon."

Caitlyn looked at her watch in surprise, "I'm sorry. Time got away from me."

The librarian laughed, "It happens to the best of us. Did you want to check out any of the books?"

"No, I don't think I have a need for them now. I found the answers to some of my questions."

After picking her and Scott up supper, she headed back to the plantation. On her way back, she reviewed what she learned today. Was there some sinister plot by Andre Picou to get the land from Marguerite? Not that it would matter if it were true, that was so long ago. Did Andre Picou have something to do with the murder of Jean Paul and Celeste? That would give the town an interesting story to tell visitors about the plantation.

***

After dinner, Scott updated his list of ever growing renovations. Unable to rest her wandering mind, Caitlyn started to dust and clean the house. It has turned into a never ending chore, but little by little, she saw that some improvements were being made.

Several hours later, she found herself exhausted and headed off in search of Scott. Soon, they would have enough of the house finished where it would be habitable. Other than a few occurrences, Caitlyn could not convince Scott that this house was haunted. So far, everything that happened, he could easily explain.

In the hallway, she heard the great pendulum of the grandfather clock as it chimed midnight. As Caitlyn headed upstairs, a slight breeze rushed past her. She looked around to see if there was a window open but saw none.

As she made her way to the second floor, a low moaning broke the quietness of the night. For a moment, she thought perhaps Scott had hurt himself. He must have thought the same of her because he came rushing out of the room he was working in.

He looked at her confused for a moment, "The wind must be picking up outside. Are you ready to call it a night?"

Suddenly, the moaning increased in volume and echoed throughout the house. Unable to stop herself, Caitlyn ran to Scott for comfort. She became aware of a heady scent of lilac that drifted through the hall. The mournful moan intensified and reminded Caitlyn of a wailing woman. She looked at Scott, "Do you still think that's the wind?"

Scott looked down at her, "I think we are both exhausted and need to get a good night's sleep."

***

Once in the trailer, Caitlyn found sleep eluding her. As she fell asleep, she felt someone caress her cheek in the darkness. Terrified, she bolted upright in bed. She was so frightened that she couldn't move.

A figure emerged from the darkness of her tiny room. Before the apparition fully took shape, Scott came bursting into the room, "I thought I heard you cry out. Are you okay?"

"I'm sorry, I didn't mean to wake you. I'm all right. I guess the antique store owner's stories bothered me more than I thought."

He sat on the bed and pulled her into his arms. She let his embrace remove the chill from her body. Still, she looked around the room to see if she saw the apparition again. There was something familiar about the shape, but she couldn't put her finger on why it looked so familiar.

***

From the shadows of the room, he watched as the man hugged his Caitlyn. Anger moved through him at the thought of this man touching the woman of his dreams. He refused to allow another man to touch her.

Chapter 17

Morvant glanced up at his partner, Bertrand, as he asked, "How long has she been in the water?"

Morvant straightened himself back up. The killer struck again, and he answered with disgust, "The coroner believes three to four days. It is the same as before; he eviscerated her before removing her face and scalp."

Bertrand felt apprehension growing inside of him. This was the second body in a little over a month.   Bertrand has dealt with all kinds of killers, but these cases were a first for him; these women appeared to have been killed simply for their face and hair. Could that be possible?

Morvant informed Bertrand, "Doc plans to do the autopsy later on this afternoon."

If it hadn't been for the young man fishing, there was no telling how long before the body would have been discovered, especially with her snagged in some thick brush. Not too many people fish out this way because of the cypress stumps and it was easy during low tide for your boat to drag the bottom.

With the state of her body, it would be hard to identify the poor woman. Bertrand stated, "I hate this part of the job."

Bertrand walked along the bank of the bayou being careful to not disturb any potential evidence. He hoped they caught whoever did these horrific murders before he struck again. The biggest problem with the water was it tended to wash away any trace evidence, making it even harder to catch the killer.

Chapter 18

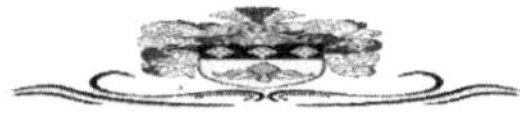

As soon as Caitlyn entered the house, she heard tapping coming from upstairs. Shrugging her shoulders, she figured Scott must be hard at work. Curious as to what he was doing, she slowly made her way upstairs to see.

She followed the taping noises to one of the back rooms. She stopped in the doorway and watched as staring out the window was a young woman. She couldn't be more than twenty years old. With her back to Caitlyn, she stood there, staring out the window. Her open palms pounded on the glass and then just rested there.

Caitlyn stood there watching the young woman. With each passing moment, the woman's pounding grew louder, more insistent. Caitlyn wondered if a ghost's hand could break the glass. Suddenly, the young lady punched the glass with enough force that Caitlyn knew it would shatter. However, the pane rattled in its frame, but never broke.

As if sensing Caitlyn's presence, the young woman turned around. She looked at Caitlyn with surprise registering in her eyes. Looking behind Caitlyn, her eyes went from surprise to fear. Caitlyn turned around to see if someone was behind her, but she saw no one. She turned her attention to the young woman once more.

Caitlyn watched in fear as the young woman's features transformed and fall apart. Her skin turned gray and cracked; her hair became limp and oily, and her eyes unexpectedly glowed yellow.

Caitlyn felt the cold air on her neck. She swallowed down the fear in her throat. She turned around to see a black shadow behind her; his dark eyes focused in on her. She felt the rage building in him as she stepped away from the shadow. She backed away, trying to avoid the hands reaching out for her.

Finding her voice, she called out, "Scott... Scott..."

The shadow heard the footsteps echo down the hall. Scott yelled out, "Caitlyn is something wrong?"

Abruptly, the shadow disappeared along with the young woman. Caitlyn rushed into Scott's arms, "I think I saw another one of Gregory's ghosts. She tried to free herself from this room, but was trapped in here."

Even though the apparitions were no longer visible, she still felt their presence. She swore they were still here, listening and waiting. For just a moment, she experienced a feeling of pure hatred in the air like a thick layer of fog floating unseen, but still present.

Letting Scott's warm embrace soothe her nerves, she took several deep breaths until her heartbeat slowed once more and her body no longer shook. "I'm starting to wish I hadn't wanted to see the ghosts of Gregory's victims."

***

That night as Caitlyn slept, she felt Scott climb in bed with her and began covering her body with kisses. As he slowly made his way on top of her, she didn't protest. His body felt good against hers. She wrapped her arms and legs around him and pulled him closer to her.

She let the stress fall away as her body relaxed. She found herself lost in his touch. Her breath quickened as he whispered in her ear, "Caitlyn…."

She opened her eyes and saw no one on top of her. She tried desperately to push the presence off of her. The voice in her ear sounded just like Gregory. She thrashed about on the bed while trying to free herself from the cold grasp of the presence on top of her.

She bolted upright from the nightmare. She sat up trying to calm her racing heart. She looked around to make sure that no one was in the room or in bed with her. She kept telling herself that it was only a nightmare and that Gregory had not been in bed with her.

Chapter 19

Lisa Duval walked up to the house slowly. Something warned her that this offer was too good to be true. No one gave anyone something for free, but with money being tight a free haircut was just too good to pass up. Besides, the man wasn't much bigger than her, and she could handle him if he tried anything funny.

He opened the door quickly, as if sensing her discomfort, "I am so glad you decided to take me up on my offer. I don't do this for everyone, but when I saw you in the store I knew you would be perfect to add as a headshot on my website. I need you to sign a release allowing me to post your picture, but other than that, we are good to go."

Lisa signed the release he had for her and began to feel better about this being a legitimate offer. She took a seat in the chair as he explained, "I need to wash and dry your hair before we cut and style it. Would you like a water, soda, or possibly coffee?"

"A soda would be perfect. Thank you so much."

He reached into the refrigerator and handed her a cold soda. She didn't even take notice that the seal had been broken as she took a long drink. As he stood behind her, he watched her every movement waiting for the drug to take effect.

He took his time preparing her hair to be washed. The drug acted fast, and her head flopped forward within minutes.

***

Sam Morales ran along the narrow trail that followed the bayou, fully aware of his burning legs, but concentrated more on his breathing than his legs. He never understood why the last mile was always the hardest, especially since he had run this particular trail for well over a month. It was easier to run on the track at the local high school. At least there, he could zone out, but this kind of running required his full attention; the terrain was uneven, and there were various hazards. The marathon he planned on running wasn't on a track either. He had to be prepared to run on any surface they threw at them. When he found this trail, he knew it was what he needed to run on.

He jumped over a fallen log and felt himself slipping on the wet leaves. He caught himself just in time and kept pushing forward. It was the perfect training for the upcoming marathon; he planned on winning this one. As he rounded the corner, he nearly tripped over an exposed root from the recent rain and swore at himself for letting his thoughts wander.

By now, his legs were on fire, yet he kept pushing forward. He picked up speed as he rounded the next bend. This time, he did trip over another exposed root. He landed in the water and knocked the wind out of his lungs. He came up sputtering the nasty, murky water.

Once he gained control of his breathing again, he found himself looking straight at what appeared to be a body. He backed away, reached for his cell phone, and let out a curse when he discovered it submerged in the water.

***

Bertrand scanned the area before heading to the body. He took in each face he saw out here; one of them could be their killer. He learned long ago that perps enjoyed watching cops work the crime scene. If he was here, it would be easy to spot him. Especially since very few people came out this way.

The officers working the scene had their backs turned away from the body, unable to watch as the coroner prepared to move what remained of the poor woman. Bertrand shook his head; this town did not need another gruesome serial killer right now.

From behind him, he heard another vehicle pulling up and let out a list of swear words. The press had caught wind of the murders. It wouldn't be long before they moved in like vultures, pushing their boundaries to get a picture.

"Keep them as far away as possible. Move the crime scene tape if you need to. I don't want them anywhere near this scene." Bertrand knew that word of the murder would spread like wildfire, and soon bystanders would flock to the area.

As he moved closer to the scene, the officers moved aside. Dr. LeBlanc quickly looked up at him as he continued his work, "I suspect he thought the alligators would drag her off. If it wouldn't have been for the runner finding her body so soon, I doubt we would have known there was another victim."

Bertrand looked across the bayou, "I wonder how many he has dropped here before now. That may be why we haven't found any bodies before these three."

"It would be the smart way to dispose of a body in this shape. The alligators would consider it a tenderized meal for them. All they have to do is drag the remains to their hidey hole and let nature do the rest of the work."

Bertrand looked at the body in dismay. He once again wondered what kind of monster could do this. Right now, though, he didn't have time to profile a killer he knew nothing about. If he wanted to get into the mind of this murderer, he must first work the crime scene. They needed to comb this area for any evidence. Every piece of evidence, no matter how small, must be preserved, collected, and documented. Nothing could be overlooked.

He looked up at the morning sky. They would be here at least until lunchtime. Point Creole had another serial killer at large.

***

Bertrand took his tablet and took notes while Morvant talked to the young boy who found the body. He was still pale and shaken up, but coherent enough to answer questions.

All around him, the crime scene techs collected evidence and took pictures. You would think they were old pros with this now. He held his tongue, reminding himself that they knew what to do. It's just that outside crime scenes were the worst. There were so many areas where the clues could hide or they could have already blown away. Every piece of trash must be collected; it took one good clue to lead them to the killer. They could at least be thankful that it hadn't rained yet, so some of the scene had been preserved.

Every person working the scene had a varying shade of grim on their face, few looking in the direction of the body. He understood how they felt. He found it difficult to view the body as well.

Mark Girard headed up the crime scene investigations unit today. He had a sharp eye that helped to ensure no evidence went unnoticed. He had become an invaluable asset to the team.

From here, Bertrand heard Girard instruct the technicians, "I want this entire area taken in a grid formation. Everyone works in twos, and we check each quadrant twice using a different set of eyes."

Morvant walked over to Bertrand, "The witness didn't see anyone in the area this morning. Our killer probably dropped the body off up a ways, and the current carried her down until she became caught in the cypress knees."

"The killer probably hoped that an alligator would be in the mood for an early breakfast. Dr. LeBlanc is getting ready to move the body, but this was our killer. Just like the other girls, he let her bleed to death before removing her face and hair," Bertrand explained to Morvant.

Morvant let out a long sigh, "Damn, this is getting frustrating. This is a sick fuck."

Dr. LeBlanc walked over to the two detectives as his assistants removed the body, "I won't know the time of death until I get her on my table, but rigor hasn't set in. Other than the heavy scent of blood, there is no smell of decomposition, which is probably why the alligators didn't move in. His surgical work is getting better."

***

Once back at the station, Morvant asked Bertrand, "Will we ever catch a break and find some evidence that will help us stop this monster?"

Bertrand ran his hands through his hair, "Eventually, this guy will make a mistake; they all do. This asshole won't get away from us mon ami."

***

Liz Girard watched the crime scene with extreme interest. This case could be what she needed to get her noticed. CAJN may be just a small station here in Point Creole, but the story could be picked up by a larger network. That could be the boost she needed in landing a better job. Once again, she rearranged her hair and looked over at her camera man, "I'm telling you Randy, something about these murders isn't right. What are they trying to hide? Why are they stonewalling us if this is a simple murder?"

Randy Duval adjusted his video camera in case he could get a good shot of the body as it was being moved, and shrugged his shoulders, "I don't think this is a simple murder. My gut tells me that there is something the cops don't want revealed."

Liz chewed on her bottom lip, "I just wonder what on earth it may be. A few of the cops who worked the scenes looked green."

Randy smiled over at her, "Why don't you try calling the morgue or funeral home to see what they have to say about the bodies?"

Liz made a mental note to call both the morgue and the funeral home as soon as the name of the victim was released. She could always say she was a friend of the family who didn't want to bother the grieving family members and would like to send flowers. If she became friendly enough with someone from either place, maybe, just maybe, they would give her more information than they should.

Chapter 20

Caitlyn tossed and turned most of the night. Unable to sleep any longer, she decided she may as well get busy in the house. She wanted to tackle the formal living room today. Gregory had made a mess of the lovely room when he transformed it for his haunted house. Scott brought it back to its former glory, but there was still a lot of cleaning to do in there.

As she swept the floor, dust stirred around her. For a moment, she thought she saw a figure materialize in the dust. She stopped what she was doing and just watched. Terrified at first, but she became fascinated as the form of a young woman took shape. Her long black hair seemed to shimmer in the early morning light. Moaning sobs filled the room as Caitlyn's sense of time altered. The ghost's moans steadily grew louder. Could this be a lost soul who found her fate unbearable?

The ghost quickly dissipated and floated straight through her. Caitlyn's body became wracked with the sorrow that the ghost felt; it consumed her soul. She couldn't catch her breath as the blood in her body seemed to turn to ice.

It had taken a few moments before Caitlyn felt normal once again. She found herself exhausted from the brief experience; the ghost's pain and suffering were caused by the injustice done to her by Gregory.

Strangely, she did not feel threatened by the ghost itself, but by the intense emotional pain that ensnared her body.

Gregory did unspeakable, horrible, vile things in this house to the poor souls before their deaths and now, they couldn't find peace.

As she stepped onto the porch, Scott headed her way with two cups of coffee. The morning sun felt welcoming on her face and helped to rejuvenate her. As she took the coffee from him, she said, "Thanks, I was coming for a cup."

"I thought I heard you leaving early this morning."

She let out a soft sigh as she took a sip of her coffee, "I tried to be quiet as I left. I hope I didn't wake you."

As they walked inside, he informed her, "I am a light sleeper, but figured you were too restless to sleep."

She nodded her head in agreement, "I still can't get over what Gregory did here in this house and what those poor souls must have endured. I want to clean the formal living room so I can cleanse the room."

Scott shook his head at her attempts to "cleanse" the house. He had never believed ghosts walked this earth. As he entered the front room, he let out a long whistle, "Well, you have been busy this morning. This place looks better already."

"I certainly hope so. It seems like this will take us forever."

Scott had been meaning to ask her this and now may be the perfect moment, "Are you sure that you can afford to do this? I mean, it would be easier to tear down this place."

Caitlyn ran her hand over the magnificent mantel above the fireplace. "Many people have told me that would be the easiest way to handle this house, but as soon as I walked in here, I couldn't bring myself to do that. Someone lovingly built this home." Caitlyn couldn't explain it, but she felt drawn to this house. As if restoring this place was her destiny.

Scott informed her, "When I was a kid, my friends tried to convince me there were ghosts living here. We came to poke around, but as many times as I have been here I never saw a ghost."

Images from last night came rushing into Caitlyn's mind, "What about last night? Do you think the wind did that moaning?"

"I'm sure there is a simple explanation for that." As Scott listened to Caitlyn talk, he became aware of her nearness. He breathed in the intoxicating smell of her and wondered what it would be like to kiss her. As if something foreboding read his mind, a frigid gust of wind blew through him. Shaking off the feeling, he took Caitlyn's hand as he dragged her from the room. "Well, let's see what we should focus on next."

"Before we do, I want to burn sage in this room." For once, Scott didn't argue about how ridiculous that would be. Instead, he found himself willing to help her.

As they prepared to burn the sage, Scott told her, "Oh, by the way, I learned a little more about this area. It turns out during the Civil War some of the abandoned plantations were taken over by river pirates. The crops were stolen and sold to unscrupulous men, despite the embargo on Southern trade. The rumors around town were that the hauntings came from the river pirates. Everyone was too afraid of the consequences to come and check it out personally."

"That would explain some of the alleged hauntings I suppose."

"Over the years, drifters found this place useful for whatever their needs may have been at the time. With this place being right on the bayou, I am sure that during prohibition times it was used for ulterior motives as well. This poor home has been vacant more than lived in."

"Well, then it is time for this to be a happy place again. We need to dispel the shroud of gloom that hovers over this place."

Scott walked around the renovated room, thick with the scent of burning sage, "I think the new paint and trim help this room. Soon, people will flock to this place to find out about its rich history and take in its luxury."

"I hope you are right. This might make a perfect bed and breakfast."

Scott rubbed his chin as he thought about that, "If you have the money to invest, it could be very worthwhile. Haunted plantations are known to attract tourists."

"Money isn't a problem; I promise you."

Scott wondered about her comments regarding money. Curiosity had him wanting to ask just what Gregory left her, but he didn't want her to think he was interested in her for what she had.

As they left the room, Caitlyn turned around to tell Scott something and found herself in his arms instead. She felt his warmth and breathed in the manly scent of him.

Clearing her throat, she said, "I just wanted to thank you for all you are doing for me."

***

That night they ate supper on the front porch. Scott set up a small makeshift table that overlooked not only the cemetery, but the bayou as well. He lit a small candle as Caitlyn placed their plates on the table.

As they finished their supper, a movement caught Caitlyn's attention. She jumped up, knocking over her chair, "Look in the cemetery!" She hollered to Scott. He watched as what appeared to be a transparent figure moved through the cemetery.

Massive oak trees with moss draped branches reached out over the cemetery. The gravestones were old and, in the fading sunlight, had a ghostly glow to them. Even from here, she could tell that most of the headstones were broken and chipped from years of neglect. Eerie tall weeds had taken over much of the cemetery.

Caitlyn swallowed back her excitement, "Do you see what I am seeing?"

Scott watched in amazement; he knew there was a reasonable explanation for what they saw. "It has to be fog moving through the cemetery."

As the shape took more of a human form, Caitlyn shouted out, "It is a ghost. See, I told you this place was haunted."

Scott walked over to his truck and found a flashlight, "Wait Caitlyn. It may be someone walking through the cemetery looking for something specific."

As they made their way to the graveyard, Scott grabbed Caitlyn's shoulder, "Maybe, you should let me go in first."

Caitlyn shook her head, "No way. I wouldn't miss this for anything. I want to see your face when you realize that this place is haunted."

"Caitlyn, I don't think that is a ghost, but a real person looking for something."

Grabbing his hand, she pulled him closer to the cemetery, "I'm going to check this out. I know it is a ghost."

Whatever was in the cemetery must have heard their approach and darted off to the bayou, "See, a ghost would have just vanished into thin air," said Scott.

Grabbing his arm, she pulled him along, "Come on, maybe it wants us to follow it."

As they neared the bayou, whatever they were following disappeared.

***

As they entered the dark house, Caitlyn turned on lights in the foyer.

Scott asked, "Do you mind if I start a fire in the fireplace? I checked out the chimney today, and it's good to go. There seems to be a chill in the house tonight."

"A fire would be nice."

Caitlyn watched as he built a fire. The marble fireplace had an impressive rosewood mantle. Every room had a fireplace and massive hearth that was as tall as a six foot man. She had never seen a plantation built as exquisitely as this house. It would have been a shame to demolish this house. She was surprised that over the years the house hadn't been vandalized, nor the antiques stolen. Maybe the ghosts that haunted the old plantation home kept the treasures safe.

Caitlyn found an old blanket and spread it out on the floor in front of the fireplace. As Scott sat next to her he said, "The workmanship in this house is just breathtaking. The one good thing we can say about your old boyfriend is that he didn't totally destroy the beauty of the house when he made his haunted house."

A shiver ran through Caitlyn's body at the way he said "her old boyfriend." Was that how she would be forever labeled?

***

He watched from deep in the shadows and grew angry at the way these two were getting comfortable with each other. He must stop this relationship before it progressed any further. He refused to share her with another man.

***

Caitlyn looked over at Scott, "I appreciate your help. There is no way I could have attempted this monumental task without you. On top of that, you are giving up your entire personal life to stay here with me. I thought I could stay here by myself, but now, I am glad you are here. This place is unsettling at night."

As he looked at her, he found himself wanting to pull her close and kiss her. Unable to resist, he brought her into his arms. The kiss started slowly, and then progressed with a sense of urgency. The kiss ignited a fire deep inside of Caitlyn. To her, it seemed like they were long lost lovers who'd once again found each other.

Scott pulled her closer to his hard body and moved his tongue along her lips. Her body sizzled with electricity as desire flowed through her. She ran her hands through his hair as her blood turned to molten lava.

Embers of desire turned into hot need. Her head dropped back as his lips left a trail of hot kisses down her neck. She watched as his eyes gleamed with desire. Could she be falling in love with this man she wanted so much?

A low moan filled the room and a frigid burst of air blew through the room. The next thing they knew the lights in the room went out, and they were bathed only in the firelight. Scott helped Caitlyn up as they made their way to the foyer. "Something must have blown the breaker. I think I left the flashlight in the foyer."

As they walked into the foyer, Scott heard a scurrying near the stairs. Once he found a flashlight, he scanned the room. In the corner near the dining room, he saw a movement. It appeared to be a black shadow darting into the kitchen.

Scott rubbed his eyes thinking it was an illusion. Did vagrants still live somewhere in this house? He knew that in a lot of the old plantations there were secret rooms; this was a possibility they hadn't considered.

He turned back to Caitlyn, "Tomorrow morning we need to investigate this house from top to bottom and see if there are any secret rooms here. Most houses built back then had secret passages. It allowed the servants to go from room to room without being seen. However, since the house was part of the Underground Railroad I bet we find all sorts of tunnels that run under this property."

Caitlyn rubbed her hands together in excitement, "Oh, that could be fun. Just imagine all the things we could find if that is true!"

***

He watched Caitlyn sleep. Was she dreaming of him right now?

His heart raced as a small smile formed on her face. That smile was just for him; he was sure of it. Soon she would discover that he was here for her and had been here this whole time, waiting and watching.

Chapter 21

As Bertrand sat in Sheriff Savoie's office with Morvant, he felt like he was back in high school waiting for a lecture from the principal. He could tell just from the Sheriff's stance that he had grown impatient, "You mean to tell me that we have no leads."

Bertrand sighed, "For now, we still have no leads. The computer search has turned up nothing. There wasn't even a hint that this MO has shown up somewhere else. And it doesn't help that this killer has left nothing behind at the crime scenes."

Sheriff Savoie looked at the two detectives, "What is your next course of action?"

Morvant threw up his hands, feeling the weight of this case on his shoulders. "We could always look into our crystal ball to see when the killer plans to strike again."

Sheriff Savoie scolded the detective, "I don't need smart ass remarks right now. I need results that I can bring to the higher ups. They are riding my ass hard right now."

Morvant dropped his shoulders in defeat, "We are doing the best we can, Sheriff. This guy isn't giving us anything to go on."

Bertrand informed the Sheriff, "We are comparing photos of the bystanders at the crime scenes in case one particular person visited each and every scene. If the killer was at the scene, there is a chance the photographer took a picture of him."

Sheriff Savoie contemplated what Bertrand said, "I agree, but there still is a chance that even an innocent bystander was at each crime scene."

"There is that chance, but I think our killer will be watching us rather than the body. He has already seen what he did with the body; he will want to know how we take in the surroundings."

"So you are looking for people who are observing you and not the body?"

"Yes, sir."

***

For the next several days, Bertrand read the papers and watched the news to make sure none of the details of the case leaked out. He found a few articles about the murder and later the investigation, but nothing about the particular details. The articles focused on how the police weren't forthcoming with the details.

Bertrand wished that these reporters would take into consideration a murder investigation happened in stages. They spent the first twenty-four hours examining the crime scene and interviewing witnesses, if any. The next day, they reviewed the evidence in hopes of identifying a potential suspect, but if there were no witnesses or evidence, it was almost impossible to identify a suspect. The killer was more than likely already on the hunt for his next victim.

So far, their files on the murders were very slim. They had the autopsy reports, crime scene photos, interviews and a very vague timeline, but not much else to fill in the blanks.

***

Liz Girard slammed down the phone as she reached yet another dead end. There was something unique about these killings. She felt it in her gut that the police were hiding something. So far, she had been unable to find anyone who would talk to her. There had to be someone anxious to talk. Someone always liked to gossip more than the others; someone wanting the limelight.

She looked at her watch and noticed that it was almost five o'clock. If she made it to the funeral home as people left, perhaps she would find someone willing to talk to her. Before getting out of her car, she checked her makeup and hair. Satisfied that she looked more like a model than an investigative reporter, she headed into the funeral home.

Inside the funeral home, she found it cooler than expected. The scent of flowers hung heavy in the air, but even its heady scent couldn't hide the odor of death. Soft music played from unseen speakers giving the place more of an eerie feeling rather than a calming one.

There were two rooms for viewing at the mortuary and a large room with several caskets. Liz could see the funeral director, Mr. Arthur Pierron, busy polishing the caskets. His smile seemed to freeze on his face when he saw her. From the corner of her eye, she noticed a smaller man walking out the front door. He must have been curious as to who she was because he stopped to stare at her for a few minutes. She made a mental note to find out his name and talk to him; if Mr. Pierron didn't give her any information, perhaps he would. She tried to get the receptionist to speak to her, but the woman was a pit bull when it came to guarding secrets. So far, Liz had been unable to get any information from her.

"Mr. Pierron, could you give me any information on the bodies that were released to your care? Have they been identified?"

Mr. Pierron shook his head grimly, "This is such sad business cher. The police asked us explicitly not to release any information regarding the body and the families have concurred with their wishes."

His statement caught her attention, "Why don't they want you to release information about the body?"

Shaking his head, Mr. Pierron said, "I'm sorry, but we are under strict orders not to talk to anyone about these cases. This is a small town, after all, and I don't want to upset the police."

Liz wasn't going to get any information from this man. "Well, thank you for your time Mr. Pierron. I am sorry to have bothered you."

"I am sorry that I couldn't help you."

Outside, she breathed in the fresh air as she looked around to see if the man she saw earlier was still here. Disappointment filled her when she realized he had left.

Chapter 22

Caitlyn looked around the completed rooms and was proud of the job she'd done today. The kitchen gleamed as did the old hardwood floors. It had taken over six weeks, but it was starting to feel more like a home than an old abandoned house. It took a lot of work, but when you walked in the house, you no longer smelled the putrid scent of decay; instead, you were welcomed with the smell of furniture polish and fresh paint. She didn't know what she would do without Scott; he gave up a good portion of his life to stay and help her complete this project.

Darkness had fallen and once again filled the house with sinister shadows. The house still had a gloominess that lived in it. No matter how hard they cleaned and renovated the house, the evil that had moved in still pulsed throughout the house.

As she made her way upstairs to find Scott, a loud boom of thunder rattled the house. Her hair stood on end as the air around her suddenly seemed to be charged with electricity. She looked around to see if another ghost was possibly making its presence known.

Not seeing anything, she continued to walk up the stairs. As soon as she made it to the second floor, the lights went out, and she was bathed in darkness. A flash of light from the window caught her eye. Walking over to the window, she peered out into the night and saw another quick flash of light near the bayou. Maybe Scott was working outside.

She strained to see who or what caused the flashes of light when a burst of cold air whipped across her.

***

As Scott finished the grout work for the glass tile, his mind drifted towards thoughts of Caitlyn. She was one smart and very determined woman. She was not only beautiful, but had curves in all the right places. Just looking at her made him hard. It had been difficult to keep his hands off her, especially when every time he saw her he wanted to kiss those luscious, tempting lips of hers.

Scott looked around the bathroom once more, pleased with the way the tile came out. This was his second bathroom to complete, and he was proud of the renovations.

As soon as he stepped out of the bathroom to get Caitlyn, the lights went out. He looked out the bedroom window and saw that not only had night fallen, but it looked as if a storm rolled in with it. The bedroom was bathed in complete darkness and had an eerie feel to it. For a moment, he thought he heard something moving in the hall. Lightning flashed across the murky sky as thunder boomed eerily overhead, followed by lightning flashes again. It would be one hell of a storm, and Scott thought it might be safer for them to sleep in the old house instead of the travel trailer tonight.

"Caitlyn?"

He looked down the hall and caught an image near the window on the landing, "Scott? I saw a light in the woods. I thought it was you."

"I worked on the bathroom all day. I wanted to show you how it turned out, but the lights went out."

Scott looked to see if he could make out where the light was coming from. "It looks as if someone is out on the bayou. It is probably a fisherman hoping that this storm will bring out the catfish."

A strong sense of foreboding washed over her; it was as if they were being watched. Before they could move away from the window, a frightening scream echoed through the night. She jumped and landed hard against Scott's warm body, "What was that?"

As another scream sliced through the night, Scott pulled her into his warm embrace while he looked out into the night through the window. "That, my dear, was a panther from the sound of it. They are plentiful in this area."

"A panther? I didn't even know they lived in this area."

"There are only a few left, but they are here. A few black bears have even been reported."

As the scream sounded through the night once more, she said, "It sounds awfully close to the house."

Scott's baritone voice enveloped her in its warmth, "It is probably miles from here, deep in the woods. Sound carries in the swamp at night."

She leaned into him even more. He smelled heavenly, a heady mixture of musk, citrus and spice that mixed so well with his virile scent. It warmed her blood and sent desire spiraling through her. As if sensing her desire, he moved his hands up and down her arms.

Desire churned inside of her like lava in a volcano. As if reading her thoughts, he cupped her jaw, bent down, and kissed her. He smiled down at her; his thumb gently stroked her cheek.

As his hands moved up her body to caress her breasts, a jolt of electricity shot through her. She whispered his name against his heated skin.

She almost lost complete control when he feathered his thumbs over her erect nipples. His tongue teased her lips until she opened her mouth to his. She wrapped her arms around his neck and pressed her body close to his.

She quivered in his heated embrace. The feel of his hands on her body drove her wild with need. The need to feel bare flesh caused her to claw at his clothes.

She ran her hands up under his shirt, reveling in the feel of his taut muscles covered with soft hair. It reminded her of silk over steel. In one swift move, she removed his shirt.

Unable to resist touching him any longer, Caitlyn slipped her hand into his briefs and wrapped her hand around his erection. Its searing heat was sweet torture. She pushed his pants to the floor and fell to her knees. When she took him in her mouth, it was almost too much pleasure for him. He tangled his fingers in her silken hair. The feel of her lips and tongue on his burning flesh scorched him.

He pulled her up to him and kissed her. Their tongues danced as she quickly removed her clothes. Unable to take any more, he carried her to the bed. When he took one of her erect nipples in his mouth, she moaned in delight as his tongue tormented one breast and then the other. She allowed his hands to explore, to play, to kiss, and to touch.

The need building turned into an ache deep inside of her. Unable to take any more of this sweet torture, "I need you now." When he entered her, it was pure heaven.

A low groan escaped his mouth; she was like molten silk. Fireworks erupted through her body as she climaxed repeatedly. Her body quivered with delight as wave after wave of ecstasy rolled over her.

***

Watching from his hiding spot, Gregory was consumed with a vivid, destructive anger as the two of them consummated their relationship. His eyes filled with hatred as he clamped his teeth together. How could she betray him like that? He would suffer for making love with his beloved. He wanted to smash something. He wanted to shout at her that she was supposed to be with him. What a mess this had turned into. His whole being trembled with rage.

Gregory screamed a long, terrible wail of rage and despair that echoed throughout the house. Caitlyn and Scott bolted upright in bed. Both unsure of where the wail came from.

***

The tall trees loomed before him. Excitement coursed through him as he peered through the tree's moss draped limbs. As he stared at the plantation in front of him, it looked more like a ghostly multi-column illusion that seemed to rise out of the bayou.

Every step took him closer to her. He had to be patient though. Tonight was simply to find access points and escape routes.

He had to wait until she was alone. That man seemed to hang around her constantly. He had to get her alone. His body hummed with energy at the thought of claiming her. She was the masterpiece he had been waiting for. She would be his forever.

***

With every streak of lightning casting eerie shadows and the thunder shaking the house, Caitlyn couldn't fall asleep. Making sure not to wake Scott, she slipped out of bed and quietly walked downstairs.

Maybe a cup of hot tea would help her relax. She placed a cup in the microwave and leaned against the counter to watch the seconds slowly count down as she prepared to catch the timer before it went off.

Once her tea was ready, she sat down at the makeshift table in the kitchen. They moved inside the house two weeks ago, and she still wasn't all that comfortable moving about the house at night by herself. As she sipped the hot tea, she felt the warmth rush into her chest, and her body relaxed.

She glanced around the kitchen as she drank her tea. She thought about how beautiful this kitchen would be when it was done. As she finished her drink, a movement by the pantry door caught her attention. Her pulse quickened as she watched the dark shadow just stand there staring at her.

Voices filled the room. They talked at once; she couldn't understand what they were saying. Suddenly, a man's voice pierced through the conversation, "Enough, she is mine."

Caitlyn leaped up from her chair in horror. Without once turning around, she ran to her room, locked the door, and ducked under the covers. It may be a childish reaction, but for now, she wanted to hide under the covers and prayed the ghosts left her alone.

Chapter 23

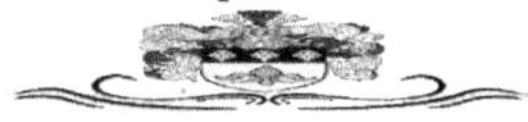

Bertrand saw the article in the paper and wanted to throttle that damn reporter. He carefully read it one more time:

Women, you need to lock your doors and please take the necessary precautions. Men, you need to watch out for your wives, girlfriends, daughters, sisters, and mothers. There is a chance that a serial killer is once again terrifying our small town. Three bodies have been found so far, and until the police catch this madman, there is no telling who his next victim may be.

He let out a string of curse words before storming out the door. Where the hell did she come off saying that there may be another serial killer running loose? Three murders did not mean they had a serial killer; even though he was certain of it.

She jumped the gun on this one, and her article would cause mass panic. The phones would ring nonstop today. Everyone would want to know exactly how the police department planned to protect the citizens of Point Creole.

He agreed that people should be wary, and the public had the right to be informed of the murders, but there was no reason to put fear into everyone. Life was returning to normal. But now, because of these killings and this damned article, people would be afraid to leave their houses once again.

It didn't appear that the victims were from here. They still had to identify the last body and were combing through missing persons' reports from various cities across the state. So far, they had had no luck, but Bertrand refused to give up. Somewhere out there, someone was missing this girl and wondering what happened to her.

Sure enough, when he walked into the station, phones were ringing off the hook. The poor receptionist looked hassled. Bertrand heard the Sheriff call for him and Morvant, "Get in my office now."

As soon as they walked into his office, the Sheriff closed the door, "It isn't even eight, and the place is a madhouse! Can you imagine what it will be like by lunchtime?"

Bertrand was just as pissed as the sheriff. He hated that Morvant and he were the unfortunate recipients of his anger.

"I want y'all to find this murdering son of a bitch before this turns any more chaotic. This town does not need another serial killer."

They replied in unison, "Yes, sir."

"Do either of you have any idea how she got her information?"

Bertrand answered, "Not yet, sir, but I intend to find out."

"Well, let me know as soon as you do and I'll take care of it," the Sheriff said angrily.

"Yes, sir."

Then the Sheriff asked, "Do we have any more information yet?"

Bertrand continued, "No, sir. It looks as if the same person committed all three murders. Each of the women had their face and scalp removed after death. None of the bodies had trace evidence to help pinpoint a killer. The women were killed some place other than where they were discovered. So far, we have been unable to identify either of the last two victims, but we doubt either woman was a local."

Chapter 24

Scott peeked in on Caitlyn and saw that she was still asleep. He quickly snuck out and headed into town. They deserved a treat for breakfast, and he ordered them each the hungry man's breakfast from Roni's Diner. On the way out, he picked up a paper and hoped he made it to the house before Caitlyn woke up.

***

He waited in the shadows as the intruder to Caitlyn's life left. He slipped into Caitlyn's room and watched her sleep. He noticed that she kicked off the covers. He wondered what dream tormented her enough to thrash about. However, he was grateful for this small favor. She slept in the nude last night.

She was such a beautiful creature. Her gorgeous auburn hair cascaded over the pillow and covered her face. He went to move her hair from her face without thinking but caught himself. He shouldn't wake her. Now was not the time to let her know he was coming for her. Instead, he stood here reveling in the beauty of her naked body. She turned over slightly, giving him a better look at her voluptuous breasts. He waited in utter anticipation, hoping that she rolled on her back completely and gave him a total view of her glorious body. He felt himself growing larger and more rigid as he continued to watch her.

She let out a soft sigh as she curled up into a fetal position, reaching for the covers. He slipped deeper into the shadows of the room just in case she woke up as she reached for the covers. Her sudden movement freed her face from the confines of her hair. Even without makeup, she was beautiful.

***

The smell of bacon and scrambled eggs woke Caitlyn. She looked over at the clock to find that it was almost seven. Anxious to see what Scott was up to, she walked out of the small bedroom to find him pouring two cups of coffee. "Good morning."

"Good morning, sleepyhead. I thought I would surprise you with breakfast this morning."

Caitlyn's stomach let out a loud growl as she peeked over his shoulder, "I didn't even realize how hungry I was until you mentioned breakfast."

"Let's sit down and eat before we go exploring."

As she dug into the scrambled eggs and bacon, "That sounds like a plan to me." Involuntarily, she let out a sigh, "Oh my goodness, this breakfast is delicious. It sure beats a bowl of cereal."

"I thought you would enjoy it. A man can only live on cereal for so long."

Caitlyn let out a small laugh, "I guess I should work harder on feeding you then shouldn't I?"

"That's not what I meant. You and I have both been putting in so much time on this house so I figured we deserved a break."

"Well, I am glad you thought of this. I may have to go into town more often for breakfast or learn how to cook eggs."

"By the time we are done with the kitchen, you may be inspired to learn how to cook. We should update it into a gourmet kitchen. That way, no matter what you decide, sell or turn it into a bed and breakfast, it will be something that appeals to everyone."

"I agree. I am also lucky that almost all of the bedrooms have their own bath. Those with adjoining bathrooms can be rented out as family suites."

"You are very lucky that when Jean Paul built the house he had the foresight to think of individual baths. That was a true luxury back then."

Caitlyn agreed, "I bet there may be passages from the bedrooms. If he kept his family hidden from everyone, he would want to have it where, if needed, they could move about the house comfortably without fear of being seen. That would include the bedrooms and possibly the bathrooms."

"I wonder if back then citizens of Point Creole wondered why a single man had such a large extravagant house."

"I am sure that they did. Even back then, people liked to gossip."

As soon as they finished their breakfast, they began to examine the house for secret passages. They started in the kitchen by checking around the walls for any type of lever or button. In the dining room, Caitlyn noticed that there was a beveled edge around the wall panels. She called out to

Scott, "Look at this. Why would they need such extravagant work on these panels?"

Scott felt around, "I think this may be just what we are looking for." He checked each area to see if they moved. He let out a sharp breath as he discovered hinges. "Look here. There has to be a latch somewhere to open the panel."

Caitlyn looked at the panel, "What if it is one that you push on to open? A latch may have been too conspicuous."

Realizing that she was probably right, he pushed on the panel. The woodwork gave as stale and musty air escaped from the old passageway. "Wait right here and let me grab us some flashlights." Not only did he grab his flashlights, but he tucked a 40 caliber he kept in his truck into his waistband, "Just for protection," he told Caitlyn. "There is no telling what we will run into."

Before stepping into the darkness of the passageway, Caitlyn took one of the heavy dining room chairs and propped it up against the panel. "To make sure that we don't get locked in here with no way out."

As soon as Scott turned his flashlight on, the passage turned out to be a narrow, windowless corridor. "With the amount of dust down here, I don't think this passageway has been used in a long time."

At the end of the passageway was a narrow stairway. "Do you want to go up or down?" Scott asked Caitlyn.

"Let's see where this takes us first."

"As you wish, my lady." As they crept up the stairs, Scott tested each step first. "The floors seem to be solid wood." They had to brush away several cobwebs that hung overhead. Caitlyn almost screamed when a spider landed right in front of her face; he seemed to be warning her not to go any further. The further up they went, they found the odor turned more foul, "It is almost like something died up here," stated Scott.

"Ugh, thanks for that image."

Scott informed her, "We need to check the kitchen and other areas for trapdoors. They would not only want hidden doors, but something that gave them fast access to the outside as well. Something tells me this was simply a secret passage to give them added security. I don't think this is the main passage we are looking for. This may have been built for Celeste to travel around the house unseen."

Caitlyn grabbed Scott's shoulder to stop him, "Look, there are footprints in the dust."

"Well, I don't know about you, but I don't see a ghost having to leave behind footprints." He bent down to inspect the footprints, "These appear to be quite recent."

"Maybe Gregory found the passageways when he worked on the house."

Scott scratched his head, "That could be but then they would be covered with at least a thin layer of dust. No, these are more recent than when Gregory was in the house. Perhaps he told his attorney about the passageways, but, if so, why didn't the lawyer tell you?"

As Caitlyn looked at the prints, "Scott, why do you think they just appear here?"

"That's a good question. We need to feel around. There has to be another door around here."

They began pushing the walls where the footprints appeared. Caitlyn caught sight of what seemed to be a large ring on the wall. Pushing against the wall, Scott found that the door opened with complete ease, "Someone oiled the hinges on this door. Unlike the other door, it didn't screech in protest."

Caitlyn and Scott found themselves in the bedroom where the door slammed shut on her the other night. Scott stated, "See, I told you there was an explanation for the door slamming shut. I think someone wants to scare you away from this place."

In the adjoining room, Caitlyn cried out, "Scott, I found another secret door. It is built into the closet." Instead of venturing into the passageway, Scott stated, "I want to check the parlor. When we were renovating it, I didn't think of looking for hidden doors."

Scott and Caitlyn headed downstairs and as soon as he felt around, he found what he was looking for, "They built it into the bookcase in here." As they opened the secret door, several loose pages that had remained hidden for years fell from the opening. Caitlyn picked them up and placed them on one of the wingback chairs. She told Scott, "I want to read those later."

As they ventured into the hidden passageway, Caitlyn found more papers scattered on the floor and told Scott, "I want to come back and pick these up. I am anxious to see what they say." As they continued through the passageway, they found another staircase that led to the second floor. Caitlyn found another door that led into the master bedroom. A shiver swept through her; there was something cold and forbidding about this room. Was this where Gregory slept?

Scott broke the silence, "I think this was another emergency escape." To show her, he closed the door in the bedroom. It blended in with the paneling. "It is like the one in the dining room. Old Jean Paul was ingenious in how he hid the doors. If anyone came barging in here looking for secret doorways, they would look for the obvious signs. I bet no one considered pushing on the paneling."

They made their way back into the passageway, wanting to explore more of it. They spent the rest of the day exploring the various passageways and making mental notes on all the secret doors. As they made their way back to the dining room, Scott said, "I say tomorrow we check out the underground passages."

"I agree; besides, it will be dark soon, and I have worked off that big breakfast from earlier. I don't know about you, but a nice hot shower sounds good to me."

"I say we test the showers in this old place. I checked the plumbing, and it appears to be in good working condition."

When Caitlyn turned on the hot water, the pipes made a loud protesting noise, but soon hot water pulsated from the shower head. She was impressed with the water pressure in the house. Even with the pulsating water, it took a while to remove the ancient dust and cobwebs from her hair.

Once Caitlyn was done with her shower, she headed off in search of Scott. She found him seated at the massive mahogany desk in the library. Caitlyn told him, "I'm glad that Gregory didn't destroy this furniture and built his props around it instead."

She walked over to see what he was reading, "I found some more secret doors behind the bookshelves in here along with a few more papers."

"The library could be one of the most impressive rooms in this place once it is cleaned." One wall was floor to ceiling mahogany bookshelves, stained to match the ornate desk. There was a large fireplace in here as well. She noticed some leaded Victorian lamps that weren't here before, "Where did these come from?"

Scott answered, "I found those tucked away in the room behind the bookshelves. There are a few more pieces of furniture that you may want to look at. It looks as if someone may have used the room back there as their hidden office. I also found some Persian rugs rolled up and stashed in there. Something tells me that Gregory was behind that though. He probably didn't need the furnishings in this room, but didn't want them destroyed. He evidently knew quality when he saw it and the value in the décor."

As Caitlyn listened to Scott talk, she peered out the massive window. The view was breathtaking from this room. It overlooked the bayou, "I can just see Jean Paul sitting here working and watching as the boats passed."

"He made sure he designed this room well. From this desk, he could oversee what was being loaded onto the barges. Perhaps he was paranoid about his secrets being discovered. There are very few windows in any of the rooms that they would have frequented."

"Back then, their love was forbidden, so I am sure they lived in constant fear. Just think what would have happened if the two were discovered."

Scott asked, "What, that they would be hung and shot?"

She gasped, "You think someone found out about them don't you?"

"I'm beginning to think so. I also believe that someone is still using this house and may be trying to scare you."

"But who? It's not as if anyone knew I was moving out here. I didn't even tell the attorney my plans until the last minute. He wanted me to demolish the place."

"Why did he want you to demolish the house?"

"He told me he felt that was the best way for everyone to forget about the horrors here."

***

After a quick supper of leftover gumbo, Caitlyn decided to read the newspaper that Scott had picked up in town. She gasped when she saw the front page, "Scott, did you see this?"

"See what?"

She pointed to the article, "There was a body found in the bayou."

Scott took the paper from her, "Let me see that."

The surrounding air turned to ice as they read the paper. She whispered to Scott, "Do you feel that?"

"Why are you whispering?"

"I don't know, but I swear the air around us just turned ice cold." To prove her point, Caitlyn blew out a short burst of air and they watched as it turned into a fine white mist. "Do you think this murder has something to do with the figure we saw down at the bayou?"

"I'm starting to wonder. I know Detective Bertrand though, perhaps I should give him a call."

Picking up his cell phone, he called Bertrand directly, "Bertrand."

"Tony, it is Scott. Mon ami, I am renovating that plantation where the dude had the haunted house. Something strange is going on here."

Bertrand let out a long sigh. This was the last thing he needed on his plate right now. "Look, Scott, I am tied up at the moment, but I can send an officer to check on things for you. You should have known to expect problems. Everyone around here will tell you the ghosts don't want you messing with the house."

Scott let out a chuckle, "It's not the ghosts I'm scared of Tony. Look man, I wouldn't bother you if I didn't think it was anything serious. Hell, it may be nothing, but last night we saw a man down by the bayou. When I went to check it out, the person took off. At first, I just thought it was someone snooping around, but I just read the paper about the body being found in the bayou. It got me to thinking that perhaps the killer used this area as his disposal site. I have seen some mighty big alligators here; they may have a few hidey holes in the bend they use. This guy may know that as well."

Bertrand was all ears now, "Are you sure you saw someone by the bayou? What about a vehicle?"

"I didn't see a vehicle, but they took off into the woods. If it was a ghost, it wouldn't have to take off into the woods. Mais non, a ghost could just disappear."

"If it is okay with you, and the owner, of course, I would like to send someone out in the morning to search the area where you saw the person."

Scott looked over at Caitlyn, who nodded her head in agreement, "She said that is fine. There is one more thing; we found a secret passageway in the house. It looks as if someone may have recently been in the house."

"Why don't you show the officers that tomorrow as well? They can dust for fingerprints."

As they hung up, Detective Bertrand said a quick prayer that they may have a lead to follow up on finally. That old abandoned plantation would be the perfect place to drop the bodies in the bayou.

***

Scott turned to Caitlyn, "Tony will send someone in the morning to look over things."

Caitlyn wrapped her arms around herself in an attempt to settle her nerves, "Do you think that was the murderer we saw the other night?"

Scott pulled her over to him, wrapping his arms around her, "It could be nothing, but I would rather have the police check it out just in case."

Caitlyn rested her head on Scott's shoulder, "I am so glad that you are here right now. Ghosts I can handle, but a possible killer lurking these grounds again is unnerving."

Scott tilted her head up to his and kissed her. What started out as a light kiss to help calm her nerves turned into a passionate kiss that neither of them wanted to end.

He nuzzled her neck to taste her flesh and his hands caressed her breasts with fingers that teased her nipples until they were taut with desire. She squirmed beneath his body; her body prickled with excitement.

She ran her hands over the muscled contours of his back. He eased her tank top off of her shoulders. As his mouth closed over one taut nipple, she moaned in delight and sank her hands into his hair.

He picked her up and carried her off to her bedroom. They discarded their clothes in a heated fury. Hot shivers went through her as pleasure built up deep inside; she had never been with a man who brought her such joy, such pleasure. Her body felt as if it was made for him; it responded only to him. This was what love should do to a woman. It made her weak, but also strong.

She looked into his eyes and saw desire in them. As she slid onto him, she stayed perfectly still, unmoving. She enjoyed him filling her so completely. She felt the flames of lust as well as love build up inside of her. She loved the feel of their lovemaking and how connected she became with his body. They were joined heart and soul. Wave after wave of pure satisfaction washed over her body as they found their release together.

***

He watched through the window as the two kissed. Rage built up deep inside of him. He would have to take care of this new budding relationship sooner rather than later. Caitlyn was HIS! He refused to share her with any man. Soon, Caitlyn would discover that love was a powerful emotion that transcended even time. True love was forever.

How he missed her so. Soon, they would never be apart again.

***

After a quick shower, Caitlyn and Scott went walking hand in hand toward the bayou. Caitlyn had changed into a pair of tight fitting jeans and form fitting T-shirt that showed off her slim figure and her full breasts. For once, Caitlyn was glad she decided to wear a pair of old tennis shoes for the trip.

As they walked along the bayou, their bodies occasionally bumped into each other. Caitlyn felt the heat radiating from Scott. As they reached the pier that overlooked the bayou, Scott took Caitlyn in his arms once again. His breath caressed her cheek, and Caitlyn breathed in the clean, musky scent of him. A slight breeze from the bayou tousled her hair as she reveled in the strength of his arms around her. Caitlyn was drawn to this man, more than any other before.

The gently flowing water of the bayou reflected the moonlight and stars twinkling above. One could not ask for a more romantic setting. "It's so beautiful out here. I hate that such evil has touched this place."

He tilted her face up to his, and looked directly in her eyes. "You know that you can't blame yourself for what Gregory did, don't you?"

"I keep telling myself that, but when people look at me as if I am part of that monster, it wears on me."

Unable to resist, Scott took Caitlyn's lips in his. The kiss became more fervent as she pressed her body close to his. Caitlyn couldn't explain it, but she felt as if she had known this man forever. As the kiss continued, she became consumed by the sensual pleasure of his embrace.

***

As they walked back to the house, a dark figure emerged in front of them. Caitlyn was frozen with fear as she stared at the apparition in disbelief. The figure in front of them looked just like Gregory, except that his face seemed to be contorted and disfigured with the hideous mask of rage. Before either could react, the apparition reached out to grab Caitlyn. A piercing moan moved through the woods. Ghostly white images floated around them before they began attacking the dark shadow in front of them. A large gust of wind whipped through the area, taking the apparitions with it.

Caitlyn looked over at Scott, "I swear that was Gregory's image, but he is dead. That couldn't have been his ghost, could it?"

Scott was at a complete loss for words, "Until now, I would have told you there was no such thing as ghosts. Now, I am not so sure. I'm not sure what was in front of us, but I think we may want to confirm that Gregory is dead. If he is alive and roaming these grounds, we need to let the police know. That could explain the dead bodies."

Even though it was late, Scott would feel better if Tony confirmed that Gregory was dead and buried. "Tony, I know it's late, but the strangest thing just happened out here. Caitlyn swore that she saw Gregory Ferris. Is there any way you can confirm he is actually dead and buried?"

Tony had to shake his head to clear his mind, "Wait a minute, I'm not sure I heard you correctly. You said that the owner swore she just saw Gregory Ferris out there on the property?"

Scott cleared his throat, "Hell man, I'm not even sure what it was we saw. This man appeared in front of us, and Caitlyn swore that it was Gregory. I've never met the man so I'm not sure, but he was pissed. Mon ami, I don't believe in ghosts, but this was creepy as hell."

***

The last Tony had heard about Gregory Ferris was that he committed suicide in his prison cell, but what if it had been an elaborate stunt? Lord knew the man had enough money to bribe someone into helping him fake his death.

It was too late to make any calls, but in the morning, he would call the coroner's office, the funeral home, and anyone else who had contact with Gregory Ferris's body. If it meant obtaining a court order and having Gregory Ferris's body exhumed, so be it. He had to confirm that he was dead and buried.

***

Scott asked Caitlyn, "So you believe that was Ferris's ghost?"

"I don't know what to think anymore. I can't explain what just happened. The image looked like Gregory, except it had so much malevolent hatred. I swore that he looked at us with contemptuous disgust. Whoever in the hell it was out there, it gave me the creeps. I don't understand why there was so much anger coming from him and why it was directed at me. If he hated me that much, why leave me everything in his will?"

As Scott considered everything she asked, he had a feeling if he was right then she wouldn't like the answer. "If this was his ghost, it could be he didn't like the fact that I am here with you."

She shook her head, "That doesn't make any sense either. We didn't know each other that long. None of this makes any sense. I still don't know why he left me everything. Even if he did not have any family, he had close friends. Even Thomas, his best friend since kindergarten, couldn't explain why Gregory did what he did."

"Do you think it was possible that someone helped Gregory fake his death?"

A chill of pure terror ran through Caitlyn as she considered what Scott just said, "Is that even possible?"

"I've never asked you how much money Gregory left you and that's not what I am asking you now, but did Gregory have enough money to bribe someone to help him do just that?"

"Lord, yes. But wouldn't he have to pay a lot of people off?"

"That's what makes this difficult to believe. It would take an elaborate plan, and I am not sure if he could pull it off in prison. I do think it is something to look into."

***

As they neared the plantation, a green glow came from the second floor. Caitlyn stopped Scott and pointed to the window, "Do you see that?"

"I see it and I am wondering if the house is haunted or if someone is looking for something specific. We need to research this house more."

"Maybe the papers we found in the passageway will give us some clues."

"Let's get those papers and see what they say."

"They are in my room. I planned on reviewing them tonight in bed, but we may as well go through them now. I won't be able to sleep anyhow."

Chapter 25

The next morning as Scott was busy working on the house, his phone rang, "Mon ami, did you find out anything?"

Bertrand let out a sigh, "Do you think it would be possible for Ms. Reed to come down to the office and answer a few questions?"

Caitlyn happened to walk into the room and he asked her, "I can go over there if it is that important."

"Tony, give us a few minutes and we will head over."

Caitlyn looked out the window as apprehension settled deep in the pit of her stomach. Scott could tell that she wasn't too pleased with the impromptu visit. "Tony is a good person. You don't have anything to worry about, plus he is a damn good cop. He will get to the bottom of what is going on."

As soon as they arrived, Scott quickly moved to the other side of the car and opened her door. The stark, plain façade of the building had none of the southern charm the other buildings here in town had. As they walked up the stairs, a man in a pair of tan dockers and white polo shirt headed toward them. Scott shook his outstretched hand with a broad smile on his face, "Mon ami, it's good to see you again."

Bertrand turned toward Caitlyn, "Ms. Reed, thank you for agreeing to come see me."

She shook his hand with little enthusiasm, "I'm not sure what I can tell you that will help."

He smiled warmly at her, trying to put her at ease. "I promise not to take up too much of your time."

He led them down a long hallway to a large open room with harsh overhead lights. There were several desks around the room with low wall cubicles to give them an attempt at privacy. There were a dozen or so men and women busy working at their computers; their fingers clicking away at the keyboards. As Caitlyn walked by, she felt their eyes on her, staring intently with open curiosity.

Bertrand led them to a small conference room where Caitlyn paled when she saw the pictures on the board. She felt the room spinning and sat down in a chair near the window, far away from the horrors on the board. She imagined what these poor women had endured. She had always loved Gregory's haunted houses, but when she learned what he did to living people, she became grief stricken. It was unbelievable that she, as well as the general public, had found amusement in their deaths. What would possess another human being to do this to an innocent person? How could someone take a life so violently?

Bertrand looked over at Caitlyn and saw how she paled upon entering the room. There was no way she could fake that response and he was grateful that he could scratch her name off of the suspect list. Caitlyn kept her face directed towards the floor; she did not want to catch a glimpse of the pictures even accidentally. Bertrand asked, "Can I get y'all anything to drink?"

Caitlyn shook her head, unsure if her voice would betray her. As Bertrand closed the door so they could have some privacy, Caitlyn diverted her gaze to outside the window. While she was stuck in here with these horrific pictures, the people outside scurried about to and fro.

Caitlyn felt the detective's dark eyes searching her face as if he was looking for an answer to an important question. She noticed that he had a few gray hairs in his dark, wavy hair and wondered if this case caused the gray hair. This detective was a very imposing man and she could just imagine a criminal shaking in his boots as Bertrand interrogated him. "Was that the first time you saw Gregory since his arrest?"

She let out a sigh, "Technically, he called off the relationship before the grand opening of the haunted house. He called and asked that I attend the grand opening, and I thought maybe he wanted to pursue a relationship. When I arrived, I didn't see him right away and it wasn't long after it opened that the commotion started."

Bertrand asked, "Did you have any idea what Gregory was up to?"

Tears filled her eyes as she recalled that night, "No, I was just as surprised as Thomas, his best friend. Gregory had been so charming and doting when we dated. I thought he was prince charming."

Bertrand asked, "How long did y'all date?"

"We only dated a few times."

Bertrand looked into her eyes, "And you are sure that the person you saw was indeed Gregory Ferris?"

"That's just it, I am fairly certain, but I can't guarantee it. The person I saw looked like Gregory though." More than anything, Caitlyn wanted someone to tell her that the man who plagued her dreams, and ruined her life, was indeed dead.

Scott looked over at Bertrand, "Mon ami, did you find out anything yet?"

Bertrand ran his hand through his hair, "I had hoped to have some answers by now, but so far, I haven't found anything definitive. Gregory being alive would help me with this serial killer case; we could consider him as a viable suspect. So far, the only person I managed to get in touch with was the prison warden and as far as he knew Gregory was dead. This is where it gets strange though; the doctor working for the prison quit right after Gregory's death. He stated that he was tired of dealing with the dregs of society and would be better off in private practice where all he had to fear was a malpractice suit and not being killed. However, I have been unable to find this doctor. So far, he has not come up on any of my searches. It is as if he dropped off the face of the earth."

A jolt moved through Caitlyn's body at the idea that Gregory had faked his death. She looked Bertrand in the eyes, "Do you think it is possible he faked his death?"

"If enough money changed hands, I would say anything is possible." Taking her hands in his, Bertrand asked, "Did he have enough money to pull this off?"

She closed her eyes and leaned back in the chair as she struggled to come to grips with everything. Caitlyn considered all the money Gregory had in his various accounts, "Yes, he had more than enough money to fake his death. Wouldn't he have to pay off a lot of people to help him and make sure they kept quiet?"

"I am waiting for a few more people to return my call, but until I know for sure that Gregory Ferris is dead and buried, I will not let this matter drop." *Even if he had to exhume the man's remains,* Bertrand thought to himself. The problem with exhumation was the expense and without credible evidence, he didn't see the judge signing a warrant to exhume the body. It wasn't in the city's budget, but perhaps Ms. Reed would cover the costs. His gut told him she would sign over the funds to get an answer, but what would be the point? He wasn't sure they could find dental records or DNA on the man. He more than likely had been too careful to have records kept on him anywhere. "We have a sadistic killer lurking around this town. If there is a chance the person you saw was Gregory Ferris, I want to make sure we aren't looking at someone who figured out how to escape from prison. There is also another possibility; someone may be trying to scare you. Can you think of anyone who may want to frighten you away?"

Caitlyn let out a laugh, "The list is long I am afraid. Some people believe I had no idea what Gregory was doing; yet, others believe I knew and agreed to help him. I even had to change my phone number."

Bertrand asked, "I take it you received a lot of hate mail?"

"You have no idea. I even had some sickos contact me for a relationship."

"Do you have any of those letters?"

Caitlyn shook her head, "I burned most of them, but some I just threw right into the trash." Reaching into her purse, she pulled out two keys, wrote down an address, post office box number, and her attorney's name and phone number on a scrap piece of paper. She handed them to Bertrand while stating, "I haven't checked the mail in a while, but here is the number and the key. You can have it all. You don't need a warrant. You also have the address to Gregory's main house. You are more than welcome to pillage through everything in hopes of finding answers to your questions."

Bertrand looked at her with surprise in his eyes. He had never had a witness this cooperative, "Do you want us to contact you when we go to his house?"

Shaking her head, she replied, "I have no desire to go there. The attorney has a maid service go in once a week. I believe they come in on Fridays, but you can check with the attorney if you want. His name and number are on the paper. He was a little tight lipped about the whole situation; maybe he finds it hard to believe that Gregory left everything to me as well, but he may talk to you. I have a feeling he worked for Gregory for a while. For all I know, Gregory may have confided in him about how he made his props. To be honest with you, the attorney gave me the creeps so I would rather not deal with him unless I have to."

Scott absorbed everything Caitlyn said, and he asked, "Caitlyn, who would Gregory's money and property go to if something happened to you?"

She shrugged her shoulders, "I have no family left and haven't thought about it. Gregory didn't have any provisions written in his will. I'm still surprised he didn't leave everything to his friend, Thomas. That night when Gregory's secrets were discovered, Thomas and his wife, Grace, were genuinely distraught about what happened in his haunted house. I don't believe either of them even had a clue as to what lurked inside of Gregory. When I called Thomas and told him that Gregory left everything to me, he didn't sound surprised or hurt."

As he escorted Scott and Caitlyn out of the station, Bertrand made a mental note to look into both the attorney and Gregory's friend, Thomas. He wanted to find out if they received a piece of the pie if something happened to Caitlyn, or maybe, they had an ulterior motive for wanting Caitlyn out of the picture.

"Ms. Reed, it was nice meeting you. I will be in touch."

***

On the drive back to the plantation, Scott asked Caitlyn, "Do you mind if I stop by my house and pick up another gun and some more ammunition?"

The thought of a gun in the house sent a shiver down Caitlyn's body, "Do you think another gun is necessary?"

"We know for certain a serial killer is on the loose and there is a possibility someone is running around those passageways. I would feel more comfortable if we were well armed."

Caitlyn sighed, "I suppose you are right."

He could tell she was uneasy about guns and asked, "Do you know how to shoot a gun?"

Shaking her head, "I don't think I have ever held a gun in my entire life."

"I suggest we take a little bit of time off each day and target shoot. The more comfortable you are with a gun, the less likely you will be scared of it."

Caitlyn went over her conversation with Bertrand. Had Gregory faked his death or was he haunting her in the afterlife now? Why was he watching her? What could he possibly want with her? It's not like she was after him for his money, and they only dated for a short while.

Tears filled her eyes as she thought back to when she dated Gregory. She never knew that evil lurked inside of him. What would have happened to her if she found out? What would have happened if their relationship ended on a bad note? Would she have eventually become one of his props? Could that be why he followed her now?

Scott saw the range of emotions flit across Caitlyn's face, "Don't worry. Tony assured us he would have an officer patrol the area. He is good at what he does. He will find out what is going on; I promise you."

Not trusting her voice not to shake if she spoke, she only nodded her head. She took in a deep breath to calm her nerves, "I don't understand why Gregory left me his money and property." She smiled as she recalled how romantic and charming the man had been. "He was charming and doting, but something held him back as well. I didn't want to push the relationship too hard, but when I tried, he would always tell me that he was busy with the haunted house. I came to realize that the haunted house was more important than me. He called the relationship off, stating that he wanted to wait until the grand opening to pursue our relationship further." She looked over at Scott, "For a while, I thought he just didn't find me attractive."

Scott looked at her astounded, "I always took it that your relationship was much more involved."

She let out a startled laugh, "That's what I have been trying to tell everyone. There wasn't a relationship. We had a few dates, but that was as far as it went."

"So you and he were never intimate?"

Now, she laughed, "No, we had the briefest of kisses and that was it." She remembered how when Gregory left she felt the tension of sexual frustration. She even thought there may be something wrong with her, perhaps she had lost her sex appeal.

"When you said that Gregory had enough money to fake his death, do you think he would have done it?"

Caitlyn shrugged her shoulders, "Gregory was outrageously wealthy, but it seems impossible for him to fake his death."

"But you do think it is possible, don't you?"

Caitlyn nodded her head, "I am beginning to think with Gregory anything is possible." She turned in her seat and looked at Scott, "You don't think that was a ghost we saw, do you?"

"I just don't see why a ghost would run the way it did. A ghost is supposed to be made up of vapors or something isn't it? It seems like a ghost could just disappear if it wanted."

She chewed on her bottom lip as she wondered if Gregory's ghost was indeed watching her every move. "I don't know, but I think it may be beneficial to do a little more research into ghosts. I may head back into town tomorrow and go to the library."

Scott thought about it, "If you want to go over today, I can take you."

"I considered it, but the crime scene techs should be finishing up at the house. I am anxious to see if they found anything." The crime scene techs had arrived as they were leaving and Caitlyn didn't see a reason for them to wait until they returned.

"Let's stop by my house first and then we will head back to Whispering Willows."

Caitlyn's stomach let out a soft growl, "Let's stop and get something to eat first."

They stopped by and picked up lunch from Beazell's II. Scott told her, "We can eat at the house while I pack a few more things and get the guns." Anxious to see where Scott lived, she agreed to his offer.

He lived in a small, cozy cabin right on the bayou, "I am a Cajun boy at heart." He explained. "I find it relaxing to fish after a hard day at work."

Caitlyn was surprised to hear that, "I don't recall seeing you fish at the house."

"I have been a little busy there."

She shook her head, "Nonsense, you need to bring your fishing pole and take some time off to fish. I don't want to you to think you have to work twenty-four seven just because you are staying there."

After they had finished their lunch, Scott packed himself a few more clothes, grabbed his guns, and collected a few fishing poles. Caitlyn was right; he should take time to enjoy the fishing while there. Plus, it would be nice to spend some time alone with her on the water.

By the time they arrived at the plantation, the techs were finishing up with their investigation of the house. Officer Carl Miller met them over by the car, "We just finished up with everything. Thank you for allowing us to come by while you ran into town."

Caitlyn smiled up at him, "No, I am the one who should be thanking you. I appreciate you coming out here to check on things for me."

Officer Miller kicked at the dirt, unsure of what to say about the friendly compliment, "It's not a problem. That is what we are here for, to keep you safe."

Scott moved in closer to Caitlyn, overcome with a feeling of jealousy, "Did you find anything useful?" Caitlyn looked at him surprised to hear the harshness in his voice.

"The techs did a complete search of the house, but there were a lot of fingerprints all over the house. Numerous people have been in the house lately, and a lot of cleaning has taken place as well. We have no way of knowing if any of the people working for the crime scene cleanup company found any of the hidden passageways. Unfortunately, people roamed around the house while it sat vacant."

Scott asked, "What about the passageways?"

"We dusted the passageways for fingerprints as well and, surprisingly, there weren't as many in there. I never knew this place was riddled with so many passageways. I'm sure we missed some, but I'm sure we found a few that you may have missed as well. A tech will take both of your fingerprints for the files. We need to compare Gregory Ferris's fingerprints to the prints we found in the passageways. The only problem is we have no idea when the fingerprints were left behind. At least we will know if Gregory did find the passageways."

Caitlyn informed Officer Miller, "I think he knew about the passageways. Someone stashed furniture in one of the passageways. I assume Gregory didn't want to take the time to move the pieces when he started construction on the house."

Officer Miller looked at Caitlyn, "We will continue to do patrols out here, but please do not hesitate to contact us." He reached into his shirt pocket, took out a business card and handed it to Caitlyn, "Here is my number in case you need anything. I am sure that Detective Bertrand will also stay in touch with you as well. Just remember, this old plantation has been vacant for a while. After what happened here with Gregory Ferris, a lot of people, especially kids, are curious as to whether or not this place is haunted."

Caitlyn tucked his business card into her wallet, "Thank you again for looking into this for me."

"I suggest you not leave anything of value lying around just in case."

Caitlyn almost laughed out loud at that remark. She didn't have anything of value to worry about, "Thank you Officer Miller."

Chapter 26

The front door blew open while Scott walked up the stairs, causing him to stop at the landing. He swore he closed and locked the door before heading upstairs. Once again, he walked back downstairs. This time when he pushed the door closed, he deliberately, consciously locked the door. CLICK. As he made his way to the stairs, a cold breeze blew over him. He looked around to see if there were windows open somewhere letting in a draft.

Later that night as he slept, something woke him. When he looked around and saw that it was three thirty, he let out a low groan hoping that he could fall back asleep. Instead, he just tossed, turned, and watched as the minutes on the clock slowly passed.

As he lay wide awake in bed, his thoughts drifted off to Caitlyn. He wondered if she was wide awake as well. He rolled over and punched his pillow down as he tried to force himself to go back to sleep. Thinking of Caitlyn resting in bed right across the hall didn't help him get to sleep.

Unable to sleep, he gave up and went to brew himself a cup of coffee. He may as well get his day planned out. Maybe work would help clear his mind enough to figure out what had him bothered. It was as if he forgot something important, but for the life of him, he couldn't remember what.

At his bedroom door, he froze. Heavy footsteps were coming down the hall. He had tried to be quiet enough not to wake up Caitlyn. As he listened to the footsteps, he realized they were too heavy to be from Caitlyn. He peered out the door and saw the long hall was dark and empty. Scott walked into the hall, watching and listening. He knew he heard footsteps, and he knew that he'd locked the door earlier.

Scott felt someone behind him; it was a cold breath on his neck. He whirled around only to see that the hallway was still empty, but yet, it had a menacing look somehow. The footsteps continued back down the hall leading towards the stairs. He heard whoever it was making their way downstairs and back out the door.

As Scott peered into the dark hall, he wondered if he'd finally met a ghost that haunted this house or if his imagination was working overtime. Either way, it would be best not to tell Caitlyn just yet. It would be better if she still thought he was a non-believer.

As Scott walked into the kitchen, he saw Caitlyn sitting at the bar pouring herself a cup of coffee, "Couldn't sleep either?" She asked.

A sigh of relief went through him. It must have been her he heard walking downstairs. It's just that the footsteps sounded too heavy to belong to her. Caitlyn poured Scott a cup of coffee and handed it to him. Just as they went to sit down at the bar, the basement door blew open. Caitlyn held out her hand and told Scott, "I got it. I could have sworn the door was locked."

As she went to close the door, she became paralyzed with fear. Standing on the bottom step was a man, or at least, what appeared to be a man. The face was blurry, but a figure stood there watching her. As Caitlyn continued to stare at the man, it stayed perfectly still.

There was enough light from the kitchen shining down the stairs to cast an eerie glow behind the figure, silhouetting it even more. Caitlyn stepped back automatically as the figure made its way slowly up the stairs. As it drew closer, it lifted its arms as if reaching out to her. The entire upper body of the figure shook violently. As the figure blurred, a droning buzzing noise came from it.

Scott went to see what was going on and when he stepped behind Caitlyn, the figure disappeared. She looked at Scott, "Please tell me you saw that?"

"I'm not sure what I saw, but it sounded like a nest of angry hornets buzzing around down there."

Grabbing a flashlight, he walked down the basement stairs when Caitlyn grabbed his shoulders, "What are you doing?"

"I am going to go check it out. If you do have a nest down there, we need to take care of it. That could explain a good bit of the noises we have heard."

Caitlyn joined him, not wanting to stay up near the door by herself after seeing the mysterious figure. As they reached the bottom step where the figure had been standing, a bowling ball sized orb of blue light appeared before them. Scott looked at Caitlyn in disbelief. "Where do you think it came from?" She asked.

Shrugging his shoulders, "I'm not even sure what it is."

The mysterious orb of light floated in front of them, hovering in midair. It moved further into the basement, almost as if it wanted them to follow, "Do you think we should follow it?" asked Caitlyn.

"Let's see where it takes us." Scott agreed.

The further they moved into the basement, Caitlyn felt cold air swirling around her. The orb of light led them into the room where Gregory must have performed his hideous work. Caitlyn shivered as the light continued to hover over the table in the room. She whispered to Scott, "I'm not sure about you, but this is one room that I am not ready to deal with just yet."

Scott looked at her and nodded his head, "I couldn't agree more."

"I wonder if I should find a priest or someone to come out and bless this house, especially this room."

Scott looked around and shivered at the thought of the horrors performed in this room, "It may not hurt. You may not find a church that will step foot in this place, though."

***

At nine that morning, Caitlyn began making calls, hoping to find someone to come bless the house for her. She even made attempts at several of the surrounding cities with no success. About ready to give up, she found a Catholic Church in New Orleans who referred her to a Father Marc Trahan. Unfortunately, Father Trahan wasn't available to bless the house until Thursday of next week.

"Thank you, Father Trahan. I am here all day. Is there a particular time I should expect you?"

"I should be there sometime after lunch."

Caitlyn gave him directions from New Orleans to Whispering Willows. She said a quick prayer that he could help quiet some of the restless spirits here in the house.

Caitlyn made her way to the second floor to tell Scott that Father Trahan could bless the house next week. The guest bedroom took her by surprise; the rich burgundy paint had dried nicely, and she was pleased with the outcome. It didn't dry near as dark as she feared, and it gave the room an elegance that she believed guests would love. She walked over to the fireplace and was amazed to see what Scott managed to do. The boards and bricks that someone placed over the fireplace were gone, and he'd restored the mantel.

The wood floor was still scuffed and scratched, but that somehow gave the room character. Suddenly, maniacal laughter filled the room as she noticed blood soaking through the wood floor. She slowly backed out of the room. When she looked back, the blood was no longer visible. Could her eyes be playing tricks on her?

She went to step back inside the room to see what would happen, but was met with the maniacal laughter once more. She rushed back downstairs. She kept waiting for a ghost to rush at her and knock her down the stairs. The laughter now seemed to echo throughout the second floor.

As if reading her mind, the house appeared to whisper to her, "Forgive me… Forgive me… Forgive me…"

She tried to block the laughter and voices out of her mind; she told herself it was energy left behind from the tragedies that happened here, nothing more.

Chapter 27

Gina Dupre looked at the business card once more before gathering the courage to knock on the door. Perhaps the man had been a little too eager. From the outside, the house looked clean and cared for. When he approached her about the free haircut, she readily accepted. He even promised to have lunch ready if she came. Money was tight for her; she could use all the freebies she could get. She scraped up enough gas money to get here, but she should've looked at the map closer. Point Creole was further from her house than she had thought. She hoped she had enough gas to get her back home.

***

From the window, he watched as she slowly approached the house. He was the spider waiting for an innocent fly to venture too close to his web. He was eager to begin. He opened the door before she changed her mind.

***

He secured her unconscious body in the chair. He leaned her back to wash and dry her hair. He carefully brushed it to make sure he brought it back to a lustrous shine.

He reached for his knife and sharpened it once more. The unconscious woman did not matter to him. The hair on her head was what he wanted, the prize he needed. He had waited and watched for a head of hair like hers.

It had been so easy to lure her to his salon. He promised to give her a haircut that emphasized her gorgeous green eyes. He explained to her how the perfect hair cut would make her feel like a new woman. The clincher had been when he told her he would cut her hair for free and all she needed to do was allow him take a before and after shot to display in his salon. She greedily took his business card and said she couldn't wait to be transformed.

When she arrived, they chatted about the weather and the impending hurricane season. He kept the salon warm so she would be thirsty during the visit. Unknown to her, he spiked the bottle of water he offered with sedatives that he had readily available.

Her body went limp in no time. She never had time to scream or know what hit her.

Now, she was ready to be transformed. Looking at her unconscious body, she may not be a beautiful woman by any means, but her hair was magnificent. He pulled her hair back tightly so that her scalp rose by several degrees. He watched as her hair cascaded from his fist in luxurious waves.

He placed the knife on her forehead, just above her eyes and scalped her. The razor sharp knife easily cut away the skin from her face. He then started right above the collarbone, making sure not to knick any of her skin. The face and scalp came away with perfect ease from her skull. He had done this enough times to where he had become proficient with this process. As he surveyed his prize, he noticed that her hair color was natural, and this gave him extreme pleasure.

He cleaned the face and hair so that he could place it on the mannequin head he had ready. This hair seemed to be made for the mannequin head. It fit perfectly and cascaded down with perfection and he couldn't wait to style it over and over again.

Chapter 28

Caitlyn took a bite of her eggs Benedict and moaned in delight. She was glad that Beazell's II opened on the weekends for brunch. Breakfast was her favorite meal of the day and dining here, looking over the bayou, helped to lighten the mood at the table.

Bertrand took another sip of his coffee and wiped his mouth with his napkin, "Thank you for agreeing to meet me here this morning. I have my hands full with the serial killer case."

Scott asked, "Are you making any progress on the case?"

Bertrand grimaced, "Not really. The media is giving this case around the clock attention, and we are getting pressure to bring in the FBI."

Scott raised a brow, "Who wants to bring in the FBI? It's not like y'all are a bunch of country yokels who don't know what they are doing."

"That's what I keep telling them. Now, the media and some of the locals are breathing down the mayor's neck. Men are afraid to let their wives and daughters go out at night. And a few businesses have noticed a decline in tourist sales."

Caitlyn listened to the two men talk and said, "I don't envy your job. Dealing with criminals, especially killers, has to be a nasty business. I cringe whenever I think about what Gregory did to those poor people. I have yet to bring myself

to venture into the basement for extended periods of time.
And you deal with these gruesome crimes."

Scott could tell his friend was stressing over this case. He
even noticed that he had more gray peppering his dark
head of hair, "I take it you have no leads on the murderer?"

"No, not yet." Looking over at Caitlyn, Bertrand nodded his
head, "I got in touch with the coroner regarding Gregory's
death. Although vague, he said since the doctor at the jail
declared Gregory deceased by suicide, he just pencil
whipped the body straight to the funeral home. Gregory
didn't have any family and had instructed the attorney in
case of his death to have his body cremated."

Caitlyn paled, "The body was cremated? So did the
crematorium check the body beforehand?"

Bertrand let out a deep sigh, "The police commissioner is
looking into this matter, but it appears that Gregory's body
didn't follow the proper channels. The body went straight
from the morgue to the crematorium without anyone
bothering to check paperwork, etc. The crematorium, in an
effort to save money, was performing another cremation
and did several at once. When the notice came in that they
were to do a cremation for a prisoner, they figured they
would save the state money and went ahead with the
cremation. From what I could tell, the attorney mentioned
to the warden of Gregory's wishes in case of death. I think
the attorney knew that Gregory had planned his suicide.
Instead of asking the warden to put Gregory on suicide
watch, he told the warden that Gregory feared for his life.
Gregory received several death threats, even from

prisoners. He was placed in solitary, away from the general population."

Scott had some serious doubts about Gregory's death, "What about the doctor who confirmed Gregory's death? Have you located him?"

Bertrand shook his head, "We are still looking for him, but I talked to the guard who found Gregory. He had hoped they cut Gregory down in time, but when the doctor arrived he just shook his head and said they were too late."

A shiver ran through Caitlyn, "How did he do it?"

"He hung himself with his sheet from the top of the jail cell. It appeared that Gregory knew he would have enough time to kill himself before the guard did his next round."

Caitlyn looked at Bertrand, "So, I guess we won't know any answers until you talk to the doctor then?"

Nodding his head in agreement, "We have not given up locating the doctor, especially with the body count rising here. Now that I have the police commissioner on board, I hope that we can get some answers quicker."

***

Before heading back, Caitlyn and Scott stopped by the library to pick up the information she'd requested on the plantation next door. "Thank you so much for doing this for me. I will be very careful with it and get it back to you as soon as possible."

The librarian, Mindy Bourgeois, replied, "Take your time. The information came from a Mr. Eli Fontenot. His father tended the land at Cottonwood Plantation and Mr. Fontenot grew up on the plantation. He said to stop by if you have any questions. I will warn you though that he is a nice man, but he does like to talk."

On the drive back to the plantation, Caitlyn felt as if the morning's meeting had raised more questions than answers. Scott reached out and squeezed her hand. She let out a deep sigh, "This is all too difficult to believe."

"We will get to the bottom of this; I promise you." Even with everyone's reassurances, Caitlyn still couldn't fight the apprehension of knowing that Gregory may be alive and stalking her.

As soon as she arrived back to the plantation, she threw herself into her work. After several hours of dusting, mopping and scrubbing the floors, she looked around to see what she had accomplished. After what seemed like months of exhaustive work, the renovation of the house was taking shape. The work had given her a new and invigorating purpose in life. There had been re-plastering, sanding, and wall papering; not to mention the cleaning.

***

Scott marveled at the lamp he found hidden in the far corner of the passageway. He wanted to get it in the light to inspect it before checking the wiring. By the looks of it, the lamp was Tiffany inspired. What a find it would be if it was an antique Tiffany lamp. He was clueless as to why on earth someone would tuck such a beautiful piece of history so far back in the passageway. He hoped Mr. Boudreaux could give them more information on the lamp.

As Scott walked to the large window in the room, he never noticed the long cord dangling around his legs. Suddenly, the cord was pulled taut, almost as if someone stepped on it. Before Scott knew it, he lost his balance and struck the desk with a loud thud before falling to the floor.

He looked around the room to see just how he tripped. A loud booming voice reverberated through the room, "She is mine. Leave her alone!"

Scott looked around the room to see where the voice came from. He thought he heard footsteps coming from the passageway so he called out, "Who is there?"

No voice answered him. He peered into the passageway, but was greeted with nothing but darkness. Caitlyn rushed into the room, "It sounded like something fell. Are you okay?"

"I am fine. I found something in the passageway I wanted to show you." Scott held up the lamp, "I believe it is a Tiffany inspired lamp. There are a few more items tucked far away in the corner also."

Caitlyn gasped at the beauty of the lamp, "I wonder why someone tucked this away back there? I can't wait to see what else is hidden around here." Unable to resist finding other hidden treasures, Caitlyn told Scott, "I will start pulling out the other items you found."

It took another two hours to pull the other treasures tucked away in that corner. Someone took a lot of time making sure they were safely wrapped. Suddenly tired, Caitlyn let out a long sigh, "I guess I will have to wait until tomorrow to unwrap and clean these up."

Scott stretched his tired body and yawned, "It is later than I thought."

Exhausted from the day, she fell sound asleep as soon as her head hit the pillow.

***

Caitlyn bolted upright at the sound of footsteps. Could it be Scott walking around, restless? She forced the lump of fear caught in her throat down with a gulp while praying that it was not Gregory walking the halls.

As she fell asleep, a feeling of loneliness came over her. Here she was in this ancient plantation, in the middle of nowhere, and the man she wanted to be with slept in a different room.

The footsteps sounded again. This time they were monstrously loud in the quietness of the night. Her hands clutched the blankets in fear.

Her ears strained to hear another noise, anything that may give her an idea as to who, or what, was outside her bedroom door. But all she heard was the pounding of her own heart.

She tried to talk herself into getting out of bed, but her limbs were slow to respond. She couldn't seem to make herself get out of the cocoon of warmth she found in bed.

A low moan in the darkness made her blood freeze. There was something out there. She eased herself out of bed, trying to stay quiet. As she went to open the door, she doubted her actions. Maybe, she should scream for Scott. He was across the hall and would come running.

The pokers by the fireplace grabbed her attention. She drew one out as she eased her way back to the door. Her feet were quiet as she made her way over the hardwood floor. Her fingers wrapped tightly around the still warm handle of the poker.

As she opened the door, the stark darkness of the hallway mocked her. No lights burned to lend a glow to the hallway. In front of her was nothing but a dark abyss; nothing but a sinister darkness. She hadn't noticed, until now, how cold it was.

She took a deep breath and crept forward. The silence of the house menacingly taunted her. "Caitlyn…" The voice was right next to her and it sounded like Gregory's.

Icy terror raked down her spine, and her body froze with fear. She snapped her head to the side to see who was there. There was nothing but darkness.

From the end of the hall, a woman appeared surrounded by a hazy white glow, "Leave her alone." As the figure moved closer to Caitlyn, she took in her appearance. The woman appeared to be young, maybe in her early twenties. She had shiny brown hair that cascaded down her shoulders in ringlets and the most unusual shade of hazel eyes. By the look of her nightgown, Caitlyn suspected that she probably died in the mid-1800's. Another figure appeared behind the young girl. The woman wore a stunning deep purple dress that had voluminous skirts and a high lace collar. The sleeves were bell like and revealed her dainty hands, which were covered by black silk gloves. Barely any skin showed on the woman. Could this be the mysterious wife of Jean Paul?

A black figure appeared between Caitlyn and the two ghosts. Instinctively, they stepped back. Caitlyn's hand flew to her mouth as the shadow took shape. When he turned his malevolent eyes on her, it peered right into her very soul. He reached out a hand as if to touch her. His icy cold breath sent a chill down her spine, "Caitlyn it is me. Do not be afraid."

Caitlyn was frozen in terror as Gregory moved closer to her. "It's you!" His gaze intensified as he moved even closer.

Scott's voice broke the silence, "Caitlyn is that you? I thought I heard someone."

The image immediately faded, but not before he let out a loud moan that echoed throughout the house and shook the walls. Scott came running to her, "Are you okay?"

She could barely speak; her voice shook, "That was Gregory. I know it was."

Scott began to push on the walls, "There has to be a secret passage in this hall that we haven't found."

Caitlyn reached out to him, "I don't think he needed a secret passage. Gregory is a ghost."

Scott shook his head in pure disbelief, "No, I saw him too. What I saw was the figure of a man, not a ghost. I am telling you that he is lurking somewhere in this house."

***

Gregory watched from his hiding spot. He had been so close to her. He watched as the two interacted, and he didn't care for the way this man looked at his Caitlyn. He wanted to be the one holding Caitlyn, not this man. How he missed the way she felt against his body.

He wondered if Caitlyn sensed that he came into her room and lay next to her as she slept. Someday soon, he would no longer have to hide from her.

***

Caitlyn wrapped her arms around herself at the thought of Gregory being this close to her, "Either way, I won't be able to get back to sleep. You can look all you want, but that was a ghost. There were two other ghosts who tried to warn him to leave me alone. By the looks of their outfits, I would say that they were from the 1800's."

Scott looked to see if there were any signs of ghosts or intruders lurking about. "Let's set up some cameras. Maybe, we can catch Gregory or whoever else is lurking in the passageways."

"That may work. Then I can prove to you that there are ghosts haunting this house."

"Or, I can show you that there is no such thing as ghosts and someone is trying to scare you."

Caitlyn looked up at him, "Either way, we should get some answers. Do you think anyone in Point Creole will have what we need?"

Scott shook his head, "No, we will need to order it online. Unless you want to take a trip to New Orleans, ordering online is our best bet."

"No, you may have better luck finding something online. We can have it shipped here faster than us traveling all over trying to find what you want."

"Do you have good internet service here?"

Caitlyn shook her head, "We will have to go to town to get a good signal. There is still no internet out here. The phone company said it would take a while; even the cell service is spotty at times."

"Well then, tomorrow morning, I suggest we go into town for breakfast and a little shopping."

Unable to go back to bed, Caitlyn went into the library to inspect it a little more. As soon as she stepped into the room, she felt as if she'd been transported to another time. The rugs were back on the floor and the furniture was placed around the room. The doors leading to the porch were open and a breeze blew in from the bayou.

A man, busily working, sat at the desk. A young, black girl came in, "Sir, there is a Mr. Picou to see you."

The man let out a deep sigh, "Send him in."

The young girl held the door open for the distinguished looking man to enter.

"Mr. Favre, I won't keep you. I came by once more to see if you are interested in selling. I will double my previous offer."

The man at the desk just shook his head, "Mr. Picou, my answer is still no. I have put too much blood, sweat, and tears into this house. I will never sell. I am sorry, but my decision is final."

Picou turned on his heel and stormed out of the house. As soon as this Mr. Picou left the room, everything went back to normal. Caitlyn turned around to see Scott looking at her, "What I just witnessed wasn't a ghost," she told him, "but more of an impression. It must have had a significant meaning to this house for it to be memorialized. I guess the man at the desk was Mr. Favre and a Mr. Picou came in to talk him into selling the house. This Mr. Picou was upset when Mr. Favre refused to sell the house."

"Didn't you say that a Picou had the house after the Favre family?"

Caitlyn nodded her head, "Uh huh."

Scott rubbed his chin, "Wouldn't it be something if this Mr. Picou had something to do with the deaths of Jean Paul and Celeste Favre? That could be why the impression of that conversation was left here."

"Do you think that this Mr. Picou would have killed over land?"

"If you own land, you have the power and back then this was a prime piece of property. You not only have this massive house which is enormous, even by today's standards, but you also have the land that came with this piece of property."

Caitlyn interrupted, "And then you have the bayou that leads right to the Mississippi River."

Scott finished the sentence for her, "With the dock built on the property. Mr. Favre may have been considered a mere Acadian, but he had a shrewd business mind. I've done a little research on him. From what I can tell, this man started the sugar cane syrup business here as well as the cotton mill. Both products were responsible for bringing commerce to this little town. The town folk had a lot of respect for Mr. Favre and when Marguerite, his daughter, came forward after his death, no one even bothered to question it. When she returned, that put a real kink in Picou's plans. Not only did his wife want to move out of this large, extravagant house, but a mysterious woman came into town and took everything away from him that he was finally able to obtain."

"Still, I can't see why Marguerite would run off with a man after she finally had the family plantation back in her hands."

"Some of the older people here in town wonder the same thing. It seems as if rumors have circulated since her disappearance; there were questions about there being more to it than just her running off. It turned out not long after Marguerite disappeared so did Andre Picou's wife, Evangeline. When asked about her disappearance, Andre said that Evangeline left to go visit her parents. But, she never arrived at her parents' house."

"This mystery deepens."

Scott agreed, "This makes for one hell of a story, if it is all true. The only problem is trying to solve a mystery that happened almost two hundred years ago will be next to impossible."

"Oh, but it could be a lot of fun. I am anxious to tear apart the attic and other areas of the house, hoping to find more information. I noticed the other day several boxes up in the attic; there has to be something that will give us answers. There may even be more journals."

Scott took her into his arms, "I hate to disappoint you, but you must remember that a lot of the Acadians exiled here did not know how to read or write. It was the same for slaves. If their masters felt that they knew how to read or write, they were severely punished if not killed."

"I don't know. I honestly believe that Mr. Favre was a smart man who may have taught not only himself, but Celeste and the children how to read and write."

Scott kissed her on the forehead, "I just don't want you to get your hopes up. That was a different life back then. It was probably all they could do just to survive."

As Caitlyn thought back to the vision she had earlier, she knew in her heart of hearts that Mr. Favre had been jotting something down before Mr. Picou came in. There had to be something to let her know what happened here all those years ago.

***

He listened intently in the passageway to their conversation. He had hoped to scare them away by now, but so far, it wasn't working. He almost laughed out loud at the idea of this old plantation being haunted. The rumors had helped him keep others away from the house, until now.

He grew up hearing about all the money and treasures that Andre Picou hid in these walls. No one had the courage to search for what rightfully belonged to them, but he did. Hell, after Andre Picou killed his first wife, it seemed like he cursed the whole Picou family. Nothing but misfortune followed them after that fateful day.

The Cottonwood Plantation still stood, but the family was going broke trying to keep it running. Instead of doing anything about their misfortune, though, everyone would rather just sit around and talk about their troubles. He grew up eavesdropping whenever he could and it had been easy to do in that drafty old plantation home. His momma would whack him in the back of the head whenever she caught him and his dad would do worse. But without eavesdropping, he would never have learned about the secret passageways riddled throughout Whispering Willows. No one mentioned the Underground Railroad playing an important part here in Point Creole. He wondered if anyone even knew. Probably not, that seemed to be a taboo subject, even after all this time.

He was surprised that Marguerite Favre had been accepted as Jean Paul Favre's illegitimate child. He doubted it would have worked with any other family at that time. Even back then, the locals were scared of the plantation, and when Evangeline Picou confirmed the rumors of Whispering Willows being haunted, it spread like wildfire. When Andre Picou purchased it a second time around, after Marguerite's disappearance, Evangeline refused to live here. The family was forced to sell this part of the property as their money troubles increased. Each new homeowner stayed only a short time, and the house was put up for sale once again.

He couldn't help but laugh silently when he thought back to when he first started searching for the treasures hidden in these walls. He was thirteen at the time. This old place had never scared him, but he frightened the owners so bad they left in the middle of the night. They had a moving company come the next day for their things; they put the house on the market and never returned.

The only time he could not walk these passageways had been when Gregory Ferris owned the place. Mais non, that man terrified him right from the beginning. Gregory had not skimped on the bells and whistles when he set up the alarms, and that made it difficult for him to slip in and out without detection.

He'd searched this property for almost fifty years now and had yet to find any treasure. Perhaps the existence of the Picou family treasures and haunting ghosts was nothing more than rumors.

A cold wind whisked through the passageway chilling him to the bone. For a moment, he thought he felt someone breathing down his neck. He slowly turned around fearing that someone had found his hiding place. He let out a sigh of relief when he saw nothing but darkness behind him.

Still, he couldn't shake the feeling that someone watched him with dark, menacing eyes. Maybe eavesdropping on the lady's conversation had his mind playing tricks on him. All these years that he'd searched these passageways for the treasures and he had yet to come face to face with a ghost.

***

Anxious to learn what the town librarian found, she perused the documents in hopes of discovering a few more answers. She let out a soft sigh of disappointment. There wasn't much in the documents to go on. She learned that the house next door was built in 1785 by Andre Picou, a local cotton merchant. He tried to purchase property along the bayou or even better the Mississippi River, but his wife had insisted that they buy further away from the water. It turned out she had been deathly afraid that the pirates would break into their house in the middle of the night and kill them while they slept. From the papers in front of her, Andre's money came from his wife's family, and his father-in-law would only purchase land that his beloved daughter approved.

The house had stayed in the Picou family, but due to the economy, it was slowly sold off to the point that there were only a few acres where the house remained. It looked as if hard times have befallen the old plantation house there as well.

The plantation was currently owned by Henry Picou, who inherited the family plantation after his mother's death. His mother had the old parlor turned into a beauty salon to make ends meet. Henry came back home after his mother's death and now worked at a local funeral parlor. Caitlyn looked at the picture of the plantation next door to them and wondered, could it be haunted as well?

Chapter 29

Caitlyn was relieved to see the car driving up the driveway. She had half expected Father Trahan to call and cancel. After stepping out of his car, he shook Caitlyn's hand, "Ms. Reed, thank you for asking me over to your house. It isn't too often that we get a request for a house blessing. I researched this house and was surprised to learn that many horrors happened here."

Caitlyn nodded her head in agreement, "I hope that a blessing will help. I have had no luck with cleansing the rooms or house."

Father Trahan asked, "So you have seen spirits, then?"

Caitlyn shook her head, "I am not sure if it is spirits or energy left behind. But yes, there have been a few things that can't be explained."

"Well, let's see what we can do to help." As Father Trahan looked up at the house, he sensed the evil that lived in this home. He hoped this worked, but if evil made its way into the heart of the house, an exorcism would be needed.

Father Trahan was not what she expected. Caitlyn had expected a much older priest and was surprised by his youth and handsome appearance. They had talked for a few more minutes before he proceeded with blessing the house.

Father Trahan looked at Caitlyn, "I will start at the front porch and work my way through the house. If you and any guests could please keep pleasant thoughts while I do this, it will help.”

“I will let Scott know that you are here and ask for him to keep his thoughts as pleasant as possible.”

As Caitlyn headed upstairs to find Scott, she heard Father Trahan chanting a prayer that she couldn’t understand. As curious as she was about the process, she figured he would rather work alone instead of having someone looking over his shoulder. She stopped midway up the stairs; a man stood at the top of the landing, staring at her. The apparition was only that of a dark image of a man, but she felt his eyes piercing straight through her. The hate he felt for her resonated through the house.

“You can’t hurt me.” He called out. A shiver ran through her at the sound of that voice. It had a vague familiarity to it. As Father Trahan made his way inside the house, the figure sneered at him before vanishing into thin air. Could that be Gregory?

***

Father Trahan moved through the house sprinkling holy water while saying his prayers. As he made his way through the main house, the window on the front door developed a vertical hairline crack. He frowned at the split and once again blessed the foyer.

As he moved to the second floor, he felt a presence in the air. The air around him changed and became thick with evil. He continued to say his prayers and bless the house with holy water, making sure not to miss a single inch of the house.

***

Caitlyn stepped outside as Father Trahan finished blessing the house. She saw a man again in the cemetery. For a moment, she thought she saw him smile at her. She headed to the cemetery to see if this was a ghost staring at her. As she moved closer, he once again seemed to vanish into thin air. She looked back at the house and swore that the house glared back at her with evil malice; almost as if it dared her to reenter. She wondered if Father Trahan saw the man or even felt the evil that seemed to dwell in the house.

As she made her way back to the house, it suddenly looked different. Father Trahan walked out of the front door smiling. Could it be that this had worked?

"I can't thank you enough Father Trahan for coming out here and blessing the house."

Father Trahan looked back at the house, unsure if he'd banished the evil that lived inside, "It was my pleasure. I hope that you have many happy years here."

They had talked for a few more minutes before he left. Before getting into his car, he took her hands in his, "God bless you my child. Please don't hesitate to contact me if you need further help."

As she walked back into the house, she wondered if the blessing had worked. As she closed the door, she waited to hear a ghost walking around upstairs. There was nothing but silence. She slowly opened the basement door before peering down the stairs. No apparition stared back at her, nor did she hear any moaning.

***

Over the next several days, Scott and Caitlyn were able to get a lot of work done without anything unusual happening. Scott began talking about renovating the basement. Even though they hadn't noticed any strange happenings in the house, Caitlyn still couldn't bring herself to go down there. It just gave her a creepy feeling being down there.

Chapter 30

Caitlyn woke in the middle of the night to find it freezing in her room. Even with the window unit running full blast, it was normally not this cold in the room. Yawning, she watched as her breath turned into a white misty vapor in front of her.

Why was it so cold? She pulled the blankets over her and buried her head in the pillows. The temperature in the room seemed to drop another ten degrees. When she peered out from under a small gap in the covers and saw no movement in the room, she got out of bed to check the thermostat.

It was even colder in the hall. She bit back a scream as a cold hand brushed her face. She flinched away from the ghostly hand and jumped as a door downstairs slammed shut. She went to knock on Scott's door, surprised to find his door freezing cold. Something whispered in the dark near her left side, but the words were incomprehensible. Strange noises came from the staircase and moved up towards her. Whatever was roaming the house had been toying with her and obviously never left.

One part of her body wanted to bang on Scott's door and run into his arms, but another part of her wanted to find out what made that noise. Curiosity won out, and she headed for the stairs. The first floor was cloaked in darkness. No moonlight even filtered inside.

She shook her head trying to figure out what she was doing. She shouldn't be alone in the dark of night. She should run into Scott's arms and figure this out in the light of day.

As she headed back upstairs, she felt the temperature drop even more. Her feet became numb as she walked barefoot on the hardwood floors. Her fingers became stiff from the extreme cold, and she could literally breathe icicles.

A piano played from somewhere downstairs; the music was surprisingly cheerful. It called her to follow the cheery notes. As she made her way back downstairs once again, a giggling noise came from upstairs and something bound down the stairs, blowing right past her. The front door mysteriously opened and closed.

Suddenly, the downstairs was once more submersed in silence. The air around her dropped in temperature once again. This time she feared her blood would freeze from the cold and here she wore only an oversized t-shirt.

A pair of cold hands caressed her. She went to brush them away only to find no one there. She found the light switch and blanketed the room in light. The hands that caressed her body disappeared and the room grew warmer. The house went still once again. She walked back upstairs. As she climbed back into bed, she listened for a moment to the piano music playing, but this time it was single hollow notes.

As she drifted off to sleep, a voice whispered in her ear, "I want to be with you, now. I can't wait any longer." A gentle hand slid down her neck and over her shoulder. Fingers followed every contour of her body, moving over her breasts, down to her hips, and making spiraling patterns along the way. When the fingers touched her bare skin, she shivered at the cold touch.

A voice whispered into her ear, "You are finally here." Cold lips kissed her neck. Fear moved into her body, "You can never leave me again Caitlyn."

In horror, Caitlyn struggled against the cold grasp of the person on top of her. A piercing shriek filled the room as she screamed out in horror. Scott came rushing into the room just as the dark shadow vanished into thin air.

As Scott's warm embrace calmed her nerves, she wondered if she would ever fall asleep again. The voice sounded like Gregory, but there had been a different tone to it.

Chapter 31

Sweat pooled beneath his gloves as he crouched in the closet and waited for her to come home. He'd studied her patterns long enough to know that she came home every night at six and climbed in bed by eleven. He slipped drugs in several of the water bottles she had in the fridge upon his arrival. He needed her unconscious before he made his move.

Anticipation ran through his body as he eagerly awaited her arrival. She was never this late and he feared that she wasn't coming home tonight.

As he waited, he reminisced. He enjoyed his job at the funeral parlor, but he hated that his work would be destroyed for eternity. No one would ever appreciate his work. He wanted something more satisfying.

After his mother had left him the house and salon, he thought he would be happy styling hair for the women in Pointe Creole, but that left him feeling empty. He saw them a day or so after they left his shop, and their hair haphazardly hung in a ponytail or was unkempt. It aggravated him that these women had gorgeous hair, and they did nothing to show it off to its full potential.

When the door opened, he knew his time was near. She should have come to his salon, but no, she was too good for him. She would be punished for denying him what he wanted. He would have that glorious hair of hers.

When the light came on in the bedroom, he moved deeper into the closet; he didn't want to be discovered just yet. He must wait until she passed out before he made his move. Her screams would alert the neighbors.

The muscles in his stomach tightened as adrenaline rushed through his veins. His ears stayed alert as he listened to her every move. Tonight would be perfect.

He heard the water running for her shower. He imagined her getting undressed and ready to step into the shower.

***

Tiffany Dubois struggled to find the house key as she balanced her supper and a few groceries. It had been a busy day at the store and she was dead on her feet. She dropped the groceries and supper onto the kitchen counter, kicked off her shoes, and headed for the refrigerator. She reached into the freezer and pulled out the last frozen daiquiri in a bag. These were the best inventions ever made. No more dealing with a blender. Instead, you just threw the bag in the freezer and several hours later, voilà, you had a frozen concoction.

She looked over at her cell phone and contemplated calling Jason to come over. As she removed the rubber band from her hair, she caught a whiff of the heavy smoke smell that lingered on her even after work. She would be better off taking a shower and going to bed. Besides, tomorrow was Saturday and the busiest day at the store. Her dad kept her later than normal tonight. He wanted to make sure that he had extra smoked sausage, Andouille, boudin, and hog head cheese ready for the influx of tourists they were expecting tomorrow. On top of that, he needed her to help him prepare the cracklins.

When her dad first approached his wife and family about opening up a meat market in Point Creole, they thought he was nuts. When he retired from the paper mill, they figured he would spend his days fishing or at least just relaxing. He worked hard to put his children through private school, and now it was his turn to relax and let his family take care of him. Instead, her father decided that this town needed a meat market. He had made his own meats for years since no place here sold his beloved treats and he refused to go to the larger cities for anything. As it turned out, others here in Point Creole wanted the same thing because they flocked to the store on opening day. Between the locals and the tourists, they stayed busy. The local restaurants purchased from them as well. It sure helped when other businesses and locals supported the businesses in their community. The money was steady, and sales had increased as word spread.

Her dad's business was doing better than any of them expected. But she wished he would understand that she didn't want to work at the store for the rest of her life. She had her dreams just like he did. Hell, she was lucky that he paid her a salary and let her move out of the house. As much as she loved her family, she needed a life. At least here in her small house, she could work on her designs as she pleased without anyone barging in on her. She hoped that the material she ordered would have come in today, but it didn't. When she saw the material on the fabric website the other day, she purchased it instantly. Several months back, she opened a small shop on a website she found. Ever since opening the online store, her clothing and jewelry sales had taken off. As soon as she posted something on the site, she sold it right away. Tiffany hoped that one day a design company would see her work and contact her.

As Tiffany got ready for bed, she thought she heard a rustling noise in the room. The small sound echoed in the stillness of the night. Her heart pounded as the adrenaline pumped in her body. Turning around, she looked to see if anyone was there. Even though she didn't see anything, she waited and listened. Not hearing another noise, she figured it must have just been her imagination. It was almost one in the morning, and she had to be up at five. Tomorrow would be one of those days where she lived on coffee.

As she drifted off to sleep another noise echoed through the house. She bolted upright and peered into the darkness. Her heart pounded ferociously in her chest. She couldn't see anything in the darkness, but she couldn't shake the feeling that she was not alone. As she went to lie back down, a movement near the closet confirmed her fears. Before she could react, a man pounced on her and pinned her to the bed. She struggled to break free, to scream, and to kick this person off of her.

***

He had to struggle to contain her. She must not have drunk any of the water he drugged in the refrigerator. He took his hands, placed them around her neck and squeezed. The adrenaline of the kill gave him almost superhuman strength. He took the knife from its sheath and pressed it to her throat. His breath hit the side of her face as he told her, "Stop fighting me, and I won't kill you. If you scream or say a word, you are dead. Do you understand?"

He saw the fear in her eyes. Her fear was so intense; he could smell it in the air.

***

As the words penetrated her mind, she nodded her head in agreement. Her harsh breathing filled the silence of the room, and tears filled her eyes. She heard the duct tape being pulled from the roll. He forced a pill in her mouth before taping her mouth shut; she choked on the bitterness of the medicine. She found a chance to break free when he went to tape her hands to the bedposts; however, whatever pill he shoved in her mouth had taken effect. She slowly slipped into unconsciousness. As the darkness enveloped her, she wondered what would happen to her. Was he going to rape her or worse, kill her?

His breathing was hot on her body, and he had not uttered another word. Bile caught in her throat as she waited. As he moved around the room, she said a prayer that he planned on robbing her and nothing more.

As she gave into the powerful drug, he sat on the bed next to her. He whispered in her ear, "Your hair is just too beautiful." There was a familiarity to the voice, but the fear inside of her overcame her thought process. As her mind became dark and confused, she knew that she would never see her parents again. If only she'd called Jason, then maybe she would have a chance to be rescued.

***

He carefully pulled his trophy away from her body before placing it in the cooler he had stashed. He took a deep breath to calm his nerves. As he drove away, he wondered how long it would be before someone discovered the body.

***

Collin Dubois looked at his watch for the umpteenth time and wondered once again where his daughter was. It was not like her to be late, especially this late. He had a million things to do and she promised him to be here at six in the morning, if not sooner, so they were ready for the day.

He let out an exasperated sigh. He knew that she had her own dreams and was ready to live her life, but he wasn't ready to let her go just yet. Tiffany had him wrapped around her little finger since the day she was born. She had such an angelic face, accentuated by brilliant blue eyes, and a bright smile. As she grew up, everyone in town immediately fell in love with her.

He tried to call Tiffany once more and cursed as it went straight to voicemail. *Where was that girl?* He called his wife, Deborah, "Can you come over to the store? Tiffany hasn't shown up yet and I need some help."

He heard the panic in her voice, "What do you mean she hasn't shown up for work yet? That isn't like her."

He tried to calm down his wife of forty years, "Calm down. I am going to head over to her house right now to check on her. Maybe, she just overslept. We did work until late last night."

***

Deborah said a quick novena that everything was okay with Tiffany. Perhaps, she got caught up in her designing and didn't pay attention to the time. She mentioned to Deborah yesterday that she couldn't wait for her new materials to come in for another project. She wished Tiffany would tell her dad she wanted to do something other than working in the store.

***

When Collin pulled up to Tiffany's house, he saw her car still in the driveway. A sigh of relief escaped his mouth. *At least he knew that she just slept late.* He walked up to the door and knocked loudly. When she didn't answer, he figured she was either in the shower or still sound asleep. It took him a moment to find the right key, "Tiffany, it is Dad. You awake honey?"

Not hearing an answer, he moved deeper into the house. Her bedroom door was closed so he knocked loudly on it before entering, "Tiffany, it is Dad. Come on, honey, it's time to wake up." When he entered the room, the earth opened up beneath him. His scream echoed throughout the neighborhood.

***

By the time Deborah made it to Tiffany's house, she was greeted by the multitude of police cars and flashing lights in front of the house. When her cell phone rang, she expected to hear her Collin's voice on the other line telling her that they would be there shortly. Instead, it had been a strange man's voice asking her to please come to Tiffany's house.

When she asked what happened, all he said was to come right away. Deborah made it there in record time.

With this many cop cars, Deborah feared the worst. Why hadn't Collin or Tiffany called her? She swallowed back her fear as she took notice of the yellow tape encircling the house. As she walked up to the house, Tony Bertrand walked over to her. Tears instantly filled her eyes. Tony was a detective with the police force here. He wouldn't be at Tiffany's house unless something was terribly wrong.

As Deborah listened to what happened, she couldn't contain her sorrow with the horrifying tragedy. Who did this to their daughter? She was led into the house where she fell into her husband's waiting arms. As the somber news sank into their minds, tears streamed down their faces as they comforted each other.

***

Bertrand watched as the family tried to come to grips with what had happened. He knew that it was hard for them; hell, it was difficult for any person to accept. Something like this should never be endured by anyone. Their poor daughter was taken from them; her life cut tragically short. Now, they would be deprived of the enjoyment of watching her young life blossom. Their sorrow would be replaced by pure unadulterated hatred.

As Bertrand attempted to console the family, Morvant walked over to talk to Officer Taylor, "Did you find anything?"

"We have determined that the killer entered the house from the back door. He broke out the window and reached in to unlock the door." Morvant walked out back as the crime scene techs combed every inch of the property for clues. They were leaving no stone unturned as they searched for clues; every piece of furniture was being dusted, and the floors were being inspected for shoe prints.

Officer Morales walked up to Morvant, "We have talked to all the neighbors; unfortunately, no one saw or heard anything out of the ordinary last night. One neighbor did say he saw Tiffany pull up rather late, but that was it until they were awakened by Mr. Dubois's scream."

Back in the house, Officer Taylor called out, "We found where he hid." As Bertrand and Morvant walked into the room, the officer pointed to the closet. "You can see the impression of where the man sat waiting. We will be sure to dust and photograph this area well." Officer Taylor stated, "It looks as if he was here for a while from the indentation left. Hopefully, we can get something from this."

After all their hard work examining the crime scene, they only walked away with a few clues. From the size of the shoe prints, they were dealing with a smaller man or possibly a woman and that their killer was an extremely patient person. They also knew that this killing was premeditated; there were bottles of water in the refrigerator that were carefully opened and drugged. Although there had been plenty of fingerprints found at the crime scene, they could all be accounted for.

Chapter 32

Caitlyn woke to the sound of music playing. Curious as to where the lovely music was coming from, she slipped out of bed. As she made her way to the stairs, she stood on the landing in complete disbelief. Everywhere she looked, there were people dancing. It was hard to focus on any individual face as each person wore an elaborate mask of some kind. Although the scene was somewhat hazy, she was sure that the people were happy. As she moved quietly down the stairs, the scene became clearer. The women wore dresses made of beautifully colored fabrics. The men accompanying them wore well-tailored suits. All around her was muted chatter, tinkling glasses, and the sound of a party in full swing. She cringed at the sight of the man standing in a far corner glaring at a man and woman who seemed to be the center of attention tonight.

For a moment, her vision became hazy and made it seem as though the party was dissipating like a wind blowing through a dense mist. Still, she found herself drawn to the stranger. As she neared him, the fog cleared, and she found herself a few feet away. His face was covered with a mask, but he had a coldness that resonated from his very being. She could see the tension gripping his shoulders; it made his neck stiff and tight. It was as if he was nursing anger; allowing it to fester inside of him.

The longer she stared at him, she began to feel a terrible pain penetrate to her very core. A range of emotions grabbed her, threatening to choke her. Her mind went blank as he turned to look directly at her. For a moment, she thought he could see her. When she looked into his eyes, she saw the raging torrent that lay deep inside of him. As she reached out to remove his mask, the spell was broken.

Instantly, her vision shattered. The details of the room faded into the present as she was thrown back into reality.

She found herself in Scott's arms, "I heard you calling out."

"I heard music playing and came to see what was going on. It must have been another vision imprinted into the house. It was a party, maybe a masquerade ball. There was a man in the corner who apparently hated the guests of honor. You could feel the anger radiating off of him."

Scott took her hand in his and guided her back upstairs, "Come on you. These ghosts of yours really need to bother you during the day, and not at night."

Caitlyn laughed at the silly comment, but nodded her head in agreement, "I wish you could see these things as well; then you would believe me."

"Oh, I believe that you saw something. I am not convinced that it was ghosts, but it may be as you said, impressions made at some point in time. Perhaps, this old house is trying to talk to you."

***

The next morning as Scott was busy working on the upstairs, Caitlyn started cleaning some furniture they found tucked away in one of the smaller rooms upstairs. Caitlyn was reasonably confident that this small table and mirror had hung in the foyer. Once she finished restoring them to their prior glory, she planned on placing them where she saw them in her vision.

It took Caitlyn a short while to find the nail where the mirror had formerly hung. She wondered why Gregory would have bothered moving it. It would have been a great conversation piece when you first entered the old house. They had even found the extravagant chandelier Gregory had removed. It had been a challenge to get it back up there, but they did it.

As Caitlyn was hanging the mirror, a reflection in it caught her eye and drew her in closer. The image in the mirror showed a different time. She turned around to find that once again the room was transformed around her.

All around her, the house was decorated with boughs of cedar and elegant red bursts of velvet ribbon. Children were busy twining holly through the spindles of the stairwell as a woman artfully arranged it across the window sills. There were springs of evergreen tucked throughout the house. The smell pleasantly lingered in the air, mingling with the wood burning fires. The mood was celebratory and merry.

Before she could move further into the room, the vision dissipated. But the vision confirmed at one time there had been happiness in this house. Caitlyn was certain that Jean Paul loved Celeste and she would give anything for the kind of love those two had for each other. She couldn't imagine having found your one true love only to have that person violently snatched from you.

She thought she had found that in Gregory. She had been so happy with him, even if for a short period of time. As her thoughts drifted toward Gregory, she felt a presence near her. As she looked around, she didn't see anything, but she swore that there was someone in the room with her.

***

Just as he was about to make his presence known, HE walked in. He watched in fury as Caitlyn's eyes lit up when she saw him, "Doesn't the mirror look perfect right here?"

Before Scott could answer, a frigid wind blew through the foyer. Caitlyn couldn't shake the feeling that the wind brought a force into the house, one malevolent and evil. She couldn't understand why, but she suspected those feelings were directed more towards Scott than her, but she couldn't fathom why.

A loud noise came from Caitlyn's room. Scott asked, "What in the hell was that?"

"I'm not sure, but something tells me we need to go and check it out." As soon as they walked into Caitlyn's room, she gasped. Her clothes were scattered around the room. As they picked up her clothes, the secret door in her closet opened. She looked at Scott, "Okay, that was a little creepy, even for this house."

"Do you suppose someone is trying to tell us something?"

She asked, "Like maybe we need to go explore this very minute?"

"Yes, let me grab my flashlight before we go down."

As they made their way downstairs, the smell of decay permeated the air. "What is that awful smell?" Caitlyn asked.

"I'm almost afraid to find out." They continued to make their way down the narrow corridor until Scott noticed that the door to the basement was open. "It looks as if our visitor wants us to go in here."

As they neared the door, Caitlyn started to feel dizzy; she became more lightheaded with each step. Everything spun out of control as her vision blurred.

It was as if she was walking through a murky mist. She had an overpowering urge to turn around and run from this area, but instead of running, she felt Scott pulling her deeper into the room. In front of her, there was a dark figure. He seemed to be working on something in slow motion. Light and shadows wove throughout the room.

Her whole body shook when she saw the brutal vision in front of her. She cried out, "Please stop. Don't do this."

She could barely breathe as the dark figure continued his work. She felt so helpless as he continued to hack at the body in front of him.

She felt Scott shaking her, but it took a while for everything to come into focus once more. It seemed to take a while for the past and present worlds to separate once again in her mind.

She shut her eyes tightly, trying to erase what she witnessed from her mind. Tears filled her eyes, and she turned into Scott's waiting arms, "It was awful what he did to those poor people. He deliberately disfigured them. It was a nightmare." She cried for the horrors this house had witnessed. Treachery, evil, and shattered dreams to name a few were imprinted deeply into the house.

***

Scott brought her out to the front porch and sat her on the old swing. She breathed in the fresh air as she collected her thoughts. "It is obvious someone or something wants me to know everything this house has seen."

Scott pulled Caitlyn to his body as he consoled her. "Maybe there is a mystery here and, for some reason, you are the only one who can see what the house is trying to say."

"Whatever it is, I feel as if I must be the one to resolve it."

Scott tilted her chin up to where she was looking him in the eyes, "Can you continue to live in a house where so much misery has taken place? Do you believe you can bring peace to this house or will the entities here take away your joy for life as well?"

She curled up deeper into his embrace as she thought about what he just asked her. Should she just pack up and leave?

It all became too much for her to comprehend, and she began to sob. Tears flowed down her cheeks, wetting Scott's shirt. He felt like a heel for making her face reality, "It will be okay. We will get to the bottom of this. I didn't mean to upset you. I am sorry."

Scott found himself overcome with emotions as this woman he'd just met moved deeper into his embrace. He felt her warmth against his skin. There was a vulnerability to her that he didn't know existed.

She wiped her tears as she looked up at him, "I am not normally this weepy."

"I think I may know of someone who can help you. My grandmother talked about her over the years; although to be honest with you, I never took much stock in what she had to say about this woman."

"I am beginning to think we need an actual exorcism here and not just having the house blessed."

Scott told her, "What I have in mind may not be too different from an exorcism. You tried a house blessing and it did not work, so this may be the way to rid these spirits. My grandmother used to say this woman was known as a traiteur, or faith healer. Some in town have whispered that she practices voodoo. I'm not sure what is true, but she may be just the person to help you."

"I am ready to try anything. I tried to do as the voodoo shop owner in New Orleans told me; I cleansed the rooms and burned sage, but so far, nothing helped. I am beginning to think that you are right; whatever is lurking about may be more human than ghostly."

"The cameras that I installed last week have yet to take any actual photos."

Caitlyn nodded her head in agreement, "It is as if they know where the cameras are and try to avoid them."

Scott gave her a big kiss, "Damn, why didn't I think of that? It is time to think like an intruder and do a better job at hiding them. We know that someone is using the closet in your room so let's put one in there. I will come up with a few other places to hide them where they won't be as visible."

"Do you think this will work?"

"Yes, I honestly do. It will take a little ingenuity, but we can make this work."

***

Scott was busy setting up the cameras when he heard a muffled thud behind the wall. The hairs on the back of his neck stood at attention. Another muffled thud rang out. There was someone or something behind the wall. He crept over to where he thought he heard the noise. Suddenly, a blast of icy air chilled him. The temperature in the room dropped.

A noise behind him caught his attention, but before he could turn around, pain exploded in the back of his head. He swayed as his vision blurred and everything faded to black.

***

Sleep eluded Caitlyn once again. She lay in bed and listened to the various sounds the house made. Instead of calming her, it ate at her nerves.

The bedroom was illuminated only by the soft moonlight that filtered in through the window. Ominous shadows danced across the walls. She laid in bed thinking for a moment she heard a man whisper that he needed her to help him, but she shook it off.

She found her thoughts drifting back to Scott once more. He had such a strong, commanding presence. There was something intriguing about him. She felt a connection to him that she never experienced with Gregory.

Suddenly, her bed began to shake, jolting her out of her reverie. Her fear grew to mammoth proportions as the bed levitated. Her heart was pounding inside of her chest now. The doors in the room opened and slammed shut. A loud piercing voice resonated in the room, "Go to him, now."

Apprehension streaked through her as she dashed out of her room, fearing that something may have happened to Scott. As she made her way downstairs, she saw him lying face down in the foyer. She rushed over to him and carefully rolled him over, "Are you okay?"

It took Scott a moment to focus in on Caitlyn, "I'm a little woozy, but I should be okay."

"What happened?"

"I'm not sure. I thought I heard someone in the passageway, but that was the last thing I remember."

Caitlyn felt the back of his head, "I believe someone knocked you out. Let's get you into the parlor, and then I'll get you some ice for the knot. You have a large goose egg on the back of your head."

After she got the ice and placed it on his head, she stated, "I sure hope I am not making a mistake by staying here."

***

He watched through a small peephole in the wall. He hoped this scared these two out of the house. If they didn't leave, he would have to take further action. With the plantation being so far away from town, there were a lot of places to dispose of bodies in the swamp. People wouldn't even question why the two disappeared; the house was known for that type of activity. Whoever lived here seemed to disappear in the middle of the night. He made sure to keep people believing that rumor. Until he found what he was looking for, he couldn't afford for anyone to live in this house. There was a gold mine somewhere on this property, and he planned on finding it.

Chapter 33

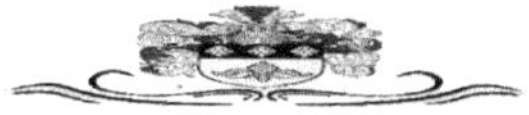

The morning sky was overcast with a dark shade of gray as Bertrand headed to the funeral home. The funeral of Tiffany Dubois was today. Her parents wanted to do something for her even though they couldn't have a proper funeral for their beloved daughter. So the casket and a life size picture of Tiffany were placed in the viewing room.

Bertrand was shocked to see that so many people turned out this early in the morning. An assortment of carnations, roses, and lilies filled the room. A soft rendition of Amazing Grace played in the background as Bertrand walked over to the police photographer. "I want to make sure that you snap pictures of every man or woman attending the funeral. Afterwards, we can compare them to the photos of the crime scenes."

Officer Morales asked, "So you think the killer will be here?"

"He won't be able to resist."

As they finished their conversation, more people arrived. Tiffany had been a well-liked young woman, as were her parents. Grief sat heavy in his heart as he watched Tiffany's parents receive condolences from family and friends before he took a moment to say a quick prayer at the coffin.

Bertrand watched as Liz Girard walked into the funeral home and he saw red. That woman better not be here to write an article about the grieving family. Walking over to her, he took her by the elbow and firmly escorted her out of earshot from everyone else.

Liz tried to remove herself from the detective's powerful grip, "I see the police are busy on the job."

In a harsh whisper, he asked, "Just what are you doing here?"

Looking up at him, she replied, "I came to pay my respects just like everyone else. I suspect that you are hoping the killer will stop by to pay his respects as well."

Bertrand glared down at the woman, "It would be best for you to go home."

Shaking her head, she said firmly, "I came here to pay my respects. I knew Tiffany, and I think it is a shame what happened to her. There are rumors going around that she was mutilated."

"I hope you will keep those rumors to yourself Ms. Girard."

Liz smiled at the detective slyly, "I am a reporter after all. It is my job to report the news."

"It would benefit you not to report any rumors that you may hear until they are substantiated."

Liz put her hands on her hips, getting exasperated with this detective, "And if I call to ask you to substantiate the rumors, will you?"

"Not at this time I won't."

Nodding her head, "That is what I figured. The people have a right to know what is going on in this town."

Not giving him a chance to have the last word, she turned on her heel and walked into the packed viewing room.

***

Bertrand and Morvant followed the black hearse to the cemetery. At least forty cars trailed behind them as they made the long, slow drive to Tiffany's final resting place.

Friends and family waited patiently for the coffin to be removed from the hearse and the priest to say a few words before she was laid to rest for eternity. Bertrand and Morvant made it a point to be the last to leave the cemetery, hoping the killer decided to pay his condolences. The police photographer took pictures here as well.

Sadness washed over Bertrand as the casket was lowered into the grave. Morvant said, "I hope she can rest in peace."

"She may be resting in peace, but I won't be able to rest until we have this son of a bitch behind bars."

By the time they made it back to the police station, the pictures were being developed. Bertrand crossed his fingers that they found at least one bystander who was at every crime scene and the funeral.

***

He watched as family and friends stopped by the parents to express condolences. How he would have enjoyed bringing Tiffany to watch these people grieve over her death. There was something exciting about having the police in the same room with him. They had no idea he was the one responsible for this. They didn't even suspect him, no one did. They considered him as nothing more than an insignificant person at the funeral home.

As the women made their way into the room, he looked at their hair. Perhaps, his next masterpiece was in this room right now just waiting for him.

Chapter 34

Bertrand let out a deep sigh as he surveyed the murder board once more. They had centered their investigation on the victims and their lives; trying to find a connection, but so far they had had no luck. They talked to friends and family members of each victim to see if anyone noticed anything out of the ordinary before their deaths, but no one did.

Hell, none of the victims shared the same physical characteristics, except for long hair. What kind of killer has a fetish for hair?

Bertrand did a search to see if a black market for hair existed. Most crimes involving hair were complaints that someone came up from behind and cut away a large section of hair. Very few crimes involved killing the victim for their hair, and those that did were not to this extreme.

He despised that they were at a complete loss for these murders. They had found no significant clues. None of them could stand having to wait for another person to be killed in hopes of finding evidence finally being left behind.

As far as the duct tape used in the crime, it was available at any store around the country, so that wasn't any help either. A small amount of DNA was found on the duct tape when the killer used his teeth to cut the tape, but, unfortunately, not enough to go on.

So far, they had no suspects and the trail grew colder with each passing day. The killer had obviously done his homework and covered all bases for these murders. Regardless of the lack of clues, Bertrand planned on continuing forward as best as he could with this investigation.

They were looking into each person who recently moved to Point Creole, hoping to find someone with a history that needed to be looked into further. But so far they had found no one who fell into that category. A few people moved into the town recently, one being Caitlyn Reed, and a few individuals moved back to town after living away for several years. The only person catching Bertrand's interest was Caitlyn Reed. She had a prior relationship with Gregory Ferris, a known serial killer; however, after talking to her, he didn't picture her committing these murders. Unless she was one hell of an actress, she had been too distraught over what Gregory did to suspect her of committing such heinous crimes as these.

Chapter 35

Caitlyn's eyes snapped open as the dark interior of her bedroom came into focus. She wasn't sure what woke her, but something did. She looked at the closet door to make sure it was still closed. The storm predicted for later in the morning seemed to be moving in fast because she thought she heard the distant rumble of thunder.

For a moment, her heart caught in her throat. She felt a cold breath on her shoulder and turned to see no one there.

She strained to hear any noises coming from the house, but the house appeared quiet. Once again, she felt a cold breath on her shoulder. She turned and looked around the room once more, but she was alone.

She turned on the lamp and looked around the room. The book she had been reading was still where she left it. Unaware that she had been holding her breath, she gently released it. She laughed at herself for being scared over nothing.

As she settled back in bed, another noise caught her attention. It was a low, ominous creaking sound. The closet door slowly opened. She was frozen in fear as the door continued to open. When the footsteps began and moved towards the bed, Caitlyn somehow found her voice and screamed.

Scott came running into the room and scooped Caitlyn's trembling body into his arms. She pointed to the closet

door and stuttered, "Someone just opened the closet door.
I heard footsteps."

Scott looked into the closet and could tell that someone, or
something, had opened the closet door. "They must have
been in too much of a hurry to bother shutting the door."

Horrible thoughts rushed through Caitlyn's mind, "You don't
think that was a ghost do you?"

"I would rather sleep in the trailer where we know there are
no secret passageways."

Caitlyn nodded her head, "I think that may be a great idea."

***

Once in the trailer, Caitlyn found that she still couldn't
sleep. She knocked on Scott's door, "Do you mind if I sleep
in here with you?"

He threw back the covers, "Come on. I figured you would
either be pacing all night or wanting company." She curled
up into his warm embrace and fell sound asleep.

***

The next morning as Caitlyn cleaned the master bathroom,
the front door opened. She called out, "I have a fresh pot of
coffee made if you want a cup."

Caitlyn was surprised that Scott didn't answer her, and she
listened to see if he was coming upstairs. The hair on the
back of her neck rose when she heard Scott's saw outside.
She knew the front door opened; she just heard it.

She poked her head out the bedroom door, but was greeted with silence in the house. As she turned back into the bedroom, the front door opened again. She waited to hear footsteps on the wood floors or the stairs creak, but there was nothing but silence.

"Caitlyn…" A voice called out. Her heart pounded in her ears as she realized that voice sounded just like Gregory. Stepping into the hall, the voice called out again, "Caitlyn…"

It sounded like it came from the room where Scott slept. She knocked on the door before quietly opening it. As she went inside, she noticed the room was dark and empty.

"Caitlyn…" She swallowed hard before looking back. This time, the voice came from behind her, but no one was there.

"Caitlyn…" This time the voice came from her room. Once again, she followed the voice and found her bedroom empty. Panic welled up deep inside of her; her heart skipped a beat, and her breath caught as she turned to dart downstairs. Nothing stopped her dash out the front door and down the porch steps. Once in the driveway, she turned to look at the house expecting to see someone chasing her out the door.

Instead, there was nothing there. No figures loomed at her from the windows and no eerie glow came from the house. As she calmed her racing heart, she looked at the house once more. She dared something to show itself. When nothing happened, she decided it was safe to enter. Besides, maybe she didn't hear a voice call out her name.

Just then, Scott walked over to her, "What are you doing out here?"

Laughing, she replied, "I thought I heard you come inside, but then I heard you sawing outside. I thought perhaps someone else was here."

"I haven't seen anybody. I had left the back door open, maybe a gust of wind blew the door closed."

"Maybe so." She smiled up at him, "I made a fresh pot of coffee."

Opening the front door for her, he replied, "After you, mademoiselle."

Over coffee, they talked and laughed about their childhood. All thoughts about the voice calling out to her earlier were forgotten. After lunch, Caitlyn decided to help Scott by finishing painting one of the bedrooms on the second floor.

Once done, she was covered in flecks of paint. Miraculously, she managed to get it on her and the wall, but none on the floor. She headed to her bedroom and showered before cooking supper.

She lathered up and scrubbed at the specks of paint on her skin. As she rinsed off the soap, she inspected her arms to make sure she'd removed the paint.

She lathered her hair and stepped into the pulsing water to rinse away the shampoo. She winced as a stream of soapy water ran into her eyes. She put her face into the stream of water, hoping to rinse the soap out of her eyes, but instead she caused it to burn even more. Thankfully, she had a towel hanging from the shower rod and reached for it. As she rubbed her eyes, a chill swept over her and goose bumps crawled up her skin.

She cautiously peered through the shower curtain to see a young woman staring at her. She had part of her face missing, and her lower body looked to be almost shredded. Out of fear, Caitlyn jumped back, slipped on the tub floor, tumbled backwards, and knocked her head on the edge of the tub as she fell.

As she blacked out, she saw the apparition crawling towards her. Caitlyn couldn't even summon the strength to scream.

***

Cold water pulsating on her lower extremities woke her. Still dizzy from the knot on her head, she eased herself out of the tub. She wrapped her robe around her wet body and stepped out of the bathroom in a haze of confusion. She searched for the lady once again as she headed out of the bathroom and into the bedroom.

Still unsettled from the fall in the bathroom, she fell onto the bed and stared at the ceiling. She had hoped to see the ghosts of those Gregory killed; now, it looked as if they were letting their presence be known.

Chapter 36

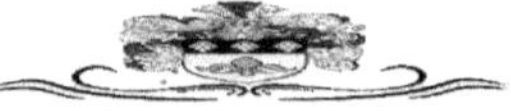

As Alex Hamilton waited for the Cessna plane to carry him off to Point Creole, he observed his surroundings. Airports no longer held any allure to Alex Hamilton; he had sat in more bars, lounges, and cafes than he cared to admit. He had spent most of his life in airports across the United States. It had been over three years since he left the FBI and now he offered his expertise, free of charge. He hoped to stop some of the most vicious of killers. His books were doing so well that he didn't need the money. Even if he did need the money, he doubted he would charge them for his help. Most of the time, he helped over the phone after he reviewed a file that was sent. But this case bothered him. He reviewed the files again, but needed to visit the crime scenes first hand.

Since he worked from home, he didn't have to spend his time waiting on planes stuck in a holding pattern. And he no longer had to worry about waiting for his bags.

He traded his boarding pass for a wife and a family and he couldn't be happier. This case, though, had him intrigued. So far, four bodies were found eviscerated, faces removed, and hair scalped. He found it bizarre that the killer removed the whole scalp and face.

Alex picked up the recent photos and took a closer look at the victim. The figure looking back at him didn't even look real. It was a garish sight with the face and scalp missing.

The killer only wanted the scalp. The victim had not been sexually assaulted. There was rohypnol in their system, but no apparent torture other than the evisceration, scalping, and removal of the face. The killer still felt the need to restrain the victims since duct tape residue was found on the ankles and wrists of the victims; even though they were sedated.

Why did the killer find it necessary to remove the face and scalp? Could it be that he, or possibly she, was horribly disfigured and wanted to do the same to these women? Whatever the reason, their killer had a bizarre fetish. So far, none of the victims had the same hair color. They even had different lengths of hair. What was the connection other than the hair? Did they know each other or possibly know their killer? Was the killer's work completely and utterly random? What drew him to these victims? The killer couldn't just be picking these randomly; could he?

There had to be a connection. If this were a patternless, random killer selecting his victims on a whim, it would be a detective's worst nightmare. Random killers were the hardest to catch. So far, the killer had left no trail. The detectives had no clues to follow; all they had were corpses.

It was extremely difficult for him to put together a complete profile of the killer. There was no victim type, which triggered this killer.

Looking at the photos once again, he noted that there were no hesitation marks. It was done in one fluid movement. So far, these victims had one thing in common, the gruesome wounds. He found it chilling that someone was out there defacing and scalping women. Did the killer stalk his victims beforehand or were these spur-of-the-moment killings?

He leaned back in the chair and closed his eyes. He gathered his thoughts before meeting with the detectives working on the case. He kept going back to the possibility that they may be dealing with a displaced Indian who sought out his own form of retribution. There were plenty of Indian tribes around Louisiana still proud of their heritage, but scalping had never been limited to the Indians. It could be traced back to the Spanish and French rule in Louisiana. Were these killings psychological or ritualistic?

The flight to Point Creole was uneventful. When he landed, Detective Bertrand was waiting for him. They shook hands before heading to the sheriff's office.

Bertrand asked, "What do you think of the case so far?"

"It appears that you have one hell of a psycho here."

"Do you agree one person did this?"

"I do. I am still not certain if this was done by a man or a woman; although, female serial killers are rare."

Bertrand replied, "I am just thankful that you are here. I know that you will help me put this killer behind bars. I don't even care who gets the credit for the capture; I just want him stopped."

Chapter 37

Early the next morning while the coffee brewed, Caitlyn heard a noise out on the front porch. At first, she thought an intruder may be breaking in, but realized it was the sound of a rattle and someone chanting.

Caitlyn opened the front door to find an elderly woman hunched over standing on the front porch. She rushed to her side. "Are you okay?"

The old woman shook her head, "Dere is such sadness here."

"You must be Madam Adelaide Geroux."

"Mais oui. Dere is much work to be done here cher. Come, let's go sit. My old bones need rest."

Caitlyn asked, "Do you want to go inside?"

"Mais non, not yet. My old bones must rest before I can go inside, cher."

Caitlyn helped her to the swing, "Would you like something to drink?"

"I do believe I smell coffee coming from inside your house."

Caitlyn let out a small laugh, "Yes, ma'am, you do. If you give me a minute, I will be right back with two cups of fresh coffee."

Inside the kitchen, Caitlyn arranged a small tray with cream, sugar, coffee and a few of the muffins she'd baked for breakfast.

As she placed the tray in front of Madame Geroux, the old lady stated, "Merci cher. You are experiencing several phenomena here. Most houses are haunted by a spirit, but dere are some who haunt dis area dat can actually manifest itself into moving items. Dis take a lot of power, and den you have some who seem to be able to manipulate images as well. Dere is a very malevolent spirit here dat means to do harm."

Caitlyn gasped, "I thought that ghosts couldn't hurt you."

"Mais, usually dey cannot, but dis one he is powerful. Dere is a spirit dat is trapped here by guilt. Unrepentant guilt chains dis devil to dis house. Dere is guilt and curses dat plague dis house. Dere are spirits here dat want to continue to torment the living and those dat are trapped here as well. Dere are some strong spirits here dat are trying to protect you and dis house, but I fear dat dey are failing."

Caitlyn asked, "Can you help us?"

Madame Geroux leaned back in the swing, "I may, but dis be more than one spirit here. Dis may be one spirit masquerading as more dan one too. Whatever it is, dis spirit will not be easy to make go away."

Caitlyn swallowed back her fear, "I sometimes fear that there is a ghost in there that hates me."

"Mais, dat may be cher. Dis be a deadly serious spirit."
Caitlyn watched as Madame Geroux took two small pouches

out of her pocket. "One is for you and one is for your man friend. You both must wear dese at all times."

Caitlyn looked at the small bags in her hands, "What are these?"

"Dese be Gris Gris bags. It protects you from bad juju. I will be back later tomorrow tonight, sometime between midnight and the cock crow in de morning. You best be ready. Dere be a lot of work to be done."

After Madame Geroux left, Scott came outside, "I thought I heard someone talking."

Caitlyn still felt unsettled, but she handed the Gris Gris bag to Scott, "Madame Geroux came to get a feel for the house. She said that we each need to wear one of these while we are here. She will be back tomorrow night to help with the ghosts."

"Are you okay?"

"It was unsettling talking to her. She said there is a malevolent force at work here and she will help me rid the house of it if she can."

***

Caitlyn looked around the house and was pleased with the work they'd managed to get done. Scott was working hard in one of the upstairs bedrooms, "You hungry?" she asked.

"I am famished."

"Let's clean up and go into town for a nice supper, on me of course."

"You don't have to pay for my supper, but a night away sounds like the perfect idea."

After they had finished cleaning up, Caitlyn handed Scott the keys to the Range Rover, "Do you mind driving? I never get a chance just to enjoy the scenery."

Scott opened the door for her, "Not at all. Do you know where you want to go and eat?"

"My favorite place in town is Beazell's."

As they headed into town, Caitlyn recalled her conversation with Madame Geroux this morning. She was still unsettled by it. Scott must have sensed that something was bothering her; on the trip to town, he kept the conversation pleasant and away from the plantation.

Within twenty minutes, they were in downtown Point Creole. She had come to love this little town with its unique combination of charming stores, restaurants, and old homes.

Both were pleasantly surprised to learn there was only a ten minute wait at the restaurant. The maître de walked them past several couples sitting at cozy, candle lit tables. Everyone seemed to be enjoying themselves and this was what she and Scott needed tonight.

They were seated at a cozy, intimate table on the terrace that overlooked the bayou. Several people danced to a slow jazz song; just enjoying the romantic scene in front of them. As Caitlyn watched them, depression settled over her. The last man she danced with had been Gregory. Caitlyn thought she had found the man of her dreams. How could someone be so evil when they were capable of being so romantic and doting? A chill swept over her as she thought of the monster he truly was.

Scott noticed the change in Caitlyn's mood. "The restaurant is beautiful." He took in the romantic ambiance of the setting, "The owners did a good job of updating the old restaurant and turning it into something this town needed."

Staring out over the water, Caitlyn became mesmerized as she watched the full moon create a breathtaking reflection on the water as graceful ripples of shining waves moved over the dark water. She looked over at Scott and began to realize that she may be falling for him. Scott's heart raced as Caitlyn looked over at him. His breath caught as her eyes sparkled in the candlelight, "This place is so elegant. I love the one in New Orleans, but this one is so peaceful and serene."

As Scott perused the menu, he asked, "Everything looks so good. What do you recommend?"

"The barbecue shrimp is out of this world, but the crab cakes are simply divine as well. I can't decide which I would rather."

Scott winked at her with a sexy grin, "Well, I don't know about you, but I worked up an appetite today. We can split the two if that is okay with you?"

"That sounds perfect to me."

As they made up their mind about the appetizers, their waitress appeared, "I am sorry to keep you waiting. We are extremely busy tonight."

Scott smiled up at the young girl, "It does look as if you have a full house this evening."

She nodded her head in agreement, "The restaurant has been busy ever since the owners opened their doors. Have you decided what you would like or do you need a few more minutes?"

Scott replied, "I would like a Maker's Mark Manhattan, and Caitlyn would like a chocolate martini. For our appetizers, we would like the barbecue shrimp and crab cakes with the tomato-tarragon remoulade."

"Those are both excellent choices. Now, for the entrée special, the chef has prepared a pan seared redfish filet topped with a Shrimp Creole, garlic buttered popcorn rice, and roasted asparagus."

Caitlyn's mouth watered, "I am not sure about you Scott, but I will have the special. That sounds too tempting to pass up."

As Scott handed the waitress their menus, he agreed, "I will have the special as well."

"Very good, sir. That is an excellent choice."

As they waited for their cocktails and appetizers, they became absorbed in pleasant conversation.

It wasn't long before the waitress set their drinks and appetizers in front of them. As always, the food tantalized Caitlyn's taste buds and caused her to crave more. While they enjoyed the delicious food and soothing jazz music, Caitlyn relaxed from the stresses of the day.

As the waitress cleared their dinner dishes away, she asked, "Can I get you something for dessert?"

Caitlyn had been eyeing the dessert on the table next to theirs, "I am not sure what that is they are having, but it looks heavenly."

The waitress exclaimed, "That is our Chocolate Insanity Cake. It is a rich chocolate cake layered with white chocolate mousse, dark chocolate mousse, and topped with a chocolate ganache. It is a new creation by the chef. Everyone seems to enjoy it immensely."

"I have a passion for chocolate, so I have to try it. It looks too good not to try." Caitlyn looked over at Scott, "Would you care to share the dessert? There looks to be enough for two."

With a twinkle in his eyes, "I think I can make room for some dessert, but I want to hear more about your passions later."

After they finished the dessert, and Caitlyn was certain that she ate more of it than Scott; he held his hand out and asked, "Would you care to dance?"

Soon, Caitlyn found herself being swept away in his arms as they danced to the soft jazz music. As she moved against his body to the music, the troubles plaguing her dissolved from her mind. The moonlight glistening off of the dark rolling water set the mood for romance.

With Scott's arms around Caitlyn, she looked up at him. Their lips met slowly at first and quickly became passionate. As the music ended, Caitlyn moved away from Scott's warm embrace. She couldn't help but remember how he made love and she compared it to how well he danced. He completely intoxicated her, which both excited and frightened her. She fell for Gregory just as fast and look how well that turned out.

As he slipped his arm around her and guided her to the car, she stated, "This has been a wonderful evening." As they walked back to the car, the moon hung low over the river creating a breathtaking view. They strolled happily arm in arm, enjoying the starry night.

As Scott opened the door for her, he kissed her once more and Caitlyn found her arms moving up to his neck – not wanting the kiss to end. She whispered against his lips, "I don't want to spend tonight alone."

Scott looked down at her with passion in his eyes. The drive home seemed to take an eternity. As soon as they were in the door, he pulled Caitlyn close to him. He took her mouth in a gentle caress causing her breath to skirt her lips. Only when her mouth was pliant and willing did he deepen the kiss by thrusting his tongue inside to dance with hers. They kissed with such passion that it ignited a spark deep inside of her. This was what she desperately wanted; she needed to be shown what it was like to be desired.

His hands slipped through her hair and tenderly cupped her jaw. She reveled in his touch.

His lips blazed a trail to her neck and shoulders. As he unzipped her dress, it fell gracefully to the floor. Caitlyn heard his sharp intake of breath as he looked over her body.

"You are so beautiful." She loosened his pants and felt his own desire for her as it pressed against her body.

Caitlyn slowly unbuttoned his shirt, ever so slightly touching him as she worked her way down. His breath caught as she unsnapped his jeans. In one swift move, he stepped out of his pants and carried her off to his bedroom. Once they were on the bed, he moved his attention to her breasts. He rained tiny kisses over each of them, cupping them in his hands to bring them closer to his mouth. As his warm lips closed over one taut nipple, she moaned, and closed her eyes and let the sensations take over her body. Desire coiled around every inch of her body. Her hands grabbed the bedcovers as he turned his attention to her other breast, giving it the same tortuous attention. She was wet and aching with need for him.

She ran her hands over the ridges of his stomach muscles and the firm skin of his thighs. She took him in her hands and reveled in the smooth, hard feel of him. The intensity of the emotions flooding her body right now was unnamable. No one had ever shown her this much tenderness and caring for her pleasure.

One of his hands traveled down her body to find her apex of need. Her body moved in rhythm with his strokes. His gaze was all heat and never had she seen such fire in a man's gaze. Pleasure vibrated through her as his fingers worked their magic. He felt warm and solid against her body; with his arms around her, she felt the love and affection he had for her.

As he thrust deep inside of her, he kept his movements slow and steady. He felt so good inside of her, so hard and so right. Her body was awash in need and desire. She felt herself going over the edge and into gratifying oblivion. She heard his cry of release as he gave one final, sharp thrust.

***

He watched as the two lovers made their way to the bedroom, both so overcome with passion they failed to recognize his presence. Anger consumed him as she gave herself to this man. He could not bear the thought of another man touching his sweet angel.

***

Caitlyn woke to find a sky filled with the vibrant pinks and orange hues of the morning sunrise. She nuzzled in closer to Scott's warm body. Scott kissed her bare shoulder before trailing kisses to her neck. He informed her, "I believe fate brought us together. And to think I almost turned down the job."

"I guess I should stop hating Gregory for everything he did. After all, he was the one who brought us together."

As soon as she uttered those words, a frigid wind blew into the room. Scott brought her closer to him, "Someone doesn't like hearing that."

"Maybe not, but it is the truth." The room suddenly became dark as the energy around them changed.

Scott told Caitlyn, "I am beginning to think you and Madame Geroux are right. There is definitely an evil entity that lives in this house. It may even be a force of formidable power, but together, we can figure out how to bring peace to this house once more."

Chapter 38

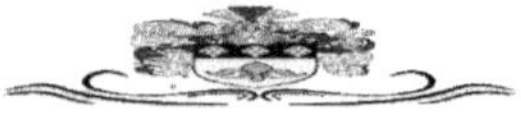

A noise caught her attention. It was a slight noise, but loud enough for her to hear. She looked behind her and saw a movement. Someone was there watching her, hiding deep in the shadows of the night. What was this person up to?

Out of the shadows stepped a figure. It took her a minute to see who was there. At first, she thought it was a short man, but she soon second guessed herself. Was it a woman or a man?

In barely an audible whisper, she heard, "I love your hair."

One of her hands went instinctively to her hair and tucked it behind her ear, "Thank you so much." She looked at the person one more time, "Do I know you?"

The person standing in front of her transformed in front of her eyes. "No, but I want your hair in my collection."

She never had a chance to scream. The knife pierced her skin before she could act. Her body slumped to the ground. He looked around before dragging her to the alleyway. He had become faster at removing his prize, so there was no reason to lure this one back to his salon anymore.

He found his hobby of taking scalps pleasurable. He left no fingerprints or DNA behind, and made sure no one saw him. He let out a laugh as he drove away; once again, he left no clues for the police to follow.

When he arrived home, he took out the small cooler and carried it into the house. He carefully removed the trophy and prepared it for the mannequin head. It would be several hours before it was ready to be displayed with the others.

***

As Charles Guillory backed into the alleyway to pick up the dumpster, he caught a glimpse of something in his rearview mirror. He stepped out of the cab of the truck to make sure that someone wasn't sleeping near the dumpster. He would hate for them to get crushed by accident when the dumpster came back down.

As he neared the dumpster, he stopped. It took a moment for the sight to register in his mind. The creature looking up at him was covered in blood and where her face should be was nothing but a gory mess.

He stumbled back to the cab of the truck and dialed 911.

The dispatcher asked, "What is your emergency?"

He stammered, "I need the police. There is a dead body between Jackson and Rue St."

"I'm sorry, sir. Did you say there was a dead body?"

He replied, "Yes, someone killed her or at least I think it is a woman. There is blood everywhere."

"Okay, sir, I am dispatching a unit your way. Can you please stay on the line? I will need to ask you a few more questions."

"Yes, of course. I will go to the street to direct them to the body."

"Thank you, sir."

In a daze, Charles walked to the street and waited for the police. It didn't take long before he heard the sirens of the police car. The noise filled the morning air. He peered down the street and saw the patrol car with its red and blue flashing lights. He waved over to the car and watched as the officers stepped out of the car.

He told the policemen, "The body is behind the dumpster. If you don't mind, I will wait here."

Officer Jim Roberts and his partner, Officer Bill Griffin, walked towards the dumpster. Officer Roberts took a step back when he saw the body. That gruesome sight would stay with him for the rest of his life.

He got on his radio and let the dispatcher know that Detectives Bertrand and Detective Morvant needed to be dispatched to the crime scene as soon as possible, "Their killer has struck again. Let them know that it appears she was scalped and killed at the same location she was found."

The dispatcher responded, "I will let them know. I will also send out the forensic techs."

Officer Roberts cordoned off the crime scene and Officer Griffin walked back to the driver to take his statement. He may have seen something without even realizing it.

***

Detective Bertrand was just stepping out of the shower when his cell phone rang. He shuddered involuntarily when he saw the dispatcher's number, "Bertrand."

"Detective, I am sorry to bother you, but there has been another murder. Officer Roberts suspects your killer struck again."

***

The drive to the murder scene took mere minutes. Point Creole wasn't that large of a town, and he only lived minutes from the crime scene. The sun had just risen, and the wet dew glistened on the grass. The early morning streets were still slick from last night's rain. Dark, ominous clouds hung heavy in the sky with the promise of more rain soon to come. They had to act fast if they hoped to preserve any evidence before the clouds opened up and washed away their crime scene.

Bertrand went up to Officer Roberts and asked, "Can you fill me in on what you know?"

"Yes, sir. The body was discovered by the gentleman over there, Mr. Charles Guillory. As he was backing up to pick up the dumpster, he saw something in his rear-view mirror. He wanted to make sure that it wasn't someone sleeping there. When he got closer, he saw the body and called 911. He swore he didn't go near the body. Forensic techs are busy working the scene, hoping to collect the evidence before the sky decides to open up."

Bertrand noticed Officer Marston taking photos of the crime scene, "Officer Marston, can you take pictures of the crowd as well? I want to see if we have anyone overly curious or even disinterested."

"Yes, sir."

Their killer was getting more brazen. He was quick and efficient in his killing, and now, he didn't care that he did it out in the open. He was getting bolder, and they may get lucky because of that.

***

Looking at the body made Morvant reconsider his decision to switch from narcotics to homicide. When working narcotics, they fought an uphill battle, but now with this killer on the loose, it seemed the same way. He learned that working homicide was not for the faint hearted.

***

As the coroner's office prepared to remove the victim, Alex Hamilton arrived. He walked over to the two detectives, "Sorry I am late. I was busy working on a profile, but this murder changes everything. He's getting more comfortable with his killing and by the looks of it, more efficient."

"I agree. I plan on asking the sheriff to increase patrols on the streets. Since he is killing these women right here on the streets, we may catch him in the act."

"I was trying to come up with a common link to the victims with little success. I hoped to figure out the killer's likes, dislikes, or even a geographic preference, but now with this murder, it throws those theories out the window."

Alex looked at the body as it was zipped up in the body bag. A chilling realization came to him. Were they dealing with a modern day Jack the Ripper that had a hair fetish?

Alex intended to come as soon as he received the call, but he couldn't pull himself away from the profile. Something nagged him about this case, and now that the killer had changed his MO, it could make it harder to catch him or possibly her.

The forensic techs made sure the hands of the victim were bagged so the nails could be clipped in case she fought back. They may even get lucky and find residue of foreign fibers or hair. As the coroner's office removed the body, the forensics cast footprints and scoured the area for any evidence that may be left behind.

Dr. LeBlanc informed the detectives, "The fatal cut to the stomach was first. It didn't take long for her to bleed out; one swift stroke of the blade was all it took. His knife is extremely sharp. The MO is the same as the others with regards to the removal of the face and scalp. It was done with one clean, concise movement."

Morvant asked, "Was this one sexually molested?"

"I will check once again when she is on my table, but I seriously doubt it. I think she is like the previous victims. He just wanted her face and hair."

Morvant asked Alex, "What are your feelings on him not sexually assaulting the victims?"

"I believe this killer strictly has a hair fetish. I am still not sure if it is a sexually motivated killing; although, our killer may be impotent. There is a possibility the killer is a woman. That would explain the lack of sexual assault."

Bertrand asked, "So you are wondering if this could be a woman?"

Alex replied, "It has always been a possibility, but the lack of sexual assault has me intrigued. Whoever removes the women's hair has a reason behind it. If I could figure out the why, maybe, we will be one step closer to figuring out the who."

Alex heard Bertrand let out a groan and looked over at him. Bertrand informed him, "The press is here."

Alex understood how he felt about the press. They may have a job to do, but they tended to get in the way of the investigation. Bertrand explained, "It is easier for us to let the Sheriff and Mayor talk to the press. Those two know how to work the press. Still, there is a chance this will ignite the whole town into a manhunt for the killer. I look for all hell to break loose with this latest murder. Everyone will be up in arms."

Alex nodded his head in agreement. This latest murder would create chaos and panic with the residents of this little town.

The forensic techs completed their work and loaded up the samples they'd gathered. It was a long shot that anything collected today would lead them to the killer, but they could always hope for a hair or a fiber in the collection that would break this case.

As they made their way back to their cars, the reporters called out to Bertrand and Morvant, "Detectives! Is it true that there was another murder?"

"Detectives, what can you tell us about the murder?"

"Detectives, can you at least let us know who the murder victim was or how she was killed?"

"Detectives, can you answer any of our questions?"

Bertrand stopped to look at the reporters. Almost immediately, they ceased bombarding him with questions and waited to hear what he had to say. A television camera focused in on him, "Sheriff Brett Savoie will make a statement shortly. Unfortunately, at this time, I don't have any information to give you."

"Come on Detective, you can't give us any information?"

Bertrand shook his head, "Not at this time."

Bertrand motioned for Morvant and Alex to move along with him. As the body was loaded into the coroner's van, camera flashes filled the air. The coroner had already informed him that as soon as he returned to the office, he would perform the autopsy. Bertrand and Morvant told Alex that they would attend and Alex wanted to be there as well. Maybe, they could learn something by being present at the autopsy instead of having to wait for the report.

As soon as Bertrand and Morvant stepped into the precinct, Sheriff Savoie was waiting for them, "Well, was it the same killer?"

Morvant replied, "It was. Dr. LeBlanc will perform the autopsy in a few minutes. We want to be there for that. Once done, we will come back here to finish our reports.

We hope that by being there during the autopsy we can get some answers sooner rather than waiting for his report."

He nodded his head, "Good, good. Let me know as soon as you hear something. I need to make a press conference as soon as possible, but I want to wait until I have some answers."

***

Later that night, Alex called his wife, Jordan, to see how they were doing. Jordan asked, "How is it going?"

"It's a bad case. This one has me stumped right now. I am fairly certain that it is a man committing these crimes, but there at times when it feels almost as if the killer is a woman."

She asked, "So, it doesn't look like you will be coming home anytime soon?"

He let out a sigh, hating that he was away from them, but the exhilaration of the case lured him here. "Not just yet. I want to get a feel for this guy. Sometimes, the only way to do that is to experience the crime scene first hand."

Jordan shuddered at how gruesome the crime scenes must be, "I completely understand. I know what you are doing is important and if that were happening here in Hope, I would want someone like you helping to catch this killer."

Alex wished he had a more definitive answer as to when he was coming home, but with this murderer he couldn't get a feel for him or possibly her. He hoped they stopped the killer before he moved on or simply stopped killing.

Chapter 39

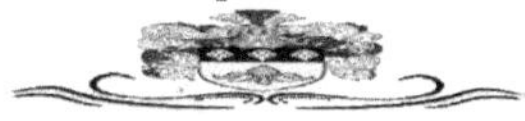

As Caitlyn was busy outside sweeping the porch, the rain began to fall. The large drops pelted the ground in front of her and a large gust of wind blew off of the bayou sending leaves across the yard. The gnarled branches shrouded with moss stretching towards the sullen sky were wary of what was to happen tonight. The swaying trees looked more like skeletons than sturdy sentinels guarding the plantation. As the fog formed over the bayou, it reminded her of a swarm of angry ghosts gliding along through the murky water.

Lightning streaked across the sky as the approaching storm bathed the old house in flashes of surreal blue light. The atmosphere around here suddenly seemed charged, threatening, and ominous.

Anxious about tonight and when Madame Geroux would arrive, Caitlyn found herself looking at her watch once more. As she was looking up, she noticed a battered Dodge truck making its way up the long driveway with its headlights barely visible in the fog rolling in.

As it pulled up to the front door, Scott ran out with an umbrella to greet Madame Geroux. As he was helping her up to the porch, she stated, "Dis be a good night for evil spirits to be lurking 'bout. Cher is you ready for dis?"

"As ready as I will ever be I suppose. It's been quiet here today." Before the three made their way inside, Madame Geroux took out a canister of salt and poured it along the entrance to the doorway. "Dis is to keep any more spirits from coming inside cher. We need to make sure we do dis to all de windows and other doors. I trust you two are wearing de Gris Gris bags?"

In unison, they replied, "Yes, ma'am."

Caitlyn noticed how chilled the house felt tonight and was glad that Scott had insisted on starting a fire. As soon as Madame Geroux began to chant, the energy in the room changed. The light coming from the fireplace created ominous, gloomy shadows that danced around the room.

Once done chanting, Madame Geroux looked over at Caitlyn, "Well, now, let's get dis started. Quelle piece a l'esprit? Which room has the spirit?"

"The spirits seem to have the run of the house. One particularly likes my room as well as the basement."

"Well den, let's see to your room first shall we?"

As they made their way upstairs, Caitlyn jumped involuntarily as a loud boom of thunder shook the house. Flashes of lightning illuminated her room and created long, deep shadows that danced around.

Caitlyn was about to go inside of the room when Madame Geroux grabbed her hand, "Wait cher. The devil spirit know dat we are here." She instructed Scott, "Bring me dat table over dere." Using her long boney finger, she pointed to a table in the far corner.

Once Scott had it in front of the doorway, Madame Geroux reached into her purse and pulled out various items, placing each on the table. Among them, Caitlyn recognized the white candles, incense, an antique looking wooden cross, and a statue of St. Gerard.

A loud moaning filled the house; Caitlyn wasn't sure if it was from the wind outside or the ghosts inside voicing their complaints about the ritual to come. Caitlyn watched with interest as Madame Geroux lit the white candles and incense.

A deep moan came from the closet in Caitlyn's room that sent chills down her back. Instinctively, she clutched the Gris Gris bag at her neck. A feeling of dread moved into Caitlyn as Madame Geroux sprinkled a substance into the room.

"Dis spirit seems to feel connected to you cher." She looked Caitlyn in the eyes, "No matter what dis spirits tries or does, do not talk to it cher."

Caitlyn nodded her head as Madame Geroux swayed side to side while chanting. The chanting became louder as the moaning coming from the closet grew louder. "Mais, der will be a confrontation tonight cher. Dere are spirits trapped here with the evil dat took dere lives. Dey want justice. Dis spirit though is not ready to leave. He wants to keep dem, and you cher."

As Madame Geroux began her chanting once again, the secret passageway way door slammed open with a loud bang. A cold breeze blew in from the passageway, carrying with it malevolence. Another flash of lightning illuminated the bedroom as the storm rolled in from the bayou.

Caitlyn felt the overpowering presence of evil all around her. A large black shadow made its way around the room. She gripped Scott's arm, "Please tell me that you see that?"

"Yes, I do."

Madame Geroux raised her finger to her lips commanding the two to be quiet as she continued to chant once more. A horrible stench permeated the air, and Caitlyn gasped as a hazy apparition materialized in the center of the room. Bones appeared from the darkness of the shadows and took form. Tendons connected to the bone that moved on their own accord as muscle and skin took on a human shape. The apparition's skin glowed with a sickly yellow demonic color.

The apparition moved towards Caitlyn, reaching out to her with its arms. Caitlyn was paralyzed in fear as he moved closer and closer to her. The apparition let out a deep moan toward Caitlyn and the room filled with a putrid stench as black shadows reached out for her from his open mouth.

The apparition of Gregory Ferris ridiculed Caitlyn, "You are nothing but a whore. You betrayed me with this man." His eyes looked down on her with palpable hatred. His glaring eyes filled her soul with gut wrenching guilt and self-loathing. Her body seemed to be swept into a tempest of emotions manifesting themselves in a vile cesspool of bitter hate. Caitlyn grasped her heart as her soul felt like it was being pulled into an all-consuming abyss of hell. She wasn't sure how much longer she could take this emotional abuse he was bombarding her soul with. Her heart was beating so fast right now that she thought it would explode out of her chest.

Then Gregory's apparition saw Scott move in to comfort Caitlyn and assaulted him as well. Scott felt the hatred this creature had for him as it seemed to consume his soul. The apparition reached out to Scott and lashed out at him with skeletal fingers. Caitlyn jumped in the way, not wanting Gregory to hurt him. She cried out as the sharp fingers of the apparition tore into her skin.

Scott felt horrified as he witnessed what was happening to Caitlyn. He couldn't believe that she jumped into the creature's path. He took her in his arms and carried her out of the creature's reach. Madame Geroux stepped in the creature's way as it attempted once more to grab Caitlyn.

Madame Geroux instructed the apparition in front of her, "I order ya to return to yar grave. Return to yar grave Gregory Ferris."

The apparition let out a loud howl that sounded guttural and unearthly. Gregory reached for Caitlyn desperate to bring her with him, "Not without her!" The lightning outside began to streak violently as thunder rumbled deep in the sky. It was as if they were trapped in an otherworldly place.

Madame Geroux stated once again, "Gregory Ferris, I send ya back to de dead. I order ya to release dese poor souls ya have trapped here. You can no longer bother dis poor girl. Back to yar grave ya debil."

In a maelstrom of violent choking hate, Gregory howled as a fire erupted in the fireplace, reaching out to drag him to the fires of hell. The air was putrid with the stench of burning flesh. Lightning exploded through the windows with pulsating light, revealing the stark emptiness of a room filled with the lonely maniacal obsession of an unrequited love. The rain outside became torrents of water as the sins of Gregory Ferris were washed away.

Madame Geroux walked over to Caitlyn, "Cher, he is gone, but de fight is still not over. Dere is another here dat must be cast into hell before de house can be cleansed." Madame Geroux walked downstairs to the foyer and called out, "Andre Picou, I command you to appear. Ya must not stay hidden like the coward ya are."

From the shadows stepped out a coward of a man. "Old woman be gone from here."

"Mais non, ya have haunted dese walls long enough. Ya are no longer welcome in dis house. It is time ya let the Favre's rest in peace."

Madame Geroux lifted her arms, "I command ye, Andre Picou, to go back to the earth as nothing more than dust. I send ye out from dis fetish and deny you all dat dwell within these walls. Be gone you. Go back to the dead!"

A raging inferno rose from the fireplace. A misty fog reached out from the center, moving towards the ghost of Andre Picou. A moment later, hundreds of wailing voices cried out as the mist took the form of a funnel cloud. Flesh torn souls of the damned morphed along the edges as their skeletal arms grabbed for Andre, as he backed away. A mouth of razor sharp teeth appeared at the opening of the vortex and lunged towards Andre.

Andre wailed and fought in sheer desperation to free himself from the horrifying creatures as he was dragged to the bowels of hell.

As the last of the evil spirits that haunted the grounds were banished, a magnificent light show took place. Tiny orbs of light floated up to the ceiling as they made their way up into the sky, "Go my lovely children. You may finally rest in peace. Dese men can no longer hurt you."

Caitlyn watched in amazement as two figures took shape in the library. Celeste and Jean Paul Favre fell into a loving embrace, kissing passionately. They held out their hands as Marguerite Favre's image took shape. She ran to grab ahold of her parents' hands. Celeste looked at Madame Geroux, "Thank you for all that you have done. Andre Picou killed not only me and Jean Paul, but my precious Marguerite as well. He was a greedy man who killed for money and power. You must be careful though. Andre found out about the passage ways and began to hide his wealth in here. He was afraid the soldiers would steal it. There is a man who must have found out about Andre's wealth concealed in these walls. Not all who walk these grounds are spirits. Be careful." Before Caitlyn could ask any questions, she watched as in a whirlwind they were whisked off into the light to find everlasting peace.

Scott looked over at Caitlyn and saw the tears forming in her eyes, "Do you think that we will see them again?"

Caitlyn let out a long sigh, "I sure hope so. I have gotten used to them walking the grounds."

As the lightning outside died down, the thunder ebbed in the distance and the horrendous rainstorm dissipated its fury into glowing hues of warm oranges and pinks in a morning sky. Scott carried Caitlyn into the parlor. He held her close as she wrapped her arms around him, kissing him passionately. "I am so sorry for bringing this all onto you. I didn't expect Gregory to lash out at you the way he did."

He looked over her body once more, "Are you hurt badly? Do we need to get you to the hospital?"

She brought his face down to hers once more, needing to feel his lips on hers. "I am fine."

They watched as Madame Geroux staggered into the room, completely exhausted. She gently lowered herself onto the chair near the fireplace. "De evil dat has been haunting you cher is gone. He is in de fires of hell. De house is finally at peace now."

Caitlyn walked over and took the elderly woman's hands in hers as she sat at her feet in front of the fireplace. "I can't thank you enough for all that you did Madame Geroux."

"Cher, please remember what Celeste told you. Dere is another presence here, but it is one of man. I cannot protect you from dis one."

She looked over at Scott, "You were right. It is an actual human being in the passageway. What do we do now?"

"I think it is time we let the cops handle this. There is still a serial killer on the loose. He may be the one lurking about. I would feel better if you took a break from this house. We can stay at my house for a while."

Caitlyn looked at him, surprised he would even suggest that. "You should know better than that. I can't leave a mystery unsolved. If there are treasures here, I would love to find them."

"But, we don't even know where to look. If this guy is moving about the house, he may be armed."

"I think it's time we fought back. He has somehow managed to keep from having his picture taken, but I say we put cameras and motion sensors throughout the passageways. He must have found a way inside through one of the old openings from the Underground Railroad. We need to find out where those outside entrances are."

Scott let out an exasperated sigh, "I would rather you let the police handle this matter, but I also know that you are too hard headed and want to solve this mystery yourself. I will help you as long as you promise me that you will call the police and tell them what you know."

She held out her hand and shook his, "That is a deal; besides, they may have a way of trapping this man."

As the two continued to plan, Madame Geroux stood up, gathering her belongings and prepared to leave, "Ye must remember dat in this life tings aren't always black and white. Dere are many shades of gray. Everything in dis universe has a purpose. It is our choice to use what God gave us, for good or evil."

They followed Madame Geroux outside and watched as she pulled away from the house before walking back in arm in arm. They walked hand in hand upstairs where they fell into each other's arms and went sound asleep.

Chapter 40

He saw the woman standing on the corner. The highlights in her hair shimmered in the moonlight. He was mesmerized by her hair as it cascaded down her back in luxurious waves. His palms were itching to style it. He came to New Orleans for a few supplies, but he would leave with much more.

***

She watched the man approach her with hesitance, or was that a woman? Soon, his stride became rushed. She smiled over at him, or again it may be a woman. This person carried himself/herself with an almost feminine quality, but she just wasn't positive from that one quality. It didn't matter to her as long as the person had cold hard cash. She was strapped and needed to earn enough to get her a hit of something to take the edge off.

"Hi honey. You want a little fun?"

In barely an audible whisper, "Sure do, cher."

"You got some money?"

She watched as he pulled out his money, "How much for an hour?"

She popped her gum as she looked this person up and down, "An hour will cost you fifty. Do you have a car?"

"Nah, I just need a quickie. How about that dark corner over there?"

As soon as they were out of sight, he took the knife and slit her throat. Next, he removed her face and scalp, being careful as he placed it in the shopping bag he had tucked in his pants pocket. As soon as he returned to his car, he would place his new head of hair delicately on the mannequin head he kept there just for this very purpose. He never knew when he would find a new model.

Chapter 41

Scott and Caitlyn were getting ready to go to bed when a loud crash echoed from outside. Caitlyn asked, "What was that?"

Scott shook his head, "I'm not sure, but with everything that has gone on, I need to check it out." As they headed downstairs, all they heard was the rain as it hit the house.

As he headed outside, she told him, "Please be careful."

He gave her a quick kiss, "I'll be right back. The storm more than likely knocked down a limb or possibly a tree." He paused on the porch to let his eyes adjust to the dark. Thunder rumbled overhead, and he figured he should check the exterior of the house once before heading back inside. There may not be any dangerous ghosts to worry about, but someone could be using the passageways in the house to get around. He didn't want to leave Caitlyn alone in the house too long in case something happened.

***

Caitlyn curled up on the couch, beneath a blanket, in the parlor and waited for Scott to come back inside. Thunder booms shook the house as the wind howled against the windows. A sudden burst of cold air sailed over her, causing fear to lodge in her throat. She sat up, wondering where the breeze had come from. The front door was closed, as were all the windows. Her body trembled as she looked around the room. She didn't see any ghosts, or intruders for that matter.

The house was silent except for the sound of the rain outside. She swallowed back her fear and tried to find out where the cold breeze had come from. The sound of one of the passageway doors opening echoed through the house. Terror quickly swept over her as her heart pounded in her ears.

She grabbed the poker from the fireplace and walked into the foyer. Shadows danced eerily across the walls, reminiscent of roaming ghosts. From the window, she watched as lightning streaked across the sky. The moaning of the wind made the hair on her neck stand at attention. And she jumped when thunder rocked the house.

Outside, the howling wind sounded like a woman in pain. Another cold blast of air swept across her. A floorboard creaked behind her as a shadow moved in front of her. She gave the poker a hard swing and heard a loud grunt as the poker met flesh. She must have hit the intruder harder than she realized. A streak of lightning illuminated the house, and she saw blood dripping down the man's face. She prepared to swing the poker once more and made contact once again, surprising the man.

***

Scott had heard Caitlyn scream and rushed back inside to see what happened. He found her swinging once more at a man dressed all in black. As soon as Scott recognized the man standing in front of Caitlyn, he hollered out, "What the hell are you doing here?"

Scott's low growl resonated through Caitlyn. He instructed the man in front of him, "Move away from her now." Scott stood in front of the man and narrowed his eyes, "How did you get in here?"

The man swallowed hard, "There is an entrance near the bayou. I found it one day while fishing. I swear I didn't mean any harm."

"Uh huh, you thought the house was vacant, right? You didn't hear anyone talking about how someone had moved into the house?"

***

He shuffled his feet as he fingered the painful lump on his head. That woman had whacked him hard. The skin was broken and it would be difficult to hide the bruise. As bad as the cut bled, it would probably leave a scar. If she pressed charges, his chances of getting into the FBI would be nothing but a dream. "I may have heard something to that effect, but I didn't mean any harm. I swear Scott."

***

Grabbing a flashlight as he headed out the house, Scott instructed the man in front of him, "I want you to show me where this entrance is. I have a good mind to call the sheriff and let him handle you."

Officer Gavin Armistead paled at the mention of anyone telling the sheriff what transpired here, "Honestly, I didn't mean any harm. I heard the woman was staying in the travel trailer. I became concerned when I saw someone else using the same entrance. I didn't have any plans on even entering the house tonight, but I thought maybe I should check it out when I saw the other person going in."

Scott stopped in mid stride, "Wait a minute. You saw someone else going into the passageway tonight?"

"I'm not sure since it was dark out, but I thought I saw a shadow near the entrance way while I was out there fishing. That little hole has some of the best catfish around and with the rain; I knew they would be plentiful."

Scott headed back to the house, "Damn. I hope you are wrong and no one else is in that passageway."

"Wait up mon ami. Don't you want to see where that entrance way is?"

"Later. If you are right, whoever was in that passageway could be in the house and Caitlyn is all alone."

***

Caitlyn settled herself on the sofa in the parlor, watching as the fire flickered. The room had grown dark and the fireplace's bright orange glow created a surreal aura in the room. She had a hard time keeping her eyes open. They could go searching the passageways tomorrow, but tonight she was ready to crawl under the covers and sleep.

The hairs on her neck bristled and a jolt of adrenaline made her hypersensitive to her surroundings. She had the distinct impression that she was being watched. A noise behind her caught her attention. She let out a small gasp, "Why, Mr. Boudreaux I didn't even hear you knock."

Mr. Boudreaux walked around the room, gently touching the antiques, "Did you know you are sitting on a gold mine here cher? These antiques could fetch you a pretty penny.

For years now, I have been secretly removing them, doing it a little at a time and placing them in my shop."

A chill of apprehension washed over her, "Mr. Boudreaux, how did you get in here?"

"I told you that my family lived here for years. What I didn't say was that my father had been in charge of working the fields over at the old Cottonwood Plantation. The family there was so wrapped up in their misfortune that they never bothered to help themselves or others. They knew that my father was a mean old son of a bitch who beat his kids, but they did nothing about it. No, they liked to instigate matters instead. They would tell my poppa awful lies. Well, one day I heard them talking about how old Andre Picou had squirreled away most of his money at Whispering Willows Plantation. I knew that was my chance to get the hell out of my poppa's house."

Caitlyn asked, "You knew that Andre Picou hid money here?"

Rage could be seen in Mr. Boudreaux's eyes, "That money is mine you hear. I know that you found it when you were renovating. If it wasn't you, then it was that boyfriend of yours. You owe me that money. I have searched these grounds all these years for it; it is mine, I tell you."

Caitlyn stepped back, "Mr. Boudreaux, we haven't found any money or hidden treasures, I promise. I have no idea if Gregory found it. He never mentioned anything to me."

"Not that boyfriend. That one there was more interested in torturing those poor people than finding wealth inside these walls."

"You knew what Gregory was doing and did nothing?"

He scoffed at her, "I didn't know exactly what he was doing here, but I knew he was up to no good. He had so many damn alarms in this place that I couldn't get near this place that whole time. No, I'm talking about your other boyfriend. He must have found it while renovating this place. That has to be why I haven't found it."

Caitlyn shook her head, "Have you ever considered that there is no treasure?"

He pulled out a gun and pointed it at Caitlyn. "Well, girlie all I can say is you better ask them ghosts that you talk to show you where that treasure is if you want to live."

Caitlyn swallowed down the fear caught in her throat, "I don't talk to the ghosts; besides, in case you didn't hear, Madame Geroux helped the spirits move on."

"Well, cher, that does not help you, now does it?"

Caitlyn prayed for a divine intervention. How could she get this man to realize she had no idea where the hidden treasures were? A sudden burst of cold air blew over them just as Scott came barging in. As Mr. Boudreaux turned around waving the gun at Scott, she made her move. Without thinking, Caitlyn lunged for the armed man, knocking him down. Caught by surprise, he lost his grip on the gun and it went flying across the room.

Officer Armistead grabbed the gun and pointed it at Mr. Boudreaux, "I suggest you stay right there, sir." Looking over at Scott, "Do you have something we can restrain him with until the sheriff gets out here?"

Scott walked into the kitchen and found the zip ties and duct tape. They sat Mr. Boudreaux on the stairs in the foyer and waited for a squad car to come take him away. The whole time Mr. Boudreaux kept mumbling incoherently. Now and then they could make out how this wasn't fair and that the treasure was his.

Scott felt a small bit of sympathy for the old man. He was searching for something that probably didn't exist and that search ruined his life. If it hadn't been for the fact that he had scared Caitlyn these last few months and pointed a gun at her, he would have suggested that they go easy on the old man. However, right now, he wanted the man to suffer for putting her through what he did.

Chapter 42

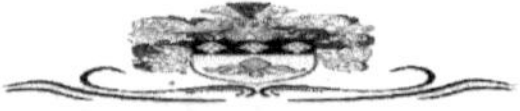

Officer Valerie Falgout walked into the Point Creole Sheriff's Office not knowing what to expect. She'd just finished with the police academy and tomorrow would be her first official day on the job. She could barely contain her excitement. She fully understood that she would be strictly working the beat for a while and had to prove herself capable in order to make rank. All she wanted was to make rank as a homicide detective as fast as possible.

Valerie hadn't known what she wanted to do with her life until her best friend was murdered. That was a wake up call for her. Valerie found out the hard way that life was short.

She stopped by the station to get her uniform and a feel for the place. She was so glad to be done with the police academy. The whole time there she kept wondering if this was what boot camp was like.

Sheriff Savoie saw the striking young woman walk into the station and wondered who she was. He walked out of his office to greet her, "Good afternoon, I am Sheriff Savoie. Can I help you with something?"

Valerie took his extended hand and gave him a firm handshake. "Valerie Falgout. I am supposed to check in tomorrow, but I wanted to get my uniforms, if possible, and get a feel for the place."

Sheriff Savoie looked over his new charge and feared he may have his hands full with this one. She had a head full of wavy auburn hair and the most striking green eyes. There was nothing Cajun about this one, mais non.

"If you don't mind me asking, what made you get into law enforcement?"

"My best friend was murdered by Gregory Ferris. After that, I constantly thought about how I should have done something to protect her. I eventually want to make my way to homicide."

"It is very admirable that you want to protect your friends, but some things are out of our control. We were all surprised by what happened. He had been doing this for years without ever being suspected of something so gruesome. Homicide is not for the faint hearted. You will be going after people who have no compassion for human life."

She nodded her head, "Yes, sir, I realize that. After what happened, I want to learn as much as I can about the criminal mind and how to stop them. At first, I thought about going into psychology, but I soon came to realize that as a psychologist, I wouldn't be able to stop the criminals. I want to work where I will have the biggest impact."

Sheriff Savoie listened intently to everything this young, eager woman had to say, but he hoped she didn't have her hopes set too high when it came to actual detective work. Give her a few months on the job and she would become jaded just like the rest of them.

"Let's go see Rosie over in human resources to get your identification, gun, and uniform."

Valerie felt the excitement inside of her bubbling up. Now, that she knew what she wanted to do with her life she couldn't wait to get started. She hated that it took losing her best friend to get her life to come together. If Sandy hadn't been murdered, she would still be working at Pop's Diner as a waitress and more than likely for the rest of her life.

***

When they walked into Rosie's small office, Sheriff Savoie made the appropriate introductions. Valerie had known Rosie Fontenot all of her life. Rosie and Valerie's mom, Cheryl, had been best friends since kindergarten. Rosie smiled over at Valerie, "Mais, I still couldn't believe when your mom called me crying over the fact that you wanted to be a cop of all things. Me, I am not sure whether I should try to beat some sense into you or pat you on the back for wanting to do something with your life."

Valerie gave Rosie a big hug, "This is what I want to do. I'm sure that Momma will come to accept that I am a cop."

She heard Rosie let out a tsk, "Mais, I don't think she will be accepting that fact anytime soon. Non, she will be worried sick about you."

Sheriff Savoie informed her, "You will be partnered with Officer David Lopez until you get the hang of the ropes."

"Where will I find him?"

"He is more than likely in the conference room. Detectives Bertrand and Morvant are going over the latest case. There was another murder, which is one of the reasons I am able to hire more officers. Suddenly, our nonexistent budget has funds available."

As she followed Sheriff Savoie to the conference room, she felt every eye in the room on her. Right now, she had two strikes against her. First, she was young and still wet behind the ears, and secondly, she was a woman.

Chapter 43

It was just after midnight when Tessa McKnight walked to her car through the dark office parking lot. The day flew by, and tomorrow would be another caffeine saturated day, but she loved every minute of this.

She reached up and freed her long, auburn hair from its confines. It cascaded down her shoulders in long, waves. She hurried across the parking lot, still lost in thought about the details of her latest case. Even at this late hour, she was too excited to sleep.

Swirls of fog danced in the air as litter blew across the deserted parking lot. At this ungodly hour, the surrounding stores and businesses were closed with their owners tucked away safely at home. The dark figure hid in the fog and shadows, watching his prey.

Tessa was a local and decided to open her practice here after graduating from law school. She had always been very goal oriented and dreamed of being a successful trial attorney. This case she just landed could be the biggest case of her career, one that recently started nonetheless.

She never suspected a case like this could even exist in her small town. A shiver of fear ran through her as the reality set in. Too many people in this town were sick, very sick; all dying from cancer. They just started to put the clues together.

Albert Bissette had esophageal cancer, Renee Duval had breast cancer, Fay Gagnon had ovarian cancer, and Brent

Girard had lung cancer, and he never smoked a day in his life. The list continued on as she went over the names in her mind.

Her first plan of attack was to hire a consultant to come in and take samples of the soil and water to check for contamination. She also planned on making a few phone calls to the EPA, Environmental Protection Agency, to see if they'd had any complaints regarding this area.

So far, most of these consultants required money up front to perform these tests, money that she didn't have. She hoped to convince one that there was a case here and they would be paid as soon as the money started to come in. If she needed to obtain pictures and samples she would do it. Something was making the citizens of this town sick and she was determined to find the cause.

She had become obsessed with all the small details that needed to be handled. This one case could consume her every waking moment. She had always been good at multitasking, and now, she was glad of her obsessive compulsive tendencies. She was good at formulating strategies and researching precedents of previous decisions. She would leave no stone unturned.

The fog parted and cleared a path for her. As she walked, her hips swayed back and forth rhythmically as her high heels clipped the cement. As she made it to her car, she noticed how dark it was out here. Her heart began racing with anxiety. She chastised herself, women were warned of a possible killer on the prowl. *Just let your eyes adjust and you will be fine.*

She ransacked her purse searching for her keys, which she should have taken out ahead of time. She let out a soft sigh of relief when she found them. As she unlocked the car door, she saw something out of the corner of her eye. A long, dark shadow appeared out of nowhere and moved across the pavement. Everything happened in slow motion; fear penetrated her mind and goose bumps made their way up her arms, her heart pounded violently in her chest and she found herself frozen in sheer horror.

A pair of headlights broke through the darkness. She waved furiously at the cops coming on the scene. She pointed to the end of the parking lot where she saw the dark figure approaching her.

***

Officer Falgout took out her flashlight, gun and started in pursuit as she had been trained. Her partner, Officer David Lopez, instructed the witness, "Please lock yourself in your car and call the 911 operator. Tell her we are in pursuit of a suspect and need backup."

***

Tessa swallowed her fear back down and nodded her head in understanding. She began to shake uncontrollably as the realization moved in that she may have almost become the serial killer's next victim. It didn't take long for the parking lot to become flooded with the flashing lights of patrol cars. Tessa thanked God that the officers passed when they did; she had been foolish to work as late as she did.

Chapter 44

Caitlyn stretched languidly and saw that Scott was still sound asleep. Slipping out of bed, she decided to prepare them breakfast in bed. She put on a pot of coffee and headed to the pantry to get everything to make a quiche for breakfast.

A noise from the kitchen caught her attention. Disappointed that Scott woke up, she called out, "Why don't you go back to bed? You are ruining my surprise." A cold breeze blew past her. Before she could turn around, strong arms grabbed her from behind and pulled her into the darkness of a passageway she didn't know existed.

***

Scott woke up to find the bed empty. The smell of coffee enticed him to the kitchen. He was surprised when Caitlyn wasn't there. He called out to her, "Caitlyn... Caitlyn, where are you?"

When she didn't answer, he began to search the house. By the time he searched every room, a good half hour had passed. The only places left to check were the passageways and the basement. Knowing how Caitlyn felt about the basement, he didn't see her going down there by herself, even if the house had been freed of spirits.

He opened a passageway door and called out for Caitlyn, "Caitlyn, honey, are you in here?"

Not hearing any noises, he picked up his phone, "Tony, I know you have your hands full, but Caitlyn has disappeared."

Tony let out a string of curse words. This just wasn't his week, first the killer slipped right through their fingers, and now a woman had disappeared. "I am sending some patrol officers there right now. I will be there shortly."

Scott informed him, "We need as much help as you can round up. The grounds are extensive."

"Let me see what I can do."

While Scott waited for the officers, he searched the house once more and opened the passageway doors as he went through each room. As he opened one of the passageway doors in the kitchen, he noticed a scuff mark in the dust. Grabbing his flashlight, he took note that this was a passageway they never ventured into. From the looks of it, though, someone had been through here recently. Less dust and cobwebs hung from the ceiling.

Panic settled deep in Scott's bones. Where was she? What happened to her? Did the killer somehow get in here and abduct her or was there possibly someone else he needed to be concerned about? Both of their cars were still here, so she didn't go anywhere. He called her cellphone only to hear it charging in the kitchen. He raked his hand through his hair as various thoughts bombarded his mind.

***

Caitlyn struggled against the duct tape that bound her wrists and ankles. It was too dark to see where she was.

There was a musty smell in the room. She tried to recall what had happened. She remembered waking up, making coffee, and gathering everything in the pantry. Hands came up from behind her and dragged her into the passageway. A sweet smelling cloth had been placed over her nose and mouth and after that, everything went dark.

Who could have done this? From the aches and pains in her body, she had been on the cold ground for a while now. She shivered as the cold seeped into her bones.

Once again, she strained against her bonds, twisting and pulling in hopes that the tape would budge. Judging from the smell, she must be in a secret part of the house. She prayed that she was not about to die. Not now that she found someone she loved and who loved her back.

She drew in a deep breath and screamed at the top of her lungs hoping Scott heard her.

***

Scott stopped what he was doing. He heard a faint noise, almost a screeching sound, echo through the passageway. In his haste of running to check the house, he missed what Officer Miller had found. Caitlyn had been in the pantry when she dropped the flour. The canister fell and rolled into the corner. When they started pushing on the walls, they discovered another entrance to the passageway from the pantry. It had been a stroke of luck finding that the shelves moved. Apprehension turned to full blown fear as the realization that Caitlyn had been missing for five hours sank in.

***

Caitlyn took another deep breath, preparing to scream once more when a figure stepped in front of her, "I wouldn't do that if I were you. I had hoped to wait until dark to move you out of here, but it looks as if the search party is smarter than I thought. They already found one of the hidden passageways."

The voice sounded familiar, and Caitlyn desperately tried to place it. Before she could react, a cloth was held over her mouth and nose. She thrashed about as she tried to turn her head away from the sweet smelling rag; it was the same smell she remembered from the kitchen. She attempted to hold her breath and not breathe in the scent. Unable to resist any longer, she drew in a breath as her world went black.

***

Scott and the cops met in the study once more. Bertrand looked at his friend, "Mon ami, our only choice is to bring in Mr. Boudreaux. He knows these grounds better than any of us. I called the District Attorney and the warden of the jail where Mr. Boudreaux is currently being held. The DA has offered Mr. Boudreaux house arrest if he agrees to help us." Bertrand looked at Scott to see if he would say anything, "In all honesty, I believe the old man would have helped us without the bargaining chip."

Scott ran his hands through his hair. All he cared about was finding Caitlyn, "Mon ami, I don't care if the DA lets him walk. I just want to find Caitlyn."

At that moment, Mr. Boudreaux walked in the door. Scott reached over and took the old man's hands in his in a firm handshake. "Thank you so much for helping us."

Mr. Boudreaux looked at the people in the house, "Did you search the underground tunnels?"

Scott looked at him with shock, "There are actual underground tunnels here?"

"Mais oui. Let's go find that pretty young thing of yours. She is kind to me. Even after my arrest, she came to visit me." He turned to one of the officers, "If you get me a piece of paper, I will map out the tunnels and where the entrances are. You must be very careful though. The bayou wiped out a few of the tunnel entrances and some areas the ground is caving in. Make sure you have working phones or walkie talkies, guns, and flashlights." He looked at each of the volunteers, "I would not fire a gun or make any loud noises unless it is necessary. These tunnels are ancient, and I cannot guarantee their stability. I used the tunnel entrance closest to the house, but there is one long one that runs under the old Cottonwood Plantation."

Scott's gut told him that was where they should look. "I'll take that tunnel."

Bertrand grabbed ahold of his shoulder, "I will go with you."

As Scott and Bertrand made their way to their tunnel, the other volunteers split up. Mr. Boudreaux called out to Bertrand, "I am coming with you. That tunnel is riddled with escape routes that they can use. I believe this was how old Jean Paul freed so many slaves around here."

In the basement, Scott was surprised to learn that of another hatch. "I never thought to look for another trap door." Mr. Boudreaux nodded his head in agreement, "Mais, I believe that was one of the reasons old Jean Paul never got caught as an important player in the Underground Railroad. It was rumored how the disappearance of slaves slacked off after his murder. After his daughter Marguerite arrived, slaves disappeared once again, but old Andre Picou could never prove that the Favres had anything to do with it."

The deeper they went into the tunnel the worse the smell became. "Mais, I haven't been down here in years, but I don't remember the stench being this bad." Mr. Boudreaux exclaimed.

Bertrand hollered out, "Be careful mon amis, the floor is getting slippery."

Scott shined his light on the ground and noticed a dark black sludge covering the ground, "It looks as if the bayou water may be getting into the ground here."

Mr. Boudreaux shook his head, "Mais non, that is not bayou water. The bayou is the other way."

Mr. Boudreaux dipped his fingers into the sludge, "Mais, I think I know what this is and I pray I am wrong."

As they moved deeper into the tunnel, they came to a complete block. Scott slammed his fist against the makeshift wall of dirt and boards, "Ah damn. They didn't come this way."

Bertrand looked at the pile of old pipe and barrels; some leaking sludge into the ground, "Mais, if this is getting into the bayou, we have a major problem."

Mr. Boudreaux paled, "Mon Dieu, I think it may be. There is a tunnel near the bayou that I used for years, but I came one day and found it caved in. Mais, what if whoever is doing this caved it in? Have you noticed how many people are coming down sick and with cancer lately? A good friend of mine, Harry Aucoin, went and talked to that pretty new lady lawyer in town."

Bertrand looked at the old man with surprise, "Wait a minute, people are talking to an attorney?"

"Mais oui. A few people compared notes and wondering if their illnesses could be related. One of them knew Tessa McKnight's family and went to talk to her. She is looking into the case for them. She even found someone to come out and take soil and water samples."

Bertrand wondered if it was the serial killer or the person responsible for the disposal who tried to attack Ms. McKnight. He picked up his cell phone and called Miller, "Get someone to go check on Tessa McKnight please. She may still be in extreme danger. Tell whoever you send to call me as soon as they have her and to not let her out of their sights."

Miller called out to Officer Pascal to come toward him, "What's going on Detective Bertrand? I have Pascal headed that way now."

Bertrand updated Officer Miller on what they'd discovered and gave him further instructions. Once he hung up, he exclaimed, "Son of a bitch, I never expected something like this to happen here. Pascal is on his way to check on McKnight. Miller is calling the EPA to see if they can help us get this area cleared out. Now, we need to find another way Caitlyn may have been taken."

Mr. Boudreaux called out, "Help me push on this." Scott saw what could be another trapdoor. The old man smiled at the two men, "I told you that this place is riddled with escape hatches. This was not only for slaves, but in case there was a breach in the tunnel, whether by cave in or man, they could get out."

By the time they made it above ground, dusk had set in. Looking around, Scott found that they were not far from Cottonwood Plantation. Bertrand put his finger over his mouth and pointed. Up ahead was a slow moving dark figure. The shadow appeared to be hunched over as if he was carrying something. Scott's heart rate started to pick up. He prayed that it was whoever had Caitlyn.

As they charged the figure, disbelief took over Scott's mind. Bile filled his stomach as he stared at the figure in front of them. Bertrand, acting quickly, grabbed his handcuffs and restrained the man pinned to the ground. He called out to Scott, "I need you to hold him down while I get Miller on the phone."

Scott kept looking at the body in front of him, searching for any distinguishing marks to tell him if this was Caitlyn or not. He fought the overwhelming urge to beat the truth out of the sniveling man in front of him. He heard Bertrand order Miller to send a car and officers to the Cottonwood Plantation, "It looks like we caught the killer."

Miller let out a sigh, "Were we in time to save Ms. Reed?"

"Call the coroner and tell him to bring his van out. We have a body for him."

With a deep grimace, Miller responded, "Yes, sir."

He walked over to Scott. "Mon ami, I am so sorry."

Scott looked at Bertrand and Mr. Boudreaux. The old man still looked woozy from the discovery, "This isn't Caitlyn. I can make out the image of a tattoo on the girl's chest."

Bertrand carefully moved the shirt that was cut open, "You are correct. There is a tattoo of some sort. I'm not sure if it is permanent or temporary."

Scott exclaimed, "It doesn't matter. Caitlyn doesn't have a tattoo. This person isn't the right body size as her either."

Bertrand picked the man up and glared into his eyes, "Who is this woman?"

He just snickered at the detective, "What are you doing out here? This is private property after all."

"Listen here you sniveling little bastard if you don't tell me who this is I may just feed you to the alligators before the cop car arrives. I am sure that neither of these two men would say a damn thing either."

Scott looked over at Mr. Boudreaux, "Did you see Detective Bertrand arrest anyone tonight?"

"Mais non, not me. We were too busy looking for your cher, mon ami. I think we need to get back on the trail and let Detective Bertrand handle this himself."

Bertrand started to drag the man back to Whispering Willows, mumbling, "I know where there is an alligator's nest. Saw it the other day while I was out here."

As the two men walked off in the other direction, Henry Picou started hollering, "No, no please don't leave me alone with him. I beg of you. This isn't your woman anyway."

Scott grabbed the man by the shirt collar, "Have you seen Caitlyn?"

Shaking his head, "Mais non, I saw this cute young cop searching the grounds and couldn't resist. I just had to have her hair for my collection."

Bertrand looked down at the body and rage filled him, "She is a cop?"

Cowering in a ball, "Yes, I am so sorry. I just couldn't resist when she came knocking on the door asking if I had seen anything out of the ordinary. It was as if fate had sent her to me."

Bertrand balled up his fist, trying to control the rage building inside of him. "You son of a bitch. You will pay for this."

Picking up his cell phone, he called Miller once more, "Detective Bertrand, the car should be arriving any minute now."

"That's good son, but you need to send over the crime scene techs to the Picou plantation. He just confessed to murdering Officer Falgout over there this afternoon."

Miller let out a loud gasp, "That can't be sir. She was here not long ago, I am sure of it."

"I am afraid it is true, son. He mentioned that he just had to have her for his collection. Something tells me we will find out exactly what he has been up to."

After hanging up with Miller, he told Scott, "I need to oversee this investigation. I hate to leave you shorthanded though."

Scott hated that he wouldn't be able to join in the search, but he understood, "Go take care of this, but we will keep looking for Caitlyn. He has to be keeping her in one of the tunnels. We would have heard a car pull up."

Mr. Boudreaux stated, "Unless he came over by boat."

Scott shook his head, "No, the motion sensors would have kicked on from any movement out there. When we suspected the killer may be dropping the bodies off at the dock, Caitlyn had me install the lights. If anything moves out there, they turn on."

Picou sneered, "Well, she didn't have to send that mambi pambi attorney of hers over to the house either."

Scott grabbed him by the shirt collar once more, "What are you talking about? Caitlyn hasn't even talked to the attorney."

With hate showing in his eyes, Picou stated, "Bullshit man. That man came over here not long after she moved in and told me to steer clear of Ms. Reed and Whispering Willows Plantation if I knew what was good for me. I thought for sure he knew what I was up to. I waited to see if he had turned me in, but after a few days, I assumed that maybe he didn't."

"Has the attorney been around here before?"

Picou nodded his head, "After Gregory Ferris bought the house, he came out here a few times, but after his death, he would show up a lot. At first, I thought he was making sure those workers weren't stealing anything. He checked up on the place now and then, especially when the trucks made a delivery."

Bertrand asked, "What trucks?"

"I don't know man. Some big moving trucks would come every so often. I don't know how they accomplished moving furniture at night, but that was when they did most of their work."

"Did you see them unloading anything or just loading up?"

"Hell man, I didn't go venturing anywhere near that property unless I had to. Occasionally, I dropped off a body there, but always in the daylight. There was no way in hell you would catch me near that place at night. The ghosts there don't like Picous. Perhaps the family rumors were correct and old Andre Picou sent Jean Paul and Celeste to their graves. He probably killed the missing girl also. Some of the family even suspected him of killing his first wife. They said that Andre was a snake in the grass."

Scott looked over at Bertrand, "Something tells me that attorney of Gregory's had his hands in more than tending to Gregory's financial affairs."

Bertrand nodded his head in agreement, "He may be responsible for that mess buried in the passageways."

Scott ran his hands through his hair, "Gregory probably told him about the secret passageways. I am betting after Gregory's arrest the attorney found a way to make a little money on the side. Whispering Willows is out of the way and few people even bother to visit because everyone feared that it was haunted. Hell, he may have believed that Caitlyn would go to Gregory's mansion and leave this house alone."

Bertrand turned towards Whispering Willows, "But where in the hell is Caitlyn? I will have the New Orleans Police Department see if he is at home. If he is, it is unlikely he abducted her."

"Yeah, but how will you do that without arousing suspicion?"

Bertrand informed him, "I can have them do a wellness check on him. If they confirm that he isn't home, I will tell them my suspicions then, but only then. If he is there, there is no reason to start any rumors flying just yet."

Scott told Mr. Boudreaux, "I'm going to keep looking. Whoever has her is keeping her in one of the tunnels."

"Well, let's go son. I hope you brought a gun."

Scott patted the back of his jeans, "I have it covered."

"There is another tunnel not far from the bayou that he may have entered the house through. The tunnel by the bayou has been sealed off."

"Well, let's go check that one then."

Chapter 45

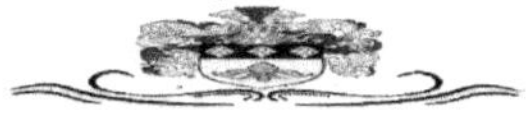

Caitlyn slowly opened her eyes, trying to adjust to the surrounding darkness. She bolted upright using her hands to steady herself on the cold ground underneath her. From the smell of the damp earth, they were still in the tunnel. In the distance, she heard a slow drip of water.

It took her a moment to realize that she was no longer bound. She slowly stood up and winced as the rush of blood entered her legs. She held on to the wall as the room swayed around her.

It took a few seconds for her vision to clear and the dizziness to subside. At the far end of the passageway, she could make out a light and at the other end was nothing but darkness. She wondered where her captor went.

She screamed out, "Help! Is anyone out there?" She continued screaming until her throat was raw. Since it wasn't doing any good standing here in the dark tunnel, she made her way towards the dark end of the old passageway. She feared that the light was a ploy.

The deeper she moved down the tunnel the darker it became, and a foul odor was in the air. A sound from behind her caused her to stop and listen. There it was again a footstep, then another. The person was getting closer. She held her breath, waiting in fear.

It seemed as if an eternity passed with no further sounds. She continued moving further down the passageway until her shoe hit something hard on the ground. She reached out and touched something hard blocking her path. Whatever it was, it had a slimy substance covering it. She continued to feel around hoping to find a way through.

Laughter sounded behind her and then a flashlight shined in her face. She gasped when she saw the man in front of her and let out a blood curdling scream. "What are you doing here? I thought you were dead."

***

Scott stopped in his tracks and looked at Mr. Boudreaux, "Did you hear that?"

"Yes, sir. I think we are on the right track. I sure hope, young man, that this is the right tunnel or we wasted precious time. This is the tunnel that is cut off at the bayou, so be warned the only way out is the way we came."

***

William Anderson grabbed her arm and pulled her close to him. He removed the mask he had been wearing, "This mask was the best money I have spent in a while."

"It was you acting like Gregory. You have been here this whole time?"

"What are you blabbering about? I only wore this once or twice. Why couldn't you just forget about this place? I should have told you this place was unlivable. I had hoped when you saw that big, beautiful mansion Gregory owned you would move in there, but no you had to come here and cause me more problems. So, I figured if you believed that Gregory was alive and stalking you here that you would leave, but instead you installed them damn security lights out back. The blasted things caused me nothing but problems. If I destroyed them you would simply repair them. No, I needed to you off this property for good."

She asked, pointing to the mass of items, "I don't understand. What is all of this?"

"This… This is my salvation. I owe some people a lot of money, the wrong people actually. After Gregory was arrested, he told me what he had done and how this place had been the perfect place for his experiments. He was a sick man. For as long as I knew him, I never suspected what he was up to. When I asked him what made this place so much better, he told me that it was easier to dispose of spare body parts and the waste left behind. When he first bought the place, he took me on a tour of the place and the tunnels he found. He figured that as the haunted house became more popular he could expand it and use the tunnels in some way to scare visitors. Upon his arrest, I had the answer to my dilemma, at least for a short time."

She pointed to the items being stored underground, "But how is this the answer to your problem?"

William ran his hands through his hair, "If I didn't come up with a solution to pay these people, they would kill me. Gregory leaving this house abandoned the way he did was my way out. While he was in prison, I tried several times to get him to sell me the place, but he refused every time. Even though he wouldn't sell it to me, I knew that I could use the land. I did some snooping and learned that no one around here came near the property at night. It became a vicious cycle for me; I would get my gambling debts paid off and then lose it all over again. As long as I let them use the land as they saw fit, they didn't care that I was doing so poorly. I made their problems go away."

She looked over at the refuse, "What is all of this?"

"I don't know and I don't care. The less I know, the better off I am, but I am sure most of it is hazardous waste material. You see, cher, I owed the mob in New Orleans a lot of money; they had clients who would pay to get rid of their problems. The regulations are getting stricter to dispose of certain materials, and they needed a way to dispose of materials without going through the proper channels. Of course, being the entrepreneur that I am, I also loaned out the land. One young man used the land to dispose of NORM material on some pipe that he had. He came at night to work so that no one would get curious and come to see what was going on here."

She let out a gasp, "But isn't that dangerous?"

"Hence my problem with you. There is to be another delivery and we couldn't do it with you here on the property. It was already becoming a problem with the killer running loose, especially with the cops patrolling this area now. With you gone, and the area once more abandoned, they would direct their efforts somewhere else."

She swallowed and backed away from him, "What are you planning on doing?"

"It's time for the serial killer to leave his body further down the bayou where they will continue their search."

With her voice shaking, "How… How do you plan on doing that?"

Pulling out his knife, he sneered at her, "I plan on giving them you, my dear. They will believe the serial killer claimed yet another victim and found a new dumping ground."

Scott stepped from the shadows, "It won't work. Detective Bertrand has already captured the killer. The EPA is surveying the area and arranging for the hazardous waste to be cleaned. There are quite a few people anxious to talk to you."

He grabbed Caitlyn and held the knife close to her throat, "I can't go to jail. The people I owe money to have long arms and can reach me even in jail."

Scott held his gun up to the man, "I'm sure they do. I am also sure that something can be done to protect you."

Scott sensed that Bertrand and the other officers had made it to where they were. He stepped out of the way without moving the gun away from William Anderson. Bertrand told him, "Put the knife down. You won't get past us and you know it."

Before any of them could react, William Anderson took the knife and slit his throat in one swift movement. Caitlyn felt the blood hit her head as it gushed from the gaping wound. She ran into Scott's waiting arms as her captor fell to the floor.

She clung to him, reveling in the feel of his arms around her. She breathed in the familiar smell of his soap and cologne.

He whispered in her ear, "I have been so worried about you. Are you okay?"

Shaking her head, still in shock over everything that had happened, "He didn't hurt me. He kept me drugged most of the time."

He kept his arms around her as he escorted her down the passageway, "Let's get you out of here. There are EMT's waiting to check you out."

"I'm fine, really."

Scott took her lips in his and kissed her, "Humor me, please. I have been worried about you. Besides, we need to make sure that there are no more drugs in your system."

As soon as Caitlyn stepped out of the tunnel and into the darkening sky, she saw all the cops and chaos around the plantation, "What is going on?"

"It turns out the good attorney used this property for a hazardous waste disposal ground."

She gasped, "That's what he was talking about. He said that he owed the wrong people money." Glancing back at his now dead body, "Why did he need to kill himself like that though?"

"He knew if the mob got to him his death would have been painful. They would have made him suffer."

Bertrand nodded his head in agreement, "That is someone you never want to owe money to. We heard they were building up their family again after the mess with St. Germaines. I wonder who is heading the family now."

Bertrand watched as the EPA supervisor made his way over to them, "It will take a good bit to clean this area. We have taken samples to see what all is tainted. Just from the sludge running into the bayou and the dead fish that float to the surface we are undoubtedly dealing with contamination. I plan on meeting with the attorney who represents several of the sick people here in town to find out what she has learned." Rubbing his hands through his hair, he went on to inform Bertrand, "I will still need you to keep an officer on her. The people who did this don't leave witnesses who can point fingers at them. If they believe she may know anything, anything at all, they will try to eliminate the problem."

"Yes, sir, I understand."

The EPA supervisor turned to Caitlyn, "I am sorry this happened on your property. It will take some time to clean the land up."

Caitlyn asked, "Can we salvage the Underground Railroad tunnels? I would hate to see that part of history destroyed."

Shaking his head, "I'm not sure ma'am. The cleanup company has mentioned that it would be easier to dig up the whole area and fill it in with new dirt."

"But it could be possible?"

Rubbing his chin, "It may be possible."

"Can you get me an estimate on what you believe the cost will be to save the tunnels and have the hazardous materials removed? I will make my decision after that."

Scott pulled her to the side, "You do realize that it may take millions of dollars to do something like this don't you?"

Caitlyn nodded her head, "If I can put Gregory's money to good use, I would feel so much better. The money means nothing to me." Looking him in the eyes, "If I gave the money away tomorrow, would you care?"

Taking her in his arms, "I love you, not the money. I am a simple man."

Bringing his head down to hers, she kissed him passionately, "I love you too. I was so afraid that I wouldn't see you again."

Epilogue

Scott and Caitlyn's romance turned into a deep and passionate love. Scott moved in permanently to Whispering Willows Plantation where they decided to open a unique bed and breakfast that not only taught about the Underground Railroad, but the trials and tribulations that occurred here at this very plantation.

As Caitlyn felt the baby kick for the first time, she smiled. Their happiness was complete, each of them had become the perfect complement to the other. They completed each other.

The evil and poisonous spirits that dwelled here for over a century were gone forever. Thanks to Scott's handiwork, the house and grounds had been restored to their once beautiful splendor.

Scott walked outside to find Caitlyn working in the garden as usual. The roses, crape myrtles, and jasmine were in full bloom.

She watched as another tour of children came in to learn about the history of this area. She loved listening to the sound of children's laughter as they explored the grounds. She caught sight of the line forming at Beazell's Bistro and was surprised to see how many locals came to eat here.

She was so glad that Scott had convinced her to talk to Beazell's into opening a small bistro here at the plantation. It turned out to be a profitable venture for all of them. The small bistro may not be as intimate as the one in town, but the food was just as good. They created a cozy atmosphere at the plantation.

The bed and breakfast was popular with the tourists and locals. Several guests swore they saw the ghosts of Celeste and Jean Paul as they walked hand in hand through the garden. Caitlyn smiled whenever she heard the stories. It brought her such great pleasure to know that she, Scott, and Madam Geroux helped to free the troubled spirits here.

Thank you!

Dear Reader,

Thank you for purchasing this book. I hope you enjoyed reading this novel as much as I enjoyed writing it.

It is crucial for me to hear what you think about the book. Your reviews give me inspiration in my future writings. You can leave a review on Amazon, Goodreads or Barnes and Noble.

Your thoughts and opinions mean a lot to me. Also, be sure to check out my website and social media sites for upcoming books and giveaways.

Sincerely,

Mary Theriot

Links

Website www.maryreasontheriot.com

Goodreads for reviews -
http://www.goodreads.com/MaryReasonTheriot

Facebook - http://goo.gl/Sd0VgY
Twitter - @Mktheriot

Google+ - +MaryTheriot

YouTube - http://goo.gl/ErM1M6
Pinterest - http://www.pinterest.com/mktheriot

Blog Page, www.maryreasontheriot.me